Dee Williams was born and brought up in Rotherhithe in East London, where her father worked as a stevedore in Surrey Docks. Dee left school at fourteen, met her husband at sixteen and was married at twenty. After living abroad for some years, Dee moved to Hampshire to be close to her family. She has written twenty-one previous novels including *Lights Out Till Dawn*, *A Moment to Remember*, *This Time for Keeps* and *All That Jazz*.

To find out more about Dee, go to her website at www.deewilliams.co.uk

C0000 002 16 227

By Dee Williams and available from Headline

Dee WILLIAMS

The Flower Girls

headline

First published in 2012 by
HEADLINE PUBLISHING GROUP

First published in paperback in 2012 by
HEADLINE PUBLISHING GROUP

1

Cataloguing in Publication Data is available from the British Library

ISBN 978 0 7553 8700 7

Typeset in Palatino by Avon DataSet Ltd,
Bidford-on-Avon, Warwickshire

Printed and bound in Great Britain by CPI Group (UK) Ltd, Croydon, CR0 4YY

HEADLINE PUBLISHING GROUP
An Hachette UK Company
338 Euston Road
London NW1 3BH

www.headline.co.uk
www.hachette.co.uk

I would like to dedicate this book to all my loyal fans who for the past 22 years have written to me and now contact me through my website to tell me how much you enjoy my books. Thank you all. I hope you enjoy this one.

Chapter 1

1926

IDENTICAL TWINS LILY and Rose Flower squealed with delight when their father Ron announced on Saturday evening, the eve of their sixteenth birthday:

'As your birthday falls on Bank Holiday Sunday this year, me and your mother are taking you to Southend for the day.'

Lily threw her arms round her father's neck and kissed him loudly on the cheek. 'Thanks, Dad.' Treats like this were very few and far between. Although both girls had been working for the past two years, their wages didn't really help the family budget.

Their mother Amy, a slim, dark-haired woman, was looking at them and smiling. Sixteen: where had all those years gone? She was very proud of her beautiful daughters. They had inherited her colouring and, like her, had wavy dark hair and big brown eyes. She had always dressed them identically till they were fourteen, but when they went out to work they found their own individual styles. Last week, Rose, to her father's alarm, had had her hair cut in the latest bob. She worked in an office that sold stationery, while Lily worked in a flower shop. She always said she never had the brains to work in an office, but she loved her job. It was a standing joke that Lily Flower worked with flowers.

'I shall wear my new white cloche hat. What about you, Lil? What will you wear?' asked Rose, who as soon as she had a few shillings would put them aside to buy new clothes. She was always poring over fashion magazines for the latest styles.

'I've got my old brown one.'

The office Rose worked in had a supervisor, Miss Evans. Rose was always full of what she wore and how she looked. She was forever saying that she wanted to be like her. Lily had seen the woman a few times when she came into the shop, and thought that she was over-made-up and rather rude and bossy, but Rose wouldn't hear a word against her.

Rose's voice broke into Lily's thoughts. 'I think it's about time you bought yourself a new hat.'

'I will when I've got the money. Don't forget, I earn a lot less than you.'

Although outsiders couldn't tell them apart till Rose cut her hair, the twins themselves knew there were big differences between them. While Lily was shy and the quieter of the two, Rose, the elder by five minutes, was full of life and ambition and longed for excitement.

'I shall go on the Big Dipper,' said Rose. 'What about you, Lil?'

'Don't know. I'll have to see how high it is first.'

Lily looked at her mum, who was busy putting the cloth on the table ready for dinner. Their father was reading the newspaper. They were so lucky they had such wonderful parents. Their father was foreman in a large tea warehouse along by the docks. They weren't well off but nor were they hard up, not like some of the people that lived round here. Parts of Rotherhithe were very poor, and there were many widows from the war.

The twins had only been four when the war started. With their father away in the army and their mother at work in the biscuit factory, they had spent a lot of time with their neighbour Mrs Perry. Mrs Perry's husband had been killed at the very beginning of the war, and she had two children. Will was a few years older than the twins, and Rose, like many of the other girls in the road, liked him; he was very good-looking. June, his sister, was about the same age as the girls. The Flowers were lucky: their father had come back from the war with just a leg injury, which had left him with a slight limp. He still had his job at the warehouse, and over the years he had been made foreman and was now in charge. Since the girls had started work, they had been helping out with their wages. Their father said it was to make them realise the value of money. The family lived in a neat two-up and two-down terraced house, and unlike many folks around here, they didn't seem to want for anything.

Lily followed her mother into the scullery. 'Thanks ever so much, Mum.'

'That's all right. We didn't know what to get you, so we thought a treat would be good. That way we can all have a nice day. Let's hope the weather stays dry.'

'I hope so for Rose's sake. She'd go mad if her new hat got wet.'

'Put the knives and forks on the table, there's a love,' said her mother, without making a comment about the hat.

Lily did as she was asked.

That night, in their sparse but comfortable bedroom, Rose was sitting on the flowery bed cover that matched their curtains. She was still talking about her new hat. 'I wish I could have afforded a coat to go with it as well.'

'You're always wanting.'

'I know. But a new coat would be nice.'

'It might have got dirty on the train, with all the sooty smuts blowing about.'

'I suppose so. What if me hat gets dirty?'

'Don't wear it. Wear an old one. Besides, it might blow off on the seafront.'

'Don't say that.' Rose moved over the table that served as a dressing table and looked in the mirror that sat on top. 'I'd die if I lost it; it cost me two and eleven. I was hoping Mum and Dad would give us some money for our birthday.'

'Why? We earn enough. Besides, it'll be nice for them to go out with us. They don't go out that much.'

'S'pose so. But I've seen a coat I'd like in Pecrys.' She patted the back of her hair. 'I really like my new hairdo. You should get yours cut.'

'Don't know.'

'I'll have to save up and buy that coat.' Rose turned to face her sister. 'Or maybe I'll get it on the never-never.'

'You can't do that!'

'Why not?'

'Because Mum and Dad don't approve of things bought weekly.'

'They won't know. I don't get it till I've paid for it, and that way I won't lose it. I'd die if they sold it. Miss Evans has got one like it; well, not really, hers looks ever so expensive.'

'Is it such a big thing? One coat?'

'Oh Lil. It's really smashing – navy with a fur collar – and it'll look ever so good with me new hat.'

Lily smiled to herself. She had heard this all before when Rose wanted something, and she knew her sister wouldn't rest till she got this new coat.

The following morning, there was great excitement in the Flower household.

'Where's Dad?' asked Lily.

'Out in the lav,' said her mother.

'Look, Mum, we've got each other the same card again,' said Lily, looking at their birthday cards. These past few years when the girls bought each other cards they were always the same.

'And I expect you've bought each other the same present,' said her mother as she parcelled up the sandwiches she'd been busy making.

Rose tore open the package her sister had given her and began laughing. 'Now how did you know I wanted a scarf?'

Lily was also laughing as she opened her present from her sister. 'And how did you know I wanted one as well?'

They hugged each other.

'Will we ever stop thinking alike?' asked Rose.

'I don't know,' said their mother.

'Well I hope so,' said Rose. 'What if we both like the same boy?'

'You'd better hope he's one of twins,' said Amy with a smile.

'Right, are you girls nearly ready?' asked their father as he walked back into the kitchen.

'Yes, Dad,' they said together.

'Well let's be off, then.'

The crowds at Fenchurch Street station were unbelievable.

'Stay close together,' said Ron Flower as the train puffed its way into the station. 'Don't want to lose you.'

'Mum, will you tell Dad to stop fussing. We're not little kids any more,' said Rose as they made their way through the crowds and on to the platform.

'He can't help being protective,' came back the answer.

'I know, but he does still treat us like children,' said Rose, smiling at a smart-looking gent.

'Rose, for goodness' sake shut up,' said Lily. 'Just get on the train.'

As the train chugged and clanked its way out of the station and they moved along the corridor looking for seats, Rose whispered to her sister, 'I would have preferred the money for a new coat.'

Lily elbowed her in the ribs and said fiercely, 'Stop moaning.' She was getting a little tired of Rose's complaints.

Children were running up and down the corridor screaming with excitement. Going to Southend for the day was a great outing for many Londoners, including Lily.

'What we got in our sandwiches?' she asked her mother.

'Some ham and some cheese. That all right?'

'Sounds lovely to me,' said Ron, patting her hand.

Rose, sitting opposite her parents, was gazing out of the window. They had left London behind and were now rushing past green fields. How she would love to live somewhere like this. She hated the dirt and the crowded houses in Rotherhithe.

One of the kids who was sharing the carriage with them came over to the window and grabbed hold of the leather strap that held it closed. As he pulled it down, the window dropped open.

'Oi!' yelled Rose as soot flew into the carriage. 'Get away, you little devil.'

'Billy, come and sit down,' said the boy's mother. Rose glared at her.

Specks of soot had landed on Rose, and the more she tried to brush it from her coat, the dirtier it became.

'Some people want to keep their kids under control,' she muttered.

The woman grabbed the boy by the hand and left the carriage.

'Rose, you've got some on your face,' said Lily.

Rose rubbed her face, causing the soot to spread. Lily laughed.

'Stop doing that, you're making it worse. Here, let me.' She took her sister's handkerchief and said, 'Spit on this.' Rose did as she asked, and Lily carefully dabbed the soot away.

Their father smiled at such a loving gesture.

The family had had a wonderful day, and as they settled back on the train home, they began to reflect on the things they'd done.

'That was really good on those bumper cars,' said their father. 'I felt as if I was driving a proper car. I'll have to think about getting one, one day.'

Amy Flower looked at him and grinned. 'If you've got that kind of money, we'll have a new three-piece first.'

'I knew you'd say that. Did you enjoy yourself, Rose?'

'Yes I did.'

'What about you, Lil?'

'It was a lovely day. Thank you, Dad.'

'That feller on the rifle range was rather good-looking, wasn't he?' said Rose.

'Yes, he was,' said Lily, as she settled back and wondered what this next year had in store for them all.

Chapter 2

1928

'GOOD NIGHT, MISS Tucker,' called Lily Flower as she
left the shop.

'Good night, Lily,' came the reply. 'See you in the
morning.'

As Lily walked home, her thoughts were full of her
twin sister Rose and the continuing arguments at home.
Next week, on Wednesday, the fourth of April, they
would turn eighteen. How they seemed to have grown up
and apart in the past two years. If only Rose wouldn't
wear so much make-up! It wasn't that Lily herself dis-
approved – after all, her sister could do what she liked –
but why did she have to make Dad so angry when she
could easily wipe it off before she got home? Lily knew
there would be more rows tonight when Rose came in.
Dad wasn't an unreasonable man, but it seemed that her
sister went out of her way to upset him. All her life Rose
had liked her own way and done what she wanted to do,
but she always wanted more.

The Flower Girls

As Lily walked down Enfield Road towards number twenty-two, she casually glanced at the row of terraced houses. She had lived here in Rotherhithe all her life. She knew most of their neighbours and had played in the street with the other kids. She smiled to herself remembering how all the girls had loved Will Perry, who'd lived at the end of the road. They would wander past his house and hope that he'd come out. He was tall, and so good-looking. Lily would grin when Rose used to tell her that she was going to marry Will one day. The family had moved away a few years ago.

From the outside, all these houses were alike. They had two bedrooms upstairs and two rooms downstairs, with a scullery at the back and a lav in the yard. The bath and the meat safe hung on the outside wall, and underneath was the mangle with its big wooden rollers and a handle that was hard to turn. It was only the state of the front steps, or the torn and grubby lace curtains at dirty windows, that told you what kind of people lived there. The Flowers' next-door neighbour, Mrs Brown, was a miserable old lady, a widow, who complained about everything and sat all day at her window watching people come and go. The kids used to call her names and poke their tongues out at her. She would shout and complain to their mothers when they walked past. Somehow she knew everybody's business, and most people tried to avoid her when she stood at her front door. Other houses held two or more families and were very overcrowded.

Lily pulled out the key that hung on a string behind the letter box and opened the front door.

'Hello, Mum. All right?' she asked as she walked into the kitchen.

Her mother was putting the knives and forks on the table. She smiled when her daughter came into the room. 'Fine. Everything all right with you, love?'

'Yes thanks.' Lily took off her brown cloche hat and, looking in the mirror that hung over the fireplace, patted her short dark hair. She too had come round to having the fashionable look. 'What we got for tea?'

'I've made a nice steak and kidney pie.'

'Lovely. I'll just go and hang me coat up.' Lily went into the passage and hung her brown coat on one of the hooks that lined the wall.

'I do hope Rose don't come in with all that make-up on. She knows how much it upsets your father,' said Amy when her daughter walked back into the kitchen.

'I know. Sometimes I think she does it on purpose.'

'And if her skirts get any shorter, they'll be indecent.'

'I think she just tries to be like the women she works with.'

'Well I can't say I approve.'

Lily didn't answer, and when she heard the front door slam, she knew that Rose was home.

'Hello, Mum, Lil,' said Rose, giving her sister a nod and putting a thick brown paper carrier bag on the table.

'You're late, where you been? And what have you got there?' asked her mother.

'Bin collecting me new coat.'

'What, another one? You've not long had that one,' said her mother, pointing to the coat Rose was wearing.

'This thing's a couple of years old now.'

'So how did you afford it?'

'I've been paying for it at Pecrys. It's taken me weeks.'

'What? You know your father doesn't approve of buying things like that. How much did it cost?'

Rose didn't answer her mother as she took off her old coat and threw it on one of the armchairs that stood either side of the fireplace. 'What d'you think?' She took a beige coat from the bag and put it on. It had a lovely thick, rich-looking fur collar. 'Well, what d'you think?' she asked again. 'Goes well with this hat and me shoes, don't you think?' Still wearing her brown cloche hat, she strutted round the kitchen. 'The collar comes off, so I can wear it in the summer.'

'It's very nice,' said her mother.

'As I said, I've been paying it off at Pecrys.'

'What did it cost?' her mother asked again.

'Not that much. Besides, paying for it weekly is a good way of saving. D'you like it, Lil?'

'It's very nice.' Lily could tell by the look of it that it must have cost at least a guinea.

'I needed a new one for when I go out with the girls from work again.' Rose winked at her sister and glanced in the mirror, running her finger over her bright red lips.

'Why don't you take some of that off?' said her mother,

taking the carrier bag from the table and placing it on the armchair.

'Because I don't want to. I like being modern and fashionable.' Rose smoothed down her beige dress. It had the latest dropped waist, with a large navy bow at the hip. Her shoes were navy too, very fashionable T-bar winkle-pickers. Everything about Rose was chic and up to date. 'Besides,' she said with a pout, 'I earn a good wage and can do as I like.'

'Not till you're twenty-one you can't.'

'You're as bad as Dad. Just let me be meself.' She picked up her coat and stormed out of the room, slamming the door behind her.

Lily went to follow her.

'Leave her,' said Amy. 'Your father will be home in a little while. I don't want any more arguments. Did you know she was buying a new coat?'

'No, I didn't. She don't tell me everything these days.' Lily took the condiments from the large dresser that lined the wall next to the fireplace and placed them on the table.

'Life was so much easier when you were little and I could dress you both the same,' said her mother. 'I was so proud of you. And the fact that nobody could tell you apart in those days.'

'We're grown-ups now, Mum; we like to be independent.'

'I know, more's the pity. Although Rose always liked to be different even when she was little. Look how she cut her hair when she was only five. Said she didn't like ringlets and looking like you. I thought your father would go mad. He was always so proud of you both.'

Lily remembered the row that had created, and how Rose had had to be taken to the hairdresser's to get it cut properly.

Her mother had a wistful look in her eyes. 'I remember that whenever we walked along with you two in the big bassinet, your dad would be grinning from ear to ear when people came up to us and commented on how lovely you were.'

'Well we're all grown up now,' said Lily.

'Yes, and grown into lovely young ladies.'

Lily went into the yard and sat on the seat that ran under the scullery window. She smiled to herself as her thoughts went back to the days when they'd laughed, giggled and played together. They had had such a happy childhood, even though Rose had always bossed her around, telling her that as she was the oldest and the cleverest, she had to be the teacher if they played schools, or the nurse if they played hospitals.

It was when they started work that Rose began to really change. Most of the women in her office were older and sophisticated and wore nice clothes. Lily often saw them when they came into the flower shop. She loved her job; working with flowers was so rewarding. At first the women from Rose's office could tell they were twins as they were so alike, but it wasn't long before Rose became more like them, with her lovely brown hair bobbed, and when she started to wear thick make-up, that was when the rows started. Lily could understand her mother's feelings; she didn't want them to grow up. Their father was even worse. They knew all about his younger sister Ann and how she used to behave, always out with different men. When she went off with a man who was married and a lot older than her, that caused a big scandal. He left his wife with two children, and when they suddenly moved away, there was talk that they had finished up in the workhouse.

Rose said she thought that story was a bit far-fetched, but as Ann wasn't around now, it was hard to dispute. Because of what had happened in the past, though, Ron Flower always said that any bloke who wanted to take his girls out had to be the best around. He was a good man and very protective. In the past year, Rose had met plenty of blokes, but she never brought them home. Tom was the latest one she talked about, and probably the reason why she'd bought the coat, though Lily doubted he was worth the expense. When they went out, Rose always tried to play the vamp like they'd seen in films; once she even tried to smoke a cigarette in a long holder. Lily told her she looked silly, but that didn't stop her; she just wanted to be grown up and look sophisticated. Their father would have forty fits if he ever saw her.

'What you doing out here?' asked Rose as she came into the yard.

'Nothing.'

'I've just got ter go to the lav, be out in a minute.'

Lily loved her sister, but wished she could be a little

more diplomatic. Why did she always strive to be different? Was it because she was a twin and wanted to be her own person? If that was the case, she was being very silly. Lily could hear her mother calling.

'Mum's calling,' she shouted to the closed lav door. 'Dinner's on the table. And Rose, Dad's home, so please wipe some of that make-up off.'

There was no reply.

Rose sat in the lav, pouting. 'If I want to wear make-up, I will,' she said out loud.

'Hurry up, Rose,' shouted her father.

'Just a minute.'

When she opened the door, her father looked at her but didn't say a word as he went in.

It was very quiet during dinner. When they had finished, Ron Flower picked up Rose's cup. 'This is disgusting,' he said, showing her the bright red lipstick mark all around the rim. 'Go and wash it off.'

Rose picked up the cup and went into the scullery.

'Ron, please don't make such a fuss,' begged Amy. 'You know what she's like. She only does it to annoy you.'

'Well she does that all right.'

In the scullery, Rose grinned to herself as she washed the cup. She knew that soon she would be able to do everything she wanted, and nobody was going to stop her.

Chapter 3

THE FOLLOWING MONDAY morning, Rose was sitting at her desk when her supervisor Miss Evans walked in. 'Good morning, girls.'

'Good morning, Miss Evans,' they all answered.

Nora Evans was tall and slim, her dark hair cut in a short style that framed her face. She was always very smart and fashionable. Rose admired everything about her, and wanted to look as sophisticated as she did. She knew Miss Evans liked her, as she was always very friendly, insisting that Rose call her Nora on the odd occasion she invited her out for lunch.

'Did you have a nice weekend?' asked Miss Evans, coming across to Rose.

'Yes thank you. Did you?'

'Wonderful. We must go out for lunch today and I can tell you all about it.'

Rose beamed.

'See you in my office at one.'

'Thank you,' said Rose, still smiling.

When Miss Evans had left the room, Betty James looked up from her typewriter and asked, 'What have you got that she's interested in?'

'She just likes good company,' said Rose, adding with a grin, 'And intelligent conversation.'

'Ooh. Hark at her,' said Molly Parker, another of the young women who worked in the office.

Rose went to the filing cabinet. She knew that one of the reasons she got on so well with her supervisor was because she never complained about any job she was given. She always tried to look smart, and as well-dressed as her budget would allow. She finished her filing and closed the drawer. Going back to her seat, she smiled to herself. She knew that one way or another, this was how she was going to get on.

'So your father made a fuss about the amount of make-up you wear?'

Rose had finished telling Nora Evans about her weekend.

'I'm surprised you stay there. If my father treated me like that, I'd leave home.'

Rose looked surprised. 'He's not that bad. He doesn't hit me or anything like that.'

'Good God, I should hope not. This is 1928, not the dark ages. Even so, I wouldn't let anyone tell me what to do.'

Rose envied Nora. She knew that she had her own flat and was very independent. She always looked immaculate, and she seemed to meet the right people. Rose would listen almost open-mouthed when she spoke of some of the places she had been to. Although she was quite a few years older – Rose guessed she was in her late twenties – she had known what she wanted in life as soon as she started work.

'Look, I'm going to a party up West this Saturday. Why don't you come with me? You can stay at my place on Saturday night. There's only a sofa for you to sleep on, but I can guarantee you'll have a good time.'

Rose stopped cutting her sandwich in half and looked at Nora. 'Do you mean it? Would you really take me with you?'

'Why not? I think it's about time you got out and saw the world. Besides, you look as if you like a good time.'

Rose giggled. 'I love having a good time and I would love to go out with you.'

'Right, that's settled. Bring your best frock and shoes and come to my flat about seven. I'll write my address down. The tube stop's quite near.'

Rose was very excited. She was going out with the sophisticated Nora Evans and staying at her flat all night. Now all she had to do was get round her mum, who then, hopefully, would get round her dad.

On her way home, Rose's thoughts were on the coming weekend with Nora. She couldn't believe the older girl wanted to take her to this party. Her biggest problem was what she would wear. Although she had some nice clothes, nothing matched Nora's. If only she hadn't spent so much on that coat, she could have been paying off for a really nice silky frock and sparkly shoes. She looked out of the bus window and suddenly felt miserable. This could be the best weekend ever and she didn't have the right clothes. She was desperately hoping that her father would give her money for her birthday. If she could borrow some from Lil, then with her wages, she might just about scrape enough together to get a new frock. That thought cheered her up a little.

That night, Lily was in bed reading a magazine while Rose sat looking in the mirror and combing her hair. All their lives the girls had loved being in their room. They could talk and giggle without being told to be quiet or to stop being silly. They felt safe and happy in here.

'Lil, do you know what Mum and Dad are giving us for our birthday?'

'No idea. Why?'

'I was wondering if you could find out.'

Lily put the magazine down. 'Why?' she asked again.

Rose turned round. 'Nora's invited me to a party on Saturday, and I was thinking that if Dad gave us some money and I borrowed some off you, I could get a new frock.'

'What?'

'Shh, keep your voice down.'

'There's plenty of frocks in there.' Lily pointed to the wardrobe.

'I know. But I fancy a new one.'

'Sorry, but I ain't going to ask Dad what he's giving us.'

'Could you just ask Mum?'

'No. And I'm not lending you any either. Look how long it took for you to pay me back the last time. Besides, you earn a lot more than me.' She picked up her magazine again.

'But you got it in the end.' Rose came and sat on her sister's bed. 'Please. This is very important. It's a very posh party.'

'Well you'll just have to make do.'

'You know, you can be very annoying at times.'

'Thanks.'

'I'm going to stay the night with Nora and I want to look really good.'

'What? Does Mum know you're staying out all night?'

'Not yet.'

'I always get the feeling that Nora looks down her nose at me when she comes into the shop.'

'I shouldn't think so. She's very nice.'

'Looks a bit out of your league.'

'Well she's not. She's older than me, and . . .' Rose stopped. She didn't want to say 'a lot wiser and more experienced' in case her sister got the wrong impression.

'Do her mum and dad know you're going to stay with them?'

'She don't live with her parents. She's got her own flat.'

'And you're going to stay there?'

Rose nodded.

'Who does she live with?'

'She lives alone.'

'That's what she tells you. Is she giving the party?'

'No.'

'So where is it?'

'I don't know.'

'Oh Rose. You could be going off into some den of iniquity.'

Rose laughed. 'You read too many novels.'

'Well it all sounds a bit sleazy to me.'

'Nora is just a nice person who wants me to go with her to a party.'

'But why?'

'Does there have to be a reason?'

'I would think so.'

Rose didn't like to say that Nora had felt sorry for her being held back by her father. 'As I said, she's just a nice person.' She put the light out and climbed into bed.

Lily lay thinking about her sister going off to a party on her own. She didn't care much for what she'd seen of Nora. The older woman also seemed to have plenty of money, and she lived alone. Did she earn all that at the office? She could hear Rose sighing. What would her mum and dad say when they learnt about the weekend? Please, not more arguments.

'Happy birthday, girls,' said their mother on Wednesday morning when she walked into the kitchen.

'Thanks, Mum,' they said together.

'Here's your cards.'

Rose opened hers eagerly and was disappointed when there wasn't any money inside.

'You'll get your present tonight when we all sit down together.'

'Thanks. It's very pretty.'

Lily gave her mother a kiss. 'Thanks, Mum.'

'Mum,' said Rose in her little-girl voice, the voice they all knew she used when she wanted something.

Her mother looked up from pouring out tea for Lily. 'Yes?'

'I was just wondering what you and Dad are getting us for our birthday.'

'You know we always wait till the evening, when we're all together.'

'I'd be just as happy with money.'

'I bet you would. What about you, Lily? What would you like?'

Lily almost dropped the cup she was holding. She hadn't expected her mother to ask her opinion. 'I don't know.'

Rose glared at her.

'As I said, you'll just have to wait and see. Now come on, look at the time, both of you. You'll be late for work.'

When they left the house Rose said. 'Thanks a lot.'

'What for?'

'For nothing. By the way, thank you for my hankies.'

'And for mine. At least they've got different initials in the corner'. As usual, they had bought each other the same card and present. 'Here's your bus.'

The Flower Girls

Lily watched her sister get on the bus, then set off for the flower shop. The rest of today was going to be very interesting. Would Rose get what she wanted and be able to go off with Nora?

Chapter 4

'HAPPY BIRTHDAY, LILY,' said Miss Tucker when she arrived at the shop.

'Thank you.'

'I'd like you to start sorting out the flowers we shall need for the bridal bouquets, and also those for the tables at the big office do this weekend.'

'Thank you.' Lily loved helping to arrange the flowers for weddings; it was a much happier task than making wreaths. She could dream about the bouquet she would have for her wedding one day. There would be white roses and sweet-smelling lavender. She gave a sigh. She hadn't even got a boyfriend, so her dreaming was just a waste of time, but she loved it when men came into the shop and asked her advice on what flowers to buy their wives, girlfriends or mothers. She hoped she always helped them make the right choice.

'Happy birthday, Miss Flower,' said Miss Evans when she walked into the office. They were always very businesslike during office hours. 'Here's a little something for you.' She handed Rose a neatly wrapped parcel and a card.

'Thank you.' Rose could feel herself blushing. She had never expected Nora to remember that it was her birthday.

'Is it your birthday?' asked Betty James.

'Yes, it is.'

'Happy birthday,' said Betty and Molly together.

'Thank you.'

'Go on, open your present,' said Molly.

Rose looked at Nora, who was smiling. She very carefully undid the ribbon and unwrapped the small box. 'Oh. This is lovely. Thank you. I've always wanted a cameo brooch, but you shouldn't be giving me such a beautiful present.'

'I thought you'd like it.'

'Thank you. Thank you so much,' said Rose again.

Molly and Betty came over to Rose's desk and peered over her shoulder.

'That's very nice,' said Molly, and went back to her desk. Rose knew there would be some comments when Nora left the room.

'Now girls, we need to get these invoices out today, so I expect you all to work through your lunch hour.'

There were groans from Molly and Betty, but Rose just smiled. She was happy to do anything Nora asked.

That evening, Rose arrived home before her sister, full of anticipation. She took her brooch from her bag. 'Look what Miss Evans gave me,' she said, holding the box out to her mother.

'Rose, that is really nice. She must think a lot of you to give you something like that.'

'Yes, she does.' Rose started to help her mother set the table. 'And she's asked me to go out with her one evening.' She thought she would introduce the subject gradually.

'That's nice of her. Hello, love,' said Amy as her husband walked in. She held her face up for a kiss.

'Hello, Dad,' said Rose sweetly, planting a kiss on his cheek. She'd wiped off her lipstick before she got home. There was no way she was going to start an argument tonight.

'Happy birthday, love,' he said, holding her close.

'Thanks, Dad.'

'Lily not home yet?' he asked.

'No, she said she might be a bit late as she was helping getting the flowers sorted for some office do and a wedding they're doing this weekend,' said Amy. 'Sit yourself down, Ron, and I'll pour you a cup of tea. Rose, show your dad what Miss Evans gave you.'

'Thanks, love,' he said, sitting in his armchair and taking off his boots. 'Been really busy today. Those warehouses are stacked to the rafters. I dread to think what would happen if there was a flood or something.'

'There'd be an awful lot of tea leaves blocking the drains,' said Rose.

Her dad grinned. 'I would say so. This is very nice,' he said, looking at the brooch.

28

'Yes, it is.' Rose took it from him and put it on the mantelpiece. 'I'll just leave it there till Lil gets home so that I can show her.'

Amy smiled at them both. She was always happy when her family were agreeable. If only it could always be like this. But their girls were growing into lovely young women and would soon want to do things their own way. She looked at Rose. She already wanted to do her own thing, but thank goodness tonight she was showing a bit of common sense.

The door burst open. 'Sorry I'm late,' said Lily. She was clutching a lovely bouquet of flowers.

'Don't worry, I thought you might be, so I haven't started to dish up the dinner just yet.'

'Thanks, Mum. D'you like my flowers?'

'They're lovely.'

'Miss Tucker gave me them for me birthday.'

'I'll get a vase. You two girls are very lucky to have such good bosses. Rose, show Lily what you got today,' said Amy, beaming. She felt as though she was overflowing with happiness.

Rose proudly handed over her present.

'This is lovely,' said Lily.

'Happy birthday, little sister.' Rose gave her a hug.

'And a happy birthday to you,' said Lily.

Both were full of anticipation as to what their parents had got them.

'I wish Dad would tell us what he's giving us,' said Rose when she and Lily were sitting outside waiting for their dinner to be dished up. 'He can be so annoying at times.'

'When are you going to tell Mum and Dad that you're staying out all night on Saturday?'

Rose shrugged. Deep down she knew this would start another argument. Why did their father have to be so protective? She was old enough to look after herself. No wonder his sister had gone off with some bloke if he carried on at her like this. 'If it is money, please, Lil, please lend me some, just enough to make up the shortfall.'

'I told you, no. Besides, how do you know how much you'll need?'

'I've seen this lovely frock in Madam Tina's shop.'

'What?'

'Shh. Keep your voice down.'

'Rose, be sensible. All her stuff is ever so expensive.'

'I know. But it's really nice: it's blue and shimmery with a petal hem, and I could wear my beige shoes with it.'

'I said no.'

Rose stood up. 'Thanks, but don't ever ask me for a favour.'

'I won't.' Lily watched her sister walk away. She knew deep down that she would end up giving her some money on Saturday.

While the girls were doing the washing-up after dinner, Rose said, 'Dad's certainly making us wait for our present. I wonder what it'll be.'

'No idea.'

'He don't normally make us hang about for so long.'

'It must be something very special.' Lily put the last plate on the draining board and wiped her hands on the striped roller towel that hung behind the scullery door. Then she took the kettle from the stove and began to make a pot of tea, while Rose put the crocks away and laid the tea things out on a tray. They had been doing this for years. It was part of the evening ritual.

Rose carried the tray into the kitchen and placed it on the table. Then she began to pour the tea.

'Right, girls,' said their father. 'I expect you're wondering what we've got you for your present.'

Rose and Lily sat quietly listening.

'Don't look so worried. I ain't gonna take you to Southend again.'

Rose gave a sigh of relief.

'We thought that on Saturday we would all go up West and have a bite to eat, then go and see that film everyone's talking about. You know, *The Jazz Singer*.'

Lily looked at Rose, who had gone pale.

'So?' said their father, smiling. 'What d'you say?'

'You don't look very pleased about it, Rose,' their mother said.

'It's a bit of a shock.'

'Well I wouldn't call it a shock,' said their father.

'Did you have something else planned for Saturday, Rose?' asked her mother.

Lily gave her sister a withering look.

'No. No I haven't,' Rose said quickly. She knew that if

she told her parents about her arrangements, it would mean more rows, and she wasn't prepared to upset them in case they didn't give her permission to stay out all night in the future.

'I thought it would be a nice change to do something together,' said their father. 'You don't have to come if you don't want to, but me and your mother would like to see this film, and we thought we could use your birthday as an excuse and all go together.'

'I think it's a lovely idea,' said Lily quickly. 'I've heard it's a really spectacular film, and it's got that Al Jolson in it. I've seen pictures of him, he's really handsome, and the talking and singing are supposed to be wonderful.' She was very pleased at the outcome.

'Well that's all right, then,' said their mother.

'It's years since we all went out together,' added Lily.

'I know,' said their father. 'One of these days you won't need us, as I expect you'll be off with your boyfriends soon.'

'Thanks, Dad.' Lily kissed her father's cheek. 'I've got to get one first, though.' Despite her cheerful words,' Lily knew that Rose wouldn't be happy about this.

'What am I going to do?' wailed Rose when the girls were alone in their bedroom.

'You'll just have to tell Nora that you can't go to the party.'

'But I desperately wanted to go.'

'Well then tell Mum and Dad that you're not going out with them.'

'I can't do that.'

'Why not?'

'I just can't, that's all.' Deep down, Rose was shocked about what had happened to her aunt Ann, and she didn't want to upset her dad. Although he was a reasonable man, he was still very old-fashioned and protective of his daughters.

'Well that's that then,' said Lily, putting her book down.

Rose was sitting on her bed clutching her knees. 'Why does everything happen on the same day?'

'Don't ask me.'

'And why did Dad decide he wanted us all to go out together?'

'Rose, I don't know. Look, all you've got to do is tell Mum and Dad that you're going out on Saturday and that you're staying all night with a friend.'

'That would go down well.'

'The choice is yours.'

'Thanks.'

'Well at least if you come out with us, you don't have to worry about getting that new frock.' Lily looked over at her sister and was surprised to see tears trickling down her cheeks. She jumped out of bed and put her arms round her and held her close. 'It's not that bad. Perhaps Nora will be invited to another party and ask you to go with her again.'

Rose sniffed. 'I hope so.'

'Now come on, dry your tears. Remember, it's unlucky to cry on your birthday, as you'll cry all the year round.'

Rose dried her eyes. 'Thanks.'

Lily got back into bed. This little scene had upset her. She hadn't realised that her sister would be so sad at the thought of missing a party. Or was it that she wanted to go out and see a different world? Rose was always the defiant one who liked to have her own way, but it looked as though she was going to back down this time. Lily was sure that her sister would be miserable on Saturday, but she herself was thrilled beyond words. She desperately wanted to see this film that everyone was talking about.

Chapter 5

Rose wasn't looking forward to going to work on Monday, as she knew Nora would be sure to tell her all about the party she hadn't been able to go to.

'Did you all have a nice weekend?' Nora asked the girls as soon as she walked into the office.

'Not bad,' said Betty.

'It's always nice to have a day off to lie in bed and do nothing,' said Molly.

'What about you, Miss Flower?' asked her supervisor.

'It was all right.'

'That doesn't sound too exciting.'

'It was all right,' Rose repeated.

'Where did you go?' asked Betty.

Rose looked at Nora. What could she say? 'Just out with the family.'

'Was it somewhere so exciting you don't want to tell us about it?' asked Molly.

Rose was getting more and more flustered. She knew

she had to tell them. 'We went to see that film *The Jazz Singer*. My dad wanted to see it.'

'Lucky you,' said Betty. 'I wish *my* dad would take me to see it. Was it wonderful? Did they actually talk? Is that Al Jolson really good-looking? And did he sing?'

Nora only raised her eyebrows.

'He's all right,' said Rose. She felt so embarrassed and wished the ground would open and swallow her. How many eighteen-year-olds went to the pictures with their parents?

At lunchtime, Nora came back into the office and said, 'Miss Flower, just a moment before you go off.'

Rose hung back as the others left. 'I'm so sorry I let you down,' she said.

'As I told you on Thursday, it's nothing to worry about. Could you file these invoices?'

Rose had been embarrassed and apologetic when she'd had to tell Nora that she wouldn't be going to the party. 'I really did want to go out with you, but I didn't think my father would be too happy after he had been looking forward to taking us out for our birthday.'

'As I said, don't worry about it.'

'I don't suppose you'll ever ask me again.'

'Don't be silly, of course I will, just as soon as we have another party. We have this little group who just love to enjoy themselves, and they like new blood. A lot of the fellas were very disappointed when I told them you wouldn't be coming.'

Rose smiled. 'You told them about me?'

'Yes. So don't worry, I'll let you know when we have another.' She patted Rose's cheek and left the room.

Rose stood for a while just grinning. Nora was going to ask her out again, and she had told her friends about her. This time Rose wouldn't let her down, and she would save up for that frock she'd seen in Madam Tina's.

Rose was very happy when she got home that evening.

'Who's put a smile on your face tonight?' asked Lily while they were washing up.

Rose twirled round the scullery. 'I had nothing to worry about; Nora said she would ask me again to one of their parties. It seems they have a quite a few.'

'So there you are then, all those tears and sulks were totally unnecessary.'

Rose didn't answer and instead got on with drying the dishes.

'Did she say how often they have these little shindigs?'

'No.'

'Could be pretty boring standing around talking to the same people all the time.'

'Oh I don't know. She did say they like new blood now and again.'

'Did she now. I don't like the sound of that, makes you sound like a lamb to the slaughter.'

'Trust you to think of something like that.'

'I was just saying, that's all.' But Lily was worried about her sister. What was it about Rose that Nora was so interested in? And what sort of parties were they? She wiped her hands on the towel that hung behind the door and began to make the tea. Was she reading too many novels? Lily couldn't help feeling protective of her sister.

As the weeks went by, Rose started to worry. Although Nora spoke to her in the office about work, she hadn't asked her out to lunch again. When they were washing up, Rose told Lily that she thought Nora didn't want to invite her to another party.

'What shall I do about that frock it if she don't ask me out again?'

'I don't know. Will you get your deposit back?'

'I don't think so.'

'Rose, you shouldn't put too much into all of this.'

'I can't help it. I want to go with her so much.'

'So that expensive frock that's hanging in Madam Tina's could be a big waste of money?'

'Don't say that. I'd just love to see how the other half lives. Besides, if I am asked to another party, then I shall be ready for it.'

Lily laughed. 'Honestly, you are a one. You never give up, do you?'

'Not where my dreams and hopes are concerned.'

It wasn't till the beginning of summer that Nora took Rose out to lunch.

'Are you doing anything on Saturday?' she asked.

'No.' Rose was almost quivering with excitement. Was

this it? Was she going to be invited to another party?

'Would you like to come shopping with me when we finish at lunchtime? I need a few things and I always like someone else's opinion.'

Although it wasn't the invite Rose was hoping for, she was still over the moon. She was going shopping with Nora. Was this the first step to greater things?

On Saturday lunchtime, when the office closed, Nora and Rose caught a bus and made their way to the West End. They wandered round the shops and Rose stood wide-eyed as Nora bought some very expensive items, including a pair of beige shoes and a beige hat that cost five and eleven. When she came out of the changing room in a beautiful green silk frock that had insert panels of satin from the waist, Rose gasped.

'That is so lovely, and it's a perfect fit.'

The shop assistant was hovering round. 'It really suits you, madam.'

'It does feel rather nice.' Nora twirled in front of the mirror. 'Yes, I'll take it.'

Rose couldn't believe that anyone would pay four guineas for a frock. It made the one she had been paying off for in Madam Tina's look very cheap, although that was twenty-one shillings, which was more than two weeks' wages.

When they came out of the shop, Nora said, 'We can get something in Lyons before we go our separate ways.'

Although Rose was hoping that she would be invited to another party, at the moment she was more worried that she was going to have to pay half the bill, and she prayed that it wouldn't be too expensive. Luckily she had been paid this morning, but she just hoped that she would have enough left to give her mother. She was relieved when Nora said she only wanted a snack.

When they'd finished their tea and sandwich, Rose sat fascinated as she watched Nora take a gold cigarette case and a long tortoise cigarette holder from her handbag.

'Would you like one?' Nora said, offering the case to Rose.

'No thank you.' Rose realised she must have been staring.

After lighting her cigarette with a gold lighter, Nora smiled. 'A present from an admirer,' she said breezily. Then she sat back and puffed smoke into the air. Everything about her looked expensive and confident; how Rose would love to behave like her.

'Now,' said Nora, leaning forward, 'I was wondering if you would like to come out with us one day.'

Rose was thrilled. 'Yes. Yes, I'd love to.'

'We shall be going to Brighton in James's car one Sunday. Would that be all right with you? Your father wouldn't mind, would he?'

'No. Not at all.' Rose couldn't believe her luck. She was going out with Nora for a whole day.

When Lily arrived home, she could see that Rose was very happy and had had a good afternoon. She was full of what Nora had bought. Lily, who had been on her feet all day, was very tired, and as soon as they had finished their cups of tea she went upstairs to bed.

She was just dozing off when Rose came into the room. 'I must tell you about this afternoon.'

'I thought you had,' said Lily.

'Only about the clothes Nora bought. Not the best bit.' Rose sat on the bed and began to tell her sister all that had happened. 'And one Sunday she could be taking me to Brighton for the day.'

'That's nice,' said Lily half-heartedly.

'With her boyfriend in his car.'

'That's nice,' said Lily again.

'Are you listening to me?'

'Yes.'

'I might meet one of her rich friends and he might whisk me away.'

'Is that what you want?'

'I want to be like Nora.'

'Is that all that woman thinks of, having a good time?'

'Yes. And I want to be part of it.'

'She must have had a very sad life.'

'Could be that it might have made her into a bit of a rebel.'

'Is that what you want to be, a bit of a rebel?'

'I wouldn't mind.'

'Don't let Dad hear you talk like that.'

'Dad's too old-fashioned.'

'Rose. Can you please be a rebel tomorrow? I feel very tired.' Lily turned over.

Rose sat and thought about her afternoon. She grinned to herself. Yes, she did want to be like Nora, and if one of her rich, good-looking young men friends took a fancy to her, she would be willing to go along with almost anything he asked, and to hell with the consequences. She just wanted to be part of that kind of life.

Chapter 6

O N MONDAY MORNING, Lily had her head down carefully arranging a table decoration when a young man behind her coughed, making her jump.

'I'm so sorry,' he said. 'I didn't mean to startle you.'

Lily straightened up and smiled. 'That's all right. It's just that I get so carried away when I'm arranging the flowers. Can I help you?'

'That's very beautiful,' he said, pointing at the decoration.

'Thank you.'

'You obviously enjoy what you are doing.'

'Yes, I do.' She wiped her hands down the sides of her overall. 'Did you want anything in particular?'

He looked round nervously. 'I'd like something for a lady.'

'Are there any special flowers or colours she likes?'

'I don't think so.'

Lily smiled. He looked so anxious. She walked over

to a display of carnations. 'I can do you a bouquet of these.'

'That would be very nice. Thank you.'

Lily began to take blooms from the container and carefully arranged them with some foliage. She looked at the young man. 'Is this all right?'

'They look wonderful. Thank you.'

Lily wrapped them and handed them to him.

'Thank you,' he said again as he paid Miss Tucker, who was busy with the display behind the cash desk.

'What a pleasant young man,' said Miss Tucker after he had left the shop.

'Yes, he was. I wonder who the lucky girl is who will be receiving those.'

'If they work for him and the answer is yes, who knows, we might be asked to do their wedding bouquet next.'

Lily laughed. It wasn't often that she wondered about their customers, but there was something about the young man that had touched her; he seemed so shy. It was probably the thought of having to walk home carrying a bunch of flowers that was worrying him, she decided.

Rose came home from work that day looking very happy.

'Mum,' she said, bursting into the kitchen, 'Nora has asked me to go with her and her friend to Brighton for the day on Sunday.'

'That'll be nice.'

Rose felt a little deflated; she'd been hoping for a

better response than that. 'I'm going in her boyfriend's car.'

'That's nice,' came the reply.

Rose went outside and sat on the seat under the scullery window, her thoughts turning to what she should wear. It wasn't long before Lily came out and sat next to her.

'And what sort of day have you had?' she asked her sister. She was pleased to see that Rose had wiped off some of her make-up. That must mean she was going to ask her father a favour.

'Wonderful. I'm going to Brighton next Sunday with Nora, in her friend James's car.'

'That'll be nice. Will she bring a friend for you?'

'She said that a bloke called Roger will be coming as well. Now my trouble is what to wear.'

'D'you know, Rose, you can be a right pain at times. Does it matter what you wear?'

'Of course it does. I want to make a good impression.'

'Why?'

'He could be my future husband.'

Lily burst out laughing.

'What's so funny?'

'You.'

'If he's got money and is good-looking, then I shall make a play for him.'

'Rose, be careful.'

Her sister stood up. 'Time will tell.'

Lily watched her walk away. She was worried about

Rose. She knew how desperate she was to find a rich man, but at what price?

It was Friday evening and almost closing time when the bell over the door tinkled and a customer came into the shop.

'Hello,' said Lily with a smile when she recognised the shy young man. 'Did your young lady like her flowers?'

'Young lady?' said the man who had bought the carnations. He looked surprised.

'I'm sorry, I shouldn't be so inquisitive, but Miss Tucker does like the customers to be satisfied.'

'Yes. Yes. She was very happy with them.'

'That's good. Now what can I get you today?'

He glanced round the shop. Miss Tucker was serving someone. 'What about those?' He pointed to a container of red roses.

'Yes. How many would you like?'

'Just one, I think. Would that be all right?'

Lily smiled again. 'It's whatever you want.' She took a rose and carefully wrapped it. 'Be careful of the thorns.'

She was still smiling when the man left the shop. There was something about him that she couldn't help liking.

It was a lovely evening when Lily finished work for the day, and as she walked along, she heard someone behind her call her name.

'Miss Flower.'

She stopped, and was surprised to see the young man with the rose coming towards her.

'Miss Flower,' he said again, raising his brown trilby. 'I hope you don't mind, but I have been trying hard to think of a way to talk to you.'

Lily smiled. 'You could have talked to me in the shop.'

'This is personal.'

Lily was alarmed. 'Were the flowers a mistake?'

'Sorry?'

'The flowers, didn't your young lady like them?'

He laughed. 'They weren't for a young lady, they were for my mother.'

'Oh,' said Lily, feeling a little foolish.

'Sorry,' he said, 'I'm not making myself very clear. You see, I wanted to talk to you. I have been admiring you for weeks. Every time I pass the shop, you always seem to be smiling. You appear to be a very happy person.'

Lily looked away quickly. She was feeling very self-conscious.

'Now I've embarrassed you. Please, take this as a peace offering.' He held out the rose.

'I can't take that. You bought it for your . . .' She hesitated. 'Your mother.'

'Now *I'm* feeling embarrassed. You see, I bought it for you. I just wanted to give you something. I'm afraid it's not very original.'

'You didn't have to do that. You could just talk to me.'

'Could I?'

'Of course.'

'Could I walk with you for a bit?'

'If it's not out of your way.'

'Do you live far?' he asked.

'Not really. I can get the bus, but I prefer to walk. It helps clear my head. Sometimes the perfume from the flowers can be a little overpowering.'

'Yes, I suppose it might be.'

The conversation was very inconsequential and Lily didn't know quite what to make of him.

'Miss Flower.'

'Please, call me Lily out of the shop.'

He smiled. 'Lily Flower. What a lovely name. Your parents must have enjoyed giving you a name like that.'

'I'm a twin and my sister's name is Rose.'

'A twin? Does she look like you? Are you identical?'

'Not to us, though at one time people would always get us muddled up. Now that we're older, we dress differently.'

'Lily, I'm not normally the sort of person who does this, but would you care to come out with me one evening?'

Lily stopped. 'Why, thank you.'

'I should have asked first, but do you have a boyfriend? Sorry, that's really none of my business. I'm not making a very good job of this, am I?'

Lily smiled. She could see this man was so very nervous. 'I don't have a boyfriend and I would love to come out with you, thank you.'

His face was beaming. 'When?'

'I don't know. What night would suit you?' Suddenly Lily was concerned. Was she being perhaps too eager to accept?

'Tomorrow. I know you work, but I could pick you up from the shop and perhaps we could have a bite to eat and then go on to the music hall.'

The thought of going to the music hall made her cast aside her anxiety. 'That would be wonderful.'

'Would it? Would it really?'

'Yes. And thank you.'

'By the way, my name is Harry, Harry Thompson.'

Lily held out her hand. 'Pleased to meet you, Harry.'

They walked quite a way, and Lily found Harry pleasant to talk to. He told her that he worked in an office just round the corner from the shop, and that he lived with his widowed mother and had an older married sister. When they were almost at Enfield Road, Lily asked him where he lived.

'Wood Street. Not that there's any woods round there.'

'But that's in the other direction to the shop.'

He only smiled.

'Your mother will be wondering where you've got to.'

'I told her I might be a little late. Besides, I am old enough to do as I please.'

Lily looked embarrassed. 'I'm sorry.'

'You didn't mind my walking with you, did you?'

'No. Not at all.' Lily knew that he would almost have to retrace his steps to get home.

He took her hand. 'I will see you tomorrow.'

'Yes. And thank you for my rose.'

'Perhaps it should have been a lily.'

Lily smiled and walked away. When she turned the

corner, she couldn't resist turning round. Harry was still watching her, and he waved. She waved back and grinned. He was rather nice, and she was looking forward to tomorrow.

When Lily arrived home, she said to her mother, 'Don't do any dinner for me tomorrow night. I'm going out.'

Rose looked up from the magazine she was reading. 'You look flushed. Who are you going out with? Did he give you that?' She pointed to the rose her sister was holding.

'Rose, don't be so nosy,' said their mother.

Lily's cheeks were red. 'He's a customer. Mr Harry Thompson.'

Her father looked over his newspaper.

Rose laughed. 'A customer who gave you a rose from your own shop? Is he some doddering old boy who wants to take a pretty young girl out?'

'He's not old and he's not doddery.' Lily was annoyed with her sister. Why couldn't she just be nice about it? After all, this was the first time Lily would be going out with a young man.

'Where you going?' asked her father.

'We're going for a bite to eat, then on to the music hall.'

'That'll be nice,' said her mother.

'I don't know what time I shall be home.'

'Well make sure it's a respectable time,' said her father. 'And no hanging about on street corners.'

'Dad, I'm only going to the music hall.'

'What do you know about him?'

'I told you, he's a customer.' Lily was getting cross with all these questions and looked at her mother.

'Don't worry about it,' said Amy. 'You go and enjoy yourself.'

'Thanks.' Lily looked at her sister. Rose would be out all day Sunday, but what time would she be home and who would she be with?

That evening, Lily was sitting up in bed hugging her knees and watching her sister remove her make-up.

'So,' said Rose. 'What's this man like?'

'He's quite tall, with brown hair, though I'm not sure what colour his eyes are. He's shy but he seems nice.'

'Is that it?'

'I know he's got an older married sister and his mother is a widow. What else do you want to know?'

'Where does he work?'

'In an office not far from the shop.'

Rose laughed.

'What's so funny?'

'You.'

'Why?'

'It sounds like you've known him for years. Not just a walk home.'

'It's just that he's so pleasant to talk to.'

Rose got into bed. 'I bet I have more to say about Roger on Sunday night.'

'I bet you do,' said Lily as she slid under the bedclothes. 'Rose, be careful. Look how Dad wanted to know all about Harry.'

Rose smiled. She knew that if Roger was good-looking, she would make a play for him, especially if he was rich, and her father could think what he liked.

Chapter 7

'MISS TUCKER, I hope you don't mind, but I am going out with Mr Thompson tonight,' said Lily when she arrived at the shop the following morning.

'My dear Lily, why should I mind? What you do in your own time is up to you.'

'But he's a customer. You know, the one who's very polite and who bought the carnations and the rose.'

Miss Tucker stopped what she was doing and smiled at Lily. 'Well, he seems a very nice polite young man.'

Lily was relieved. She didn't want Miss Tucker to disapprove. 'He's taking me to the music hall.'

'I've heard they have some very good turns there. I'm sure you're going to have a lovely time.'

All day Lily was in a happy mood and looking forward to the evening. She began to think about the questions Rose had asked last night when they were in bed. She had told her sister everything she knew about Harry Thompson.

'Sounds a bit boring to me,' Rose had said. 'And you

say he first came into the shop to buy flowers for his mother? Is he a mummy's boy?'

'I don't think so.' In the dark Lily had given a little smile. She knew that before long she would know a lot more about him.

'Well throw him over if he's a bore.'

Lily ignored that remark. Harry Thompson seemed, to be a kind, nice person, and that was what mattered to her.

It was late afternoon and almost closing time, and Lily could see Harry waiting outside the shop. She didn't want to ask him in, as Miss Tucker might not approve. She had finished the tidying up when her boss said to her:

'Lily, you can go now if you like. I can see your young man is waiting.'

Lily blushed 'Thank you.'

'Have a lovely evening,' said Miss Tucker when Lily came out of the staff room with her hat and coat on.

'Thank you.'

When she opened the door, Harry smiled. 'Are we all set?'

'Yes.'

He offered his arm and Lily took hold of it.

As they walked along, he said, 'Would you like to go to Lyons for something to eat first?'

'Thank you. That would be very nice.'

First they talked about the weather, and then Lily asked him about his mother and sister.

'Mother doesn't get out very much, but she loves

company and has many friends. And she loves it when Pat, that's my sister, comes round with her children. She has a boy, David, who's three, and a baby girl they have named after our mother, Jean. Mother loves them, although David can be a bit boisterous at times.'

Lily was warming to Harry; he seemed such a pleasant person, and he made sure he always walked on the outside of the pavement. He had very good manners. Would Rose approve of him? Was he too quiet and polite for her taste? Lily decided she wouldn't concern herself with what Rose thought; she was just going to enjoy his company.

After they had finished their egg and chips, Harry looked at his watch.

'I think we should be making our way to the theatre.'

'Of course.' Lily looked around. 'I must go and powder my nose. I won't be long.'

They left the Corner House and made their way to the theatre. Lily was really excited and very impressed when Harry said the seats were booked so they didn't have to stand in line.

They watched jugglers, laughed at the comedians, admired the dancing girls and enjoyed a host of acts that quickly followed one another. During the interval they went into the foyer.

'Would you like something to drink?' asked Harry.

'I wouldn't mind a lemonade, if that's all right.'

'Is that all?'

'Yes thank you.'

'Find a seat and I'll bring one over for you.'

'Thank you.'

Lily sat at a table and looked round at the ornate surroundings. The painted ceiling and the heavy chandeliers were very grand. Harry returned with the drinks and a box of chocolates.

'Thank you. This is very kind of you,' said Lily.

'It's so nice of you to come out with me. I must confess I don't go out very much.'

'Nether do I. I once went out with my sister to a tea dance, but we don't do that as often as Rose would like.'

'I can't dance.'

'I'm not very good. Rose can do all the latest dances.'

Harry just smiled. 'When you've finished your drink, we can make our way back to our seats, but please don't hurry, there's plenty of time.'

'Thank you so much for the chocolates, and for tonight.'

'We must do it again sometime.'

'I'd like that.' Lily felt a lovely glow.

At the end of the evening, Harry took Lily to her gate.

'Thank you for a lovely evening,' she said again.

Harry quickly kissed her cheek and walked away.

Lily stood watching him. When he stopped at the corner and waved, she waved back and waited till he disappeared from sight. Then she smiled to herself and touched her cheek.

Pushing open the kitchen door, she was surprised to see that the family were still up, waiting for her.

'Did you have a nice time?' asked her mother.

'It was lovely. Dad, you would love the music hall. All the acts and the colours. It was wonderful. We must all go together one evening.' She noticed Rose giving her a withering look at that statement.

Ron folded his newspaper and said, 'Well, come on, I want to hear all about it.'

Lily told him about the various acts she'd seen.

'And what was *he* like?' asked Rose.

Lily glanced at her mother. 'He was a perfect gentleman. He bought me a box of chocolates.'

'So he should,' said her father, grinning. 'I always gave your mother chocolates when I took her out.'

Amy smiled. 'Even if occasionally it was only a very small bar.'

'Sometimes that was all I could afford, but the thought was there.'

'I know, love.' Amy stood up. 'Who would like a cup of tea?'

'I would,' said Lily and Rose together.

'And me,' said Ron.

As Amy passed his chair, she touched his cheek. 'And I loved the chocolate.'

'I thought Dad would be more interested in Harry than that,' said Lily, who knew that once they were in bed Rose would be firing all manner of questions at her.

'So. Did he kiss you good night?' asked Rose, ignoring her remark.

'No.'

'Why not?'

'I didn't want him to.'

'Oh Lil. You're never gonna get a husband if you don't put yourself out.'

'I don't want a husband.'

'Of course you do. You don't want to be an old maid all your life, do you?'

'Rose, we're only eighteen. We've got plenty of time.'

'Well I want to get a husband quick.'

'Why?'

'So that I can lead my own life and not have Dad keep telling me what I can and can't do.'

'What if babies come along? You'll have to settle down then.'

'I don't want babies. I can't think of anything worse than changing and washing dirty nappies.'

Lily smiled to herself. We shall see, she thought.

'Who knows, after tomorrow, things might be very different.'

Lily sat up. 'Rose. Promise me you won't do anything silly.'

'Like what?'

'I don't know. Run off with this what's-his-name.'

'Do you mean Roger?'

'Yes.'

'Of course I won't run off with him.'

'What time will he be here tomorrow?'

'He's not coming here.'

'Why not?' Lily looked across at Rose. 'Where you meeting him?'

'At the office.'

'Why can't he come here?'

'Nora will be with him.'

'So?'

'I just thought it would be better to meet them at the office.'

'Are you ashamed of us?'

'No. No, of course not. It's just that people might think I'm showing off if a car came here.'

'I thought that was what you wanted.'

Rose turned over. She didn't want to say any more. She *was* ashamed of where she lived, but she would never tell her sister that.

Lily lay quietly. She guessed her sister didn't want Nora to see where she lived. Well, if she was going to go out a lot with this crowd, they'd have to find out one day that she lived in Enfield Road.

Chapter 8

WHEN LILY OPENED her eyes, she could hear Rose moving about. The sun was streaming through the curtains and it looked like a lovely morning. 'You've got a nice day for your trip,' she said in a sleepy voice.

'Oh Lil,' said Rose, putting her hand to her chest. 'You frightened the life out of me.'

'Why? What you up to?'

'Nothing. I was just trying to work out what to wear.'

'I thought you did all that last night.'

'I did, but now the sun's shining I'll have to have a rethink.'

Lily sat up. There were clothes all over Rose's bed.

'What do you think? Should I wear this hat or this one?'

'What coat are you going to wear?'

'My grey one.'

'Well wear the black hat, then.'

'It might blow off.'

'Is it an open car?'

'I don't know.'

Lily lay back down. How could such a simple thing like going out in a car cause so much fuss?

Rose still hadn't made up her mind what hat and coat to wear when they went downstairs for breakfast.

'What time you off then, love?' asked her mother.

'As soon as I'm ready.'

'They could at least have picked you up here instead of making you go all the way to the office,' said her mother.

'It's all right, I don't mind. I just thought it would be a lot easier this way; they might have had a job finding us.'

'Don't be too late home,' said her father.

As she walked out to the lav, Rose screwed up her nose and poked her tongue out.

After breakfast, she came downstairs wearing her grey coat and black hat and a lot of make-up. Her father just looked at her.

Lily was waiting for her at the front door. 'Have a good time.'

'I will.'

Lily watched her sister as she went out of the gate. What sort of day would she have?

Rose was very excited as she made her way to the office. She arrived early, but she didn't care, she was going out with Nora and her friends.

When a car finally arrived, she looked eagerly at the driver and his male passenger, who both gave her a smile. The passenger quickly jumped out and held the car door open for her. Rose could have died with pleasure when he took her hand and kissed it. She smiled sweetly and said, 'Thank you.'

'My pleasure, I'm sure.' With his slicked-back dark hair, brown eyes and thin pencil moustache, he was the most good-looking fella she had ever seen. She climbed in the back and sat next to Nora.

'James, this is Rose,' said Nora, who was looking lovely in a navy hat and coat.

'Hello there, Rose,' said James, who was the driver. Rose could see that he had a mop of brown hair pushed under a check cap. He too had a moustache, but his was thick and bushy. He had a very pleasant voice; not too upper-crust. She was worried about her London accent. She didn't speak as nicely as Nora.

'And I'm Roger,' said the other man, turning and giving Rose a smile. It was a good thing she was sitting down, as her knees had turned to jelly.

'Don't be fooled by Roger's good looks and smarmy ways,' said Nora, as if reading her mind. 'He breaks all the girls' hearts.'

'Only those who are silly enough to fall for me.'

'Right. If everybody's ready, we'll make our way down to jolly old Brighton,' said James.

The car was full of cigarette smoke and laughter as Nora and her friends reminisced about the last time they'd been out together. Rose was a little worried that Roger talked about some of his lady friends in such a mean way. Would he talk about her like that when they all went out again with a different girl? She remembered what Lily had said about being a lamb to the slaughter. Was that how they regarded people who joined their little group?

'You're very quiet,' said Nora.

'I'm just listening to all the good times you seem to have.'

Roger turned round. 'My dear Rose, how very rude of us to leave you out of the conversation. I do apologise. Now tell us all about yourself.'

'Not a lot to tell really. I live with my parents and work in Nora's office.'

'Rose's father does like to keep her under control,' said Nora.

Rose wanted to die. She had never felt so embarrassed.

Roger laughed. 'So do we have a rebel on our hands?'

Although she was upset, she knew that she had to stand up for herself. 'I could be, with the right people and in the right circumstances,' she said defiantly.

'I love a rebel,' said Roger. 'I think we could get on very well.' He gave her another wide smile.

For Rose, the journey to Brighton was intriguing. They talked about the parties they'd been to, and Roger asked Rose if she ever went anywhere exciting.

'Not really.'

'Rose was coming to Archie's party that weekend, but she had to go out with her family,' said Nora.

'That's a bit of a shame. You would have loved it. All sorts of interesting people go to Archie's,' said Roger.

'Perhaps I could come to the next party. Nora said that you have quite a few.'

'Yes, we do.'

Rose knew she was being a bit pushy, but she didn't care. She wasn't going to miss the opportunity of mixing with these people.

'I don't know when the next one will be, but you can take my word for it, when there is one, you shall come as my special guest,' said Roger.

'Thank you. I'd like that.' Rose thought about the dress waiting for her in Madam Tina's, and smiled to herself. So it wouldn't be wasted after all.

After about an hour they stopped at a pub. Rose was pleased to get out in the fresh air.

'How about a gin and tonic, Nora old girl?' asked James.

'That would be wonderful,' she said, smiling. 'He knows my little weakness,' she added to Rose.

'How about you, Rose?' he asked.

'I don't know.' She suddenly felt out of her depth. What would her father say about drinking in the morning? What should she ask for? How could she have thought she could fit in with this crowd?

'How about a port and lemon?' offered James, smiling. Rose could see he was trying to put her at her ease.

To go out with Nora was something she had wished for, so now she had to go along with them. After all, she had told them she wanted to be a rebel. 'That sounds lovely. Thank you.'

Roger came over with her drink. 'Are you all right?'

'Yes thank you. Why?'

'You seem rather shy.'

Rose looked across at Nora and James, who were laughing loudly.

'Don't worry about them. They always carry on like this.'

'And does the same go for you?'

'I can be very different if I'm with someone who is rather nice.'

Rose smiled. Her cheeks were flushed and she suddenly felt very happy.

When they had finished their drinks they were on their way again, and it wasn't long before they were driving along Brighton's promenade.

'Where shall I stop?' asked James.

'Anywhere,' said Roger. Turning to Nora, he asked, 'You going for a swim?'

'No. I haven't brought my swimwear. Look at those gorgeous beach pyjamas. I must get some of those.'

'Look at the gorgeous girls that are in them,' said Roger.

Rose was also looking at the beach pyjamas. She would like some of those too.

They got some fish and chips, which they took on to the beach, then spent the afternoon sitting in deckchairs and generally playing about. Roger chased them with wet seaweed and tried to get Rose in the sea.

'Stop it!' she yelled. 'I don't want to get my shoes wet.'

'Sorry,' he said, coming up to her, then, holding her close and in full view of everyone, kissed her long and hard.

When they broke apart, Rose felt very embarrassed. She quickly sat down next to Nora.

'Don't worry about Roger,' said Nora. 'He just likes women. Right, James and I are off for a walk.'

Rose went to stand up, but Roger sat next to her and took her hand. She didn't know whether she was pleased or annoyed. She liked him. He didn't seem to care what anyone thought of him.

He put his arm round her shoulders. 'I'm sorry if I've offended you.'

Rose tried to move away.

'No, please don't go. I like you, you seem to enjoy life.'

'My life is very dull, I'm afraid.'

'Well we will have to change all that, won't we?'

When he took her hand and gently kissed her again, she felt a thrill. He could make her life exciting and she mustn't let it pass.

It wasn't till they were on their way home that Rose began to worry about them finding out where she lived. 'Look, James, you can leave me at the office,' she said nervously.

'I shall do no such thing. Now, where do you live?'

'I've had a wonderful day, thank you, but honestly, I'm quite happy to be dropped off.'

'Rose, please let James take you home, then I shall know where to pick you up when I come calling.'

She was thrilled. Roger wanted to see her again. But she began to panic as they drove along Rotherhithe New Road. What could she do? Were there any nice large houses round here? She suddenly thought of the church a bit further up that had a very nice house next to it. 'If you must take me home, you can drop me at the church.'

'You don't live there, do you?' asked Nora.

Rose gave a quick nod.

When James stopped the car, he gave a long whistle. 'So this is where you live?'

Rose crossed her fingers and gave him a weak smile.

'Is your father a vicar?' asked Nora.

'Not exactly.'

'So is he higher than that? I don't know what they're called.'

Rose could see that Nora was intrigued. 'No. No, not at all.'

'But you live here?'

'He works for the vicar. Not in a religious way, more of a handyman.'

'No wonder he doesn't like you wearing make-up; some of that godly stuff must rub off.'

Before Rose could get out of the car, Roger had hurried to hold the door open for her.

'Can I come calling?' he asked, taking her hand.

'Not to the house.'

'Look, I'll let Nora know when we can meet up again. And I hope it will be soon.' He went to kiss her, but Rose stepped back. 'Sorry,' he said. 'I suppose we shouldn't do that sort of thing in front of the church.'

Rose smiled. 'Thank you all for a lovely day. See you in the office tomorrow, Nora.' She turned and walked up the path. Near the house she waved, and waited for them to drive away, then hurried round the back of the church.

She waited a few minutes, terrified that someone would come out and ask her what she wanted. When she was sure the car was out of sight, she began to walk home. How was she going to get out of this if Roger insisted on meeting her or taking her home one day?

Chapter 9

Rose opened the kitchen door very quietly. Although it wasn't that late, it was past the time when the family usually went to bed, so she was very surprised to see that they were all still up.

'Did you have a good time?' asked Lily when her sister walked in.

'Yes I did,' she said as she looked in the mirror and took off her hat; she had already removed most of her lipstick.

'So what car has he got?' asked her father, folding his newspaper.

'I don't know.'

'Should have given us a knock. I would have loved to see it.'

'Ron, shut up, you'll embarrass the poor girl.'

Lily knew that nothing would embarrass her sister. So why didn't she show her friends off?

'Have you had something to eat?' asked her mother.

'Yes thanks.'

'What was Brighton like?' asked Lily.

'Stony but very nice, and you should see all the fashionable women walking along the prom. A lot of 'em was wearing these new beach pyjamas that are all the rage.'

'What was Nora's young man like?' asked her sister, ignoring the remark about the fashions.

'Very nice.'

'So did she bring a bloke along for you?'

'Lily, don't be so nosy,' said her mother.

'Well I want to know who might have captured my sister's heart.'

Ron Flower stood up. 'D'you know, you girls talk a load of rubbish sometimes. You read too many silly books, if you ask me. Captured her heart indeed. She should wait a few more years before someone does that, and he'd better be a decent young man who lives round here, and not some fly-by-night with a posh car.'

Rose ignored that remark and sat at the table next to her sister. 'If you must know, he was very polite and nice.'

'Good-looking?' asked Lily.

'Lily,' said her mother sternly.

'Well yes, he was, in a Douglas Fairbanks sort of way.'

'I can't wait to see him. Are you going out with him again?'

'I don't know. We didn't make any arrangements.'

'Shame.' Lily noticed her mother giving her a look telling her to be quiet. 'Right, I'm off to bed,' she said.

'I'll be up soon,' said her sister. 'I'll just have a cup of tea first.'

'Good night,' said Lily. She knew there would be a lot more to talk about when they were alone.

As soon as Rose walked into the bedroom, Lily sat up.

'Well, come on, tell me all about him.'

'He's good-looking and I think he has a bit of money. And I don't think he's got a girlfriend at the moment.'

'What d'you mean, "at the moment"?'

'Well he didn't talk about one, and anyway, if he'd had one he would have taken *her* to Brighton.'

'Suppose so. Is he very old?'

'Not really.'

'About how old?'

'Late twenties, thirties. It's hard to tell.'

'So when are you seeing him again?'

'I don't know.'

'Will he come knocking?'

Rose sat at the dressing table. 'I don't think so.'

'Oh no. What did you say to him?'

'Nothing. He does want to see me again but he don't know where I live.'

'They brought you home, didn't they?'

'No.'

'That was a bit rotten. Where did they drop you?'

'At the vicarage.'

Lily began to laugh. 'Why?'

'They think I live there.'

'Oh Rose. You didn't tell him Dad was the vicar?'

'No, I said he worked for the vicar.'

'I don't believe you sometimes.'

'Well I couldn't let them see that I live in a dirty terraced house, now could I?'

'Don't you let Mum or Dad hear you say that.'

Rose began to get undressed. 'All these questions.'

'It's no more than I got when I went out with Harry. At least I let him bring me home. What if he goes to the vicarage to pick you up?'

'He won't do that as he knows Dad don't approve.'

'You can say that again. But how will he know how to get in touch with you?'

'He'll let Nora know.'

'You've got it all worked out, then?'

'I hope so.'

Lily lay back down and began to wonder what her sister was getting herself into.

Rose was also thinking as she lay down. Today had been very exciting. Roger had kissed her and she'd liked it. Everything about him was class and she knew she wanted to see him again. She would have to tell Nora that she liked him and try to find out more about him. If she could go to lunch with Nora tomorrow, it could be very interesting.

The following morning Rose was up and bustling about.

'You sound happy,' said Lily, opening her eyes.

'I can't wait to get to work to find out what Roger thought of me.'

Lily got out of bed. 'What are you going to tell Nora about where you live?'

'I'm just going to let her think we live in a cottage behind the vicarage. I'll tell her you can't see it from the road.'

Lily burst out laughing. 'There is no cottage behind the vicarage. You should know that. We used to play round the back of it enough times.'

'I know that and you know that, but Nora don't.'

'Well I'd certainly give you full marks for sorting things round to your way of thinking.'

'If you're going to map out your future for yourself, you've got to think about it. Coming down for breakfast?'

'I will when I'm dressed.' Lily sat on the bed. Would her sister ever really be satisfied with her life? And would she make the right decisions?

When Nora walked into the office, she gave Rose a beaming smile. After sorting out the day's work, she said quietly, 'Perhaps we could have lunch together.'

'I'd like that. And thank you so much for yesterday.'

Nora just gave a nod and walked to her office.

Rose was worried. Was something wrong? What had Roger said?

'You all right?' asked Betty. 'You've gone ever so pale.'

'I'm fine, thanks.'

'Why didn't you tell me your father worked for the church?' said Nora when they were in the local café.

'I didn't like to.'

'Now I understand why he doesn't like you wearing make-up, and I know the clergy don't like us wearing these new shorter skirts.' Nora laughed. 'Do they honestly think that the length of our skirts is going to stop a man doing what he wants?'

Rose gave her a weak smile.

Nora patted her hand. 'Now come on, cheer up. Did you enjoy yourself yesterday?'

'It was wonderful. Thank you so much. And I think your James is very nice.'

'What about Roger?'

Rose blushed and looked down. 'I think he's very nice too.'

'That's good, because he thought you were great and he wants to see you again.'

'He does? When?'

'He was wondering about one Saturday. He said he could meet you here at the office at lunchtime, then take you for a meal and perhaps to a dance.'

Rose could hardly contain her excitement. 'That would be wonderful.'

'Now come on, back to work.'

Rose felt as if the world was her oyster. She couldn't wait to tell Lily.

Lily could see that her sister had a glow about her when she walked into the kitchen. 'You look happy. Had a good day?' she asked Rose.

'Not bad.'

To Lily, that meant something good that Rose couldn't say in front of their parents.

After they'd finished their meal and were making the tea, Lily shut the scullery door and said, 'Well come on. What is it?'

'It's Roger. He wants to see me again and he's meeting me after work one Saturday and taking me for a meal and then in the evening we might go to a dance.' It was said all in one breath.

'How are you going to manage that?'

'What d'you mean?'

'How are you going to change into a frock to go dancing in?'

'I don't know. He might take me back to his place.'

'I see,' said Lily.'

'Oh don't go and spoil it. You make it sound all nasty.'

'I'm sorry, but you know me, I've got a very suspicious mind.'

Rose didn't answer. She too had wondered about that, but it wasn't going to stop her from seeing Roger again. Perhaps Nora would have some answers. If she was going along with James, perhaps Rose could go to her flat to get changed.

Lily was also happy, as she was going to see Harry on Sunday afternoon. They were just going for a walk round the park, though. So different from her sister.

Chapter 10

AFTER THEIR SUNDAY afternoon together, Lily was disappointed when weeks passed and she didn't hear from Harry. She'd thought they'd been getting on so well. Had she done something to upset him?

At the same time, Rose was also concerned that Nora hadn't said any more about Roger taking her out.

'I reckon we're destined to be a couple of old maids,' she said one Sunday as she was getting into bed. She and Lily had been discussing their love lives, or rather the lack of them.

'I think we've got a few years left yet before we have to start worrying about being old maids.'

'It could creep up on you before you know it.'

'Rose, don't talk such a load of rubbish.'

'I would have thought Harry would have been past the shop. After all, you said he only works round the corner.'

'I know. I hope he's all right.'

'Do you know where he lives?'

Lily shook her head.

'I'm going to ask Nora tomorrow if Roger's been put off by my father working at the church.'

Lily grinned. 'How you gonna get out of that one?'

'Dunno. But I'll think of something.'

They settled down, each with their own thoughts.

On Monday, the office was very busy and Rose didn't get a chance to talk to Nora. Looking directly at Rose, the supervisor told the girls she had to go to a meeting at lunchtime.

Lily was also concerned that she hadn't seen Harry, but that evening, just as the shop was closing, she was thrilled when she saw him waiting outside for her.

'Hello, Lily,' he said as soon as she walked out of the shop. 'I'm so sorry I haven't been around for a while, but my mother had a fall; she slipped on some damp grass and injured her leg. I've scarcely been to the office.'

'Oh Harry, I'm so sorry. Is she getting better?'

'Yes thank you. Mind you, it's a bit of a worry when Pat comes round, as she has to bring the children and David can be a bit boisterous.'

They'd begun to walk on but Lily said, 'Just a moment,' and hurried back to the shop.

'Miss Tucker, could I have a small bunch of the carnations,' she said quickly.

'Of course, Lily. Is something wrong?'

'Harry's mother has had a fall. I'll pay for them tomorrow.'

'I'm sorry to hear that. Do yourself up a bouquet and we'll worry about payment later.'

'Thank you.'

Harry looked surprised when Lily came out of the shop carrying the flowers.

'Would you like to give your mother these and I hope she gets well soon.'

'Oh Lily, how kind of you. You'll have to come round one day and meet her. I know you'll get on.'

'I'd like that. Now go on home and put the flowers in water.'

'I will, and thank you.' He quickly kissed her check and walked away.

Lily watched him reach the corner, and when he turned and waved, she waved back before he disappeared. Then she touched her cheek and began to walk home with a smile on her face. She did like him, and his family sounded very nice. But what would Rose think of her going to meet his mother? Would she think she was serious about him?

On Wednesday, when Rose came home from work, Lily was in the kitchen with her mother. They heard the front door shut and Rose run upstairs. Lily looked at Amy.

'Now what's she been up to?' asked her mother.

Lily just shrugged.

When Rose came into the kitchen, she looked flushed.

'Everything all right?' asked Amy.

'Yes thanks.'

'What you hiding?'

'Nothing. Why?'

'You don't usually dash upstairs straight away.'

'Just wanted to change me shoes. Me feet were killing me.' She held up her foot and they could see she had her slippers on.

Lily looked at her. What was she hiding?

'Mum, I might be going out on Saturday night. Is that all right?'

'I don't see why not. Who with?'

'Nora from work.'

'Going anywhere nice?' asked Lily.

'Don't know yet. Not sure what time I'll be home.'

'Just make sure it's not too late. You know how your father worries.'

Rose gave her mother a sickly smile.

Lily couldn't wait to get her sister alone, and walked out to the lav, hoping Rose would follow her. She was sitting on the seat under the scullery window when Rose finally came out.

'Thought I'd find you out here.' Rose had a broad smile on her face.

'Well, come on, tell me all about it. What did you take upstairs?'

Rose sat next to her. 'I'm going to a party with Roger and I managed to get my frock from Madam Tina's.'

'What? How long have you been paying for it?'

'Weeks.'

'No wonder you look so pleased with yourself. I can't wait to see it.'

'Oh Lil, I'm so thrilled. He wants to see me, and he arranged with Nora to meet me outside the office at six, then we'll go back to his place and get ready for the party.'

'I see.'

'Is that all you can say? "I see." Is that it?'

'Well I can't say I'm that thrilled at you going to his place to get changed.'

'Nora will be there as well.'

'That's different.'

Their mother banging on the window and waving them inside for their meal ended the conversation.

After they had finished their meal and done the usual chores, the girls went up to bed.

'Come on then, show me this frock.'

Rose went to the wardrobe and took a bag from the bottom. With a flourish she removed the blue dress from the bag and held it up against her.

'Rose, it's really lovely.' Lily touched the delicate material. 'How did you manage to pay for it?'

'I've only been paying off a shilling a week, just so they kept it and didn't sell it. I only had two shillings left to pay on it and I managed to save that from last week's money. Do you like it?'

'I think it's gorgeous.'

'Do you think Roger will like it?'

'I would think so.'

'These beige shoes will be good with it, don't you think?' She put her pointed-toe shoes next to it.

'They'll look smashing. What you gonna wear underneath?'

'What d'you mean?'

'Will you come home first?'

'No I'll go shopping or something. Why?'

'Well, you won't go to work in that.' Lily pointed to the dress, which was lying on the bed. 'Will you change in front of Nora?'

'I don't think so.' But Rose was beginning to be concerned. Where would she sleep? Would Roger take her to Nora's? What would she wear? She couldn't take a nightdress, so it would have to be her undies, she could sleep in those. That was it. She would have to buy some of the latest underwear she'd been admiring in the shops. 'I might have to borrow some money.'

Lily sighed. 'What a surprise. What for this time?'

'I've seen some of those camiknickers; they look really lovely and they'll go well under this. Oh Lil, I'm so happy.'

Lily smiled at her sister but she was concerned. What was this Roger like? Was he a gentleman? Well, she should know all the answers on Sunday.

The next night when Lily came home, she said that Harry had been waiting for her outside the shop and wanted her to have tea on Sunday with his mother.

'Is that all right?'

'Of course. He sounds a nice boy,' said Amy. 'Has his mother got over her accident?' Lily had told them all about that.

Lily smiled. 'Yes.' As her mother had just said, Harry was a nice boy, and she couldn't wait to meet his mother. 'I think she did something to her ankle. I shall know more on Sunday.'

Rose was getting more and more excited about seeing Roger again. Every night she took her frock out of the bag and looked at it.

'Good job it don't crease crushed up like that. Why don't you hang it up?' asked Lily when it was brought out yet again.

'What if Mum sees it?'

'She'll only ask you all about it.'

'Yes, and she'll want to know how I paid for it – you know she doesn't agree with buying things on the never-never.'

'I don't know. I give up with you.'

Rose ran her hands gently over her frock. This was something she'd love for ever, and with luck it would take her to a new world.

Lily was thinking about Harry. They had only been the once to the music hall and for a few walks in the park. She would love to go out with him more, but he did seem a bit reluctant. Perhaps when she met his mother things might be different. She really hoped so.

Chapter 11

ON SATURDAY MORNING, Lily and Rose made their way to work as usual, Rose clutching her bag with her precious frock and beige shoes inside. She thought she was going to be sick she was so excited. She was going to see Roger in a few hours. While she felt really happy, she was also a little apprehensive. Although she'd told Lily that Nora would be there, Nora hadn't said she would be. She'd have to worry about that if and when it happened.

'You left it a bit late to tell Mum that you might be staying the night with Nora,' said Lily as they walked along together. Rose had only mentioned it just as they were leaving this morning, not giving her mother a chance to ask any questions.

'I thought that was best.'

'Rose, I am worried about you.'

'You don't have to be. Here's my bus. See you Sunday.'

'I hope it works out all right for you,' called Lily as her sister boarded the bus.

* * *

'Good morning, girls,' said Nora as she walked in. 'Rose, can you stay behind for a while today?'

'Yes, Miss Evans.'

'What you been up to?' asked Betty when Nora went to her office.

'Nothing as far as I know.' Rose hoped the excitement in her voice didn't show as she put the bag holding her precious frock under her desk.

The morning seemed to drag, and as soon as one o'clock arrived and the other girls left, Rose went to Nora's office.

'You can wait in here for Roger.'

'What, till six?'

Nora didn't answer.

'Nora, are you going to this party?'

'No, and I told Roger to be here at one; I don't think it's right for you to have to wait around till six for him. Rose, I'm a bit concerned about this. He's a nice enough guy, but for you to go back to his place after the party – well, he's got a bit of a reputation.'

Rose looked at Nora. What was she trying to tell her?

'I don't want you falling out with your father over this. Does he know you're staying out all night?'

Rose slowly shook her head. 'I told my mum and my sister this morning that I would probably be staying with you. I thought you would be going to the party.'

'So did I, but . . .' Nora stopped and lit a cigarette. 'I

don't think there is a party. I asked James and he doesn't know anything about it, and as you know, he and Roger are the best of friends and do everything together.'

Although Rose was thrilled that Roger wanted to take her out on his own, she did begin to feel a little anxious and wondered where they might go.

At that moment the bell rang and Nora went downstairs to open the door.

'Rose, my darling,' said Roger as he walked into the office. 'I'm so sorry, I should have realised that you would have had to wait for me till six. Thank goodness Nora got in touch.' He was now at Rose's side and, holding her close, gave her a peck on the cheek.

'Roger, where are you taking Rose tonight?'

He stepped back. 'I'm taking her to a party.'

'Whose?'

'I'm sorry?'

'Whose party.'

'Someone at the office has invited me.'

'Why isn't James going?'

'As you know, we now work in different offices. I'm in the New York side of the business.'

Rose was looking from one to the other.

'And where is she going to stay tonight?'

'Nora, I don't really think this is any of your business.'

'It is, in as much as I introduced her to you and I know your reputation.'

Rose wanted to scream at Nora to leave her alone. This was her decision and she wanted to go with him.

'If you must know, she will be staying at Archie and Poppy's; it's their party.'

Nora raised her well-shaped eyebrows. 'Just as long as it's all above board and her father will be satisfied.'

'I can understand your concern. I'm so sorry, Rose, please forgive us.' Roger glanced at Nora. 'We have been completely ignoring you, but you must be pleased that Nora has taken you under her wing and is concerned about your welfare and reputation.'

'Yes, I am, and thank you, Nora.'

Nora smiled. Although she thought Roger's answer was plausible, she knew all about him and his philandering ways. 'So where are you going now?' she asked.

'I thought that we'd go back to my place.' He held up his hands. 'It's all above board, my dear Nora.'

Rose wanted to laugh. Nobody other than her family had worried about her reputation like this.

'It had better be. Right, come on, let me lock up.'

As they made their way down the stairs, Nora took Rose's arm. 'Please be careful.'

Rose smiled. 'Thank you. I will.'

The car outside almost took Rose's breath away. It was so sleek.

'Jump in,' Roger said as he held open the door. He gave Nora a quick kiss and walked round to the driver's side.

Rose was smiling as she gave Nora a little wave. Clutching her bag with her new frock inside, she wondered what was in store for her this weekend. Whatever it was, she was going to enjoy herself, even if she did feel a little apprehensive.

'I hope Nora didn't worry you about tonight's arrangements. I can assure you that I will be the perfect gentleman and you will have nothing to worry about.' Roger touched her hand and gave her a smile.

Rose felt her heart jump. She felt as if she loved him. Her sister would tell her that she was being silly, but she didn't care. This was the best thing that had ever happened to her, and she was going to enjoy every moment.

They were driving through a part of London she didn't know. 'Where do you live?'

'Why? Are you afraid I'm going to sell you to a white slave trader?' he laughed. Rose laughed too, but it was very half-hearted.

After a while they turned into Puffin Mews, a narrow cobbled street. Rose was stunned. The small row of houses had beautiful bay windows, and scattered around were boxes full of colourful flowers. Everything looked lovely and very expensive.

'Right. This is it.' Roger rushed round to her side and opened the car door for her.

When he opened the door to the house and they walked in, she was in awe. The hall had a large ornate mirror on one side and a heavy framed painting of a lovely lady on the other.

'This way.'

They passed a closed door and there was a narrow staircase in front of them. Rose followed Roger along a small passage into a room with a large table in the middle and four matching chairs round it. There was another door beyond that.

'This is the dining room, and that door leads to the kitchen. The lounge is on the left of the hall. There are two bedrooms upstairs, plus the bathroom. Now, is there anything you would like?'

'I would like to use your bathroom.'

'Of course. You can't miss it; it's the door with the glass fanlight over. And by the way, I gather that's your dress for tonight that you're clutching. You can lay it out on the bed next to the bathroom.'

'Thank you.'

Slowly Rose went up the red-carpeted staircase. She felt like royalty. She had never seen such a lovely house. When she opened the bedroom door, she was surprised to see a double bed. The room was very masculine: plain beige, with a dark wood wardrobe and matching dressing table with three mirrors and on top just a hairbrush with a comb stuck in it. The fireplace had a shelf over it, and on it a photo of a smiling woman. There weren't any other ornaments and the room looked very bare. There was a full-length mirror on a stand, and Rose looked at herself and felt very dowdy. Turning away, she walked over to the wardrobe. She would have loved to look inside but decided against it. Instead she took her frock from the bag and gently laid it on the bed. She put her beige shoes on the floor and stepped back. They looked so at home there.

In the bathroom, she closed and locked the door. A bathroom was something she wanted one day, with an inside lav and a white bath. Over the washbasin was a shelf, and above it a small cupboard with a mirrored door. She had to stand on her tiptoes to look in it. On the shelf were a shaving mug and a brush. She picked up the brush and pressed it to her cheek. This house was just like something out of a magazine.

She went back downstairs and into the dining room. 'You have a very beautiful house.'

'I'm happy living here.'

'Do you live alone?'

'I do have a lady who comes in every other day to clean up after me and do my washing, and some cooking if need be. She also helps out if I'm entertaining.'

The thought that was going through Rose's mind was that he must earn a lot of money to live here and have a cleaner. And who did he entertain?

'Now, I've made a pot of tea, so you see I'm not altogether useless. Do you take milk and sugar?'

'Yes please.'

He went into the kitchen and returned with a tray on which there was a tray cloth, teapot, milk jug and sugar bowl, as well as matching china cups and saucers. There was also a plate of biscuits.

'This is lovely.' Rose was trying hard not to show how impressed she was. She wanted to appear to be used to all this finery.

'I'm so glad we've got a little while to get acquainted,'

said Roger as he passed her a delicate bone-china cup and saucer. 'Help yourself to milk and sugar.'

'Thank you.' This was what she wanted. This was how she wanted to live.

Lily was just finishing off a buttonhole when she saw Harry waiting outside. She was filled with panic. He didn't work on Saturday afternoons. What if he'd come to tell her he didn't want to take her to his mother's for tea? She gave him a little wave.

At last, when she had finished and Miss Tucker said she could leave, she hurried outside. 'Harry, is everything all right?'

'Yes. Why?'

'I thought you were here to tell me I wouldn't be coming to meet your mother tomorrow.'

He smiled and kissed her cheek. 'Are they for Mother?' Lily was clutching a bunch of flowers.

'Yes, they are, but why are you here?'

'Pat has just left, and I took her to the bus stop and decided to come on and see you. I thought I could walk you home. Do you mind?'

'No, of course not.'

'I'm sorry we haven't been out, but things have been rather difficult.'

'Harry, if you don't want me round tomorrow, that's all right.'

'Lily, I do want to see you, and as it's not always been easy for me to leave Mother, this is the best way.' He took her hand. 'You don't mind, do you?'

'No, of course not.' But at the back of her mind, Lily was wondering whether Rose was right. Was Harry a mummy's boy?

When they reached Enfield Road, Lily said, 'Would you like to come in and meet my parents?'

'I'd rather not, thank you.'

Was she being a bit pushy? she wondered.

'I'll call for you tomorrow about three. Would that be all right?'

'That'll be fine. But meet me outside the shop, it will save you coming all the way here.'

'That would be better, but are you sure?'

'Yes, of course.'

'You are so sweet and understanding.' He quickly gave her a kiss and went on his way.

Lily stood for a moment watching him. Although she quite liked Harry, there was something about him she didn't understand. She knew he was shy, but this was 1928; and young men were a bit more forthcoming these days. Her thoughts went to Rose. I bet she's having a far better time than I'm going to have tomorrow.

Chapter 12

ROSE WAS STILL amazed that such a nice man could live like this and not have been snapped up. His voice interrupted her thoughts.

'Mrs B left us a few sandwiches to tide us over. There will be plenty to eat and drink at Archie and Poppy's tonight.'

'I'm really looking forward to it.' Rose was hoping this evening would be a chance to find out more about him. She took one of the sandwiches and looked at the clock hanging on the wall. She was a bit concerned: what were they going to do for the next four hours? 'I know Nora told you to collect me at lunchtime; I'm sorry about that.' She felt embarrassed. 'Did you want to go for a walk or something this afternoon, or do you have some work to do?'

He smiled. 'I'm sure we can find something to keep us occupied.'

Rose gave him a weak smile back. What did he have in mind?

After a while Roger dabbed at his mouth with his

serviette and, reaching across the table, took her hand. 'Come with me.'

'Where're we going?'

He laughed. 'Don't look so frightened. I'm only going to take you into the sitting room. There's something in there I think you'll like. I don't know if they allow this sort of thing at the vicarage.'

'I told you, we don't exactly live in the vicarage.' She kept her head down as she felt the blush of embarrassment rise up her face.

Roger opened the door and ushered Rose in. She stood for a moment or two taking in the lovely surroundings. Although the room wasn't large, it was very cosy. There was a fireplace with a marble shelf over and another photo of the woman from the bedroom. A velvet three-piece suite in a lovely rust colour displayed a woman's touch, with the cushions matching the curtains framing the bay window. In the corner stood a tall table and on it was a gramophone. Rose was amazed. She hurried across to it. 'You've got a gramophone. I've only ever seen these in the big department stores; they are very expensive.' She ran her fingers over the brass horn.

'I have a few records. Do you like jazz?'

Rose nodded and watched him take a record from the shelf underneath and wind up the gramophone. When he had placed the arm that held the needle on the record, he took her hand and they began to dance. Rose was laughing with sheer happiness as Roger tried to teach her to do the Charleston.

When the music finished, she fell on to the sofa. 'You are a very good dancer,' she said. 'How did you learn all these new dances?'

'Sometimes I have to travel to New York on business, and I go to the clubs when I'm over there.'

'Roger, you lead such an interesting and thrilling life.'

'Yes, I do, but it's not all fun. I do have to work some of the time.' He put his arm round her shoulders. 'You would love New York, it's noisy and exciting.'

'It must be wonderful to go to America,' she sighed, and as she turned her head, he kissed her. It was a long, passionate kiss, and Rose thought she would pass out with excitement. This was the man she was in love with. This was how she wanted to live. When she came up for air, he tapped the back of her hand.

'I'd better not sit here with you for too long, or I might break my promise to Nora.' He stood up and took a cigarette from the wooden box on the small table at the side of the sofa. Then he wandered over to the gramophone and put another record on. This was a slow tune. When he held out his hand, Rose stood up and went into his arms, and they moved very slowly round the room.

'Rose, I hope this doesn't sound silly,' he whispered, 'but I think I've fallen in love with you.'

Although Rose felt her knees buckle, she knew she had to sound flippant or she might end up making a fool of herself. She gave a little giggle. 'I bet you say that to all your girlfriends.'

'I've never felt this way about anyone before.'

'I'm very flattered, but you've only seen me a couple of times.' Rose was trying so hard not to give in to her feelings. She loved him but knew she had to control herself. She couldn't bear to think of what her father would do if she ever got into trouble.

Roger kissed her again, and this time she broke away. 'I'm sorry,' he said. 'I think we'd better play a game of cards or something to keep us occupied.'

Rose wanted to laugh at such a suggestion to cool his ardour.

After a while Roger said, 'I think we should begin to get ready. Do you want the bathroom first?'

Rose nodded.

When she came downstairs again, Roger was still in the sitting room, smoking. He turned and stood up when she opened the door, and quickly stubbed out his cigarette.

'Rose. You look absolutely gorgeous.'

She smiled and gave a little curtsey. 'Thank you, kind sir. I do try.'

'I don't think you have to try very hard.'

'You say the nicest things.'

'It's true. You are very lovely.'

Rose blushed. She was in heaven with this man.

'I'll see you in a few moments. Why don't you play some records?'

'Thank you.'

Roger left the room, and Rose wandered over to the photograph on the mantelpiece. Was this his mother?

Then she went and wound up the gramophone and picked out a record by someone called Louis Armstrong.

When Roger walked into the room wearing an evening suit, his black bow tie a stark contrast to his white shirt, it was Rose's turn to look amazed. He was so handsome, and he was going to be her escort for the evening. 'You look very nice as well,' she said, trying to hide the fact that she was paying a man a compliment.

'Thank you, my lady,' he said, giving a sweeping bow.

Rose giggled.

'Now, I suggest we have a little snifter before we go. What do you fancy?'

Rose knew there wasn't any reason to be other than honest with him, so she said, 'I don't really know. We don't drink in our family.'

'Of course. How about something very mild to start with? I've got to get you used to drinking if we're going to go out together.'

Rose's head was reeling. He loved her and wanted to take her out again. 'What do you suggest?' she asked.

'Well, there will be plenty of champagne at the party; Poppy always drinks champagne.'

'I've never tasted champagne.'

'It's very nice, but you have to be careful not to drink too much.' He was busy opening a bottle. 'After a while you forget what day it is, but don't worry, I'll make sure you stay with us. Now, how about a gin and orange?'

'I've never had gin.'

'I can see that I've really got to look after you.' He

handed Rose a glass and she took a sip and shuddered.

He laughed. 'And I shall have my work cut out showing you our wicked ways.'

'Hello, love,' said her mother when Lily walked in. 'You all right? You look a bit down.'

'I'm fine.' Lily took off her hat.

Her father looked up from his chair and asked, 'What's this about Rose staying out all night?'

'I don't know. I was surprised when she told Mum this morning.'

'She didn't tell you?'

'No.'

'Do you know this Nora?'

'No, not really, though she comes into the shop sometimes.'

'What's she like?'

Lily could throttle Rose for leaving her to answer all these questions. 'She's well-dressed and seems to have plenty of money, and Rose thinks the world of her.'

'Well I'm not happy about it. D'you know where she lives?'

'No.' Lily was filled with panic. What would her father do when Rose came home tomorrow?

'Is she with a bloke?'

'I expect there will be some at the party.'

Her father stood up.

'Ron, leave the poor girl alone. Come on, love, sit down. I've kept your dinner hot.'

'Thanks, Mum.' Lily sat at the table and thought about her own love life, or lack of it. Was this how things were going to be every time they went out with someone? Would there always be lots of questions?

When Lily and her mother were alone in the scullery, Amy asked, 'Did you not know Rose might be staying out all night?'

'No, Mum. I didn't.'

'I don't think your father will go to bed tonight till she gets back.'

'Oh Mum. What if she don't come home?'

'I dread to think.'

When Lily went to bed that night, she wondered what her sister was up to. And if she was having a great time, would she think it was all worth it when she got home tomorrow?

They had been driving for about an hour. Rose knew they were out of London, as they had passed a sign that said they were on the Southend road. That brought back happy memories of when they'd gone to Southend for the day on their sixteenth birthday.

'Where're we going?' she asked.

'A place called Little Heath.'

After leaving the main road, Roger turned into a long drive with well-laid-out lawns on either side. There were lots of cars in front of a very large house.

'This is it,' he said as he turned off the engine and came round to Rose's side to open the door.

'This is lovely,' said Rose, taking in her surroundings. 'But it seems a long way for Archie to travel to get to work.'

'Not really, he's got a car.' Roger held out his hand. 'Mind your feather.'

Rose giggled and ducked her head. The feather in her hairband was rather long, but she did feel good and very modern.

As they walked up the steps to the large wooden door, it was flung open by a very glamorous blonde woman wearing the most beautiful frock that Rose had ever seen. It was white and all the fringes rippled as she rushed towards them, her long rope of knotted pearls swaying back and forth. She too was wearing a headband, but hers was jewelled.

'Roger, darling.' She threw her arms round his neck and kissed him on the lips. When they broke apart, she turned to Rose. 'Hello, you must be Rose.' She held out her hand. 'Welcome.'

'Thank you,' said Rose, taking her hand. She was surprised that Poppy knew her name. Roger must have been talking about her.

'I must say, Rog, you certainly know how to pick 'em.' Poppy smiled at Rose. 'Now come on in, darling.'

As they entered the wide hall, the music mixed with laughter and voices coming from one of the rooms was very loud.

'It's a good job we don't have any neighbours,' said Poppy.

Rose followed her into a very large room that seemed to be full of smoke and people. She stood and looked at the high ceiling, from which hung two of the most beautiful chandeliers she had ever seen. Not that she had seen that many.

'Rose, this is my husband, Archie.'

Rose turned to see a man of about Roger's age holding out his hand.

'Pleased to meet you. Any friend of Roger's is a friend of ours. And I must say, he's got excellent taste.'

Rose could feel herself blushing.

'Now, Pops, how about getting these good people a drink,' said Archie, patting his wife's bottom as they moved further into the room. Poppy turned and kissed his cheek.

'Champers?' she asked.

'Please,' said Roger. Rose only nodded. She was pleased that Roger was at her side, guiding her into the room. He stopped many times to shake men's hands and give them a hug; a few of the beautifully dressed ladies came and kissed him. He seemed very popular.

They made their way across to the pair of open glass doors that looked out on to a beautiful conservatory. There were a lot of people in there, laughing and dancing. It was a very happy scene, and Rose was going to enjoy every minute of it. She would have so much to tell her sister.

Roger came towards her with a glass of champagne. 'Don't drink it straight down,' he warned.

Rose took a sip and the bubbles tickled her nose. 'This is very nice.'

'Poppy likes you.'

'And I like her and her house.'

'Well her husband is a millionaire, so she will have the best.'

'I've never met a millionaire before.'

'They are just ordinary people who have made a lot of money. Let me show you the garden.'

Rose and Roger wandered round the garden and then sat down on one of the many seats that were dotted around. A waiter came over with another glass of champagne.

'Have you known them long?' asked Rose.

'A few years, since I started working for the firm.'

'Has Nora been here?'

'Once or twice, but James works in a different office. Now, tell me a bit about you. Are you an only child, or is there another gorgeous person like you?'

Rose looked into her glass. 'No, there's only me.' Why had she not told him she was a twin? Was she frightened he might prefer Lily to her? She shuddered.

'Are you cold?'

'I'm fine, thank you.'

After a while Roger said, 'I think we should wander inside; it is beginning to get a little chilly out here. How about something to eat?'

Rose giggled. 'All right.' As she stood up, she felt slightly giddy.

Roger took her arm and they made their way inside.

'Food's in the dining room, Rog,' said Poppy as they walked in.

Rose's jaws ached from smiling, but she couldn't stop. Was this all a dream? Would she wake up?

Roger gave her a plate.

'Help yourself.'

She looked at the sumptuous spread on the huge table. There were candles flickering and a wonderful centrepiece. How Lily would love these beautiful flowers. Rose had never seen so much food. She didn't know where to start. Some of the dishes she didn't even recognise. She decided to take only the things she knew and liked.

After a while, when everybody had eaten, someone began to play the piano and they started to sing all the wartime favourites.

Rose had never felt so happy, and she didn't want it to end.

Chapter 13

LILY WOKE WITH a start. She looked over at her sister's bed. It hadn't been slept in.

Where had Rose spent the night? Was it with Nora? What was going to happen when she finally came home?

There was a faint knock on her bedroom door. 'Lily, are you awake?'

'Yes, Mum.' Lily sat up and was shocked at the sight of her mother when she walked in. Amy always tidied her hair as soon as she was up, but this morning it was sticking up all over the place, while the dark rings under her eyes made her look as if she hadn't had any sleep for days.

'Mum, are you all right?'

'No. Your father has been pacing the floor all night. He's worried sick about Rose. Where is she?' Amy sat on her daughter's bed.

'Mum, you knew she might be out all night.'

'Yes, but who with?'

'She said with Nora.'

'I know, but is that the truth?'

'Why do you say that?'

'I don't know, just a feeling I've got.'

'You must let her go out. You know what she's like.'

'I'm not happy about this.'

'Well I think you should wait till she gets home, and then she can explain where she's been and who with.'

'She'll certainly have a lot of explaining to do when she finally shows her face, I can tell you.' Her mother left the room.

Lily lay back. This was going to be a very bad day. In some ways she hoped she wouldn't be here when Rose got home. She was going round to Harry's this afternoon, and she wanted everything to work out for her there.

Slowly Rose opened her eyes and quickly closed them again. Her mouth felt dry. It was daylight. Where was she? She didn't remember going to bed; in fact, she didn't remember much at all about last night, just that she'd been at a party with Roger and had a wonderful time. Again she opened her eyes. She suddenly recognised the room. It was Roger's. How had she got here? She felt the space beside her. It was empty. She lifted her head carefully from the pillow. She was alone, and when she looked under the bedclothes, she was shocked to see she was wearing only her camiknickers. Where was her frock? She turned her head, although it took a lot of effort, as it was thumping. Who had undressed her? Her frock was on a hanger that was hooked over the picture rail. She could see the photo on the mantelpiece, and it looked like the woman was smiling at her. Her thoughts filled her head. I hope I didn't make a fool of myself. He'll never want to see me again. Tears ran slowly down her cheeks. She also knew that she would be in big trouble when she got home, but she didn't care. She was so in love with Roger, and didn't want to lose him. The gentle tapping on the door startled her, and she quickly dabbed her eyes on the sheet.

'Who is it?'

'Rose, it me, Roger. Can I come in?'

'Yes.' She tried to smooth her hair down.

Roger came in with a tray and placed it on the dressing table. 'Tea?'

Rose had pulled the bedclothes up to her chin. 'Yes please.'

'Did you sleep well?'

'Yes. What time is it?'

'Ten thirty.'

'Oh my God. I've got to get home. My father will be going mad.'

'You'd better have a bath and get dressed first.'

'Roger, who undressed me?'

'I did.' He began pouring out the tea.

Rose gasped.

'Well I didn't think you would want to crease your pretty dress.'

'Did you . . . ?'

'Did I take advantage of you?' he asked as he handed her a cup. 'Two sugars, wasn't it?'

Rose squirmed. 'Thank you.' What was he going to tell her?

'If you remember, I told you I loved you. I don't know what you think of me, but I can assure you that I am no cad. I would never take advantage of a young lady.'

Rose blushed. 'So where did you sleep?'

He sat on the bed. 'In the spare room. Mrs B always keeps the bed made up, as I never know who's going to finish up here after a night out.'

'Roger, did I make a fool of myself last night?'

He smiled. 'No, but you certainly know how to dance, especially after a few glasses of champagne.'

'I am so sorry. Was Poppy cross with me?'

'No, she loves you, and she certainly wants to see you again.'

'I don't think I could ever face her again.'

'Nonsense. In fact, we have been invited over for a meal next Saturday.'

'I couldn't.'

'Why not?'

'After last night, I don't think . . .' She stopped. How could she say that she didn't think her father would let her out again?

'It will only be us. Please, Rose. I must see you again.' He took her hand. 'I suppose I shouldn't tell you this, but you could help me with my promotion.'

Rose was shocked. She quickly pulled her hand away. 'Is that the only reason why you asked me out?'

'No. No, honestly. I love you.'

'But you need me to be your, your . . .' She couldn't think of the right word.

'Please, Rose, don't be annoyed.'

'Could you please leave the room. I want to get dressed.'

He stood up and left.

Again Rose began to cry. Why was she being so silly? She loved him, and he said he loved her, but did he really? What was so wrong with him wanting to take her out, and if it might help with his promotion, what did she have to lose? In fact, it could be to her advantage if Poppy liked her. At the moment she didn't know what she wanted; she was so confused.

When Lily went downstairs, her father's face was like thunder. She had never seen him look so angry. 'Good morning, Dad.'

'Is it?'

'Please don't be angry with me.'

'You knew she was going to stay out all night.'

'Only when she told Mum.'

'I don't believe you. You two have always been in cahoots. Didn't she say anything as you walked to work?'

Lily was upset by her father's attitude towards her. 'No, not really.'

'Come on, out with it. Who is she with? Some rich playboy?'

Lily tried to suppress her grin, but she really wanted to laugh. 'Now that would certainly suit Rose, if he was rich and a playboy.'

'I don't want none of your cheek, young woman. Do you know his name?'

'No.'

'I expect she stayed the night with him. Well, you know that ruins her chances of getting married, don't you?'

'Why?'

'No bloke wants second-hand goods.'

Lily was shocked. How could her father think like that? And even if Rose had done it, surely it didn't mean the end of her life?

She went outside to the lav. Her thoughts were all over the place. If only it was afternoon and she could be at Harry's. She certainly didn't want to be here when Rose got home.

When she returned to the kitchen, she sat at the table in silence to finish her breakfast. After a while she said, 'Dad, you know I'm going to tea with Harry and his mother today?'

Ron grunted and looked up from his newspaper. 'And what time will you be rolling home?'

'I don't know, but it won't be late.'

'It better not be. I'll be going to bed early tonight to make up for the sleep I missed last night.'

Was this how their lives were going to be? Why was

their father so strict? If it was because of what his sister had done, she certainly had a lot to answer for.

'Rose. Please. I must see you again.' They were in the kitchen and Roger was holding her hand.

When she looked at him standing there looking handsome but sad, her heart melted. 'Roger, I do want to see you again, but it could be very difficult.'

'I understand. Let me come and talk to your father.'

Rose was shocked. What could she say? 'I don't think that's a very good idea.'

'If he's a man of the cloth, I'm sure he would understand. I'll tell him that I haven't violated his daughter.'

Rose was beside herself. Why had she told those lies? 'Roger, he isn't a man of the cloth. I told you, he's just a labourer.'

'I know, but he must be quite religious, and he obviously wants to protect his only daughter.'

'Please, take me back to the office.'

'No. I'm going to take you home.'

Rose felt her knees begin to buckle. 'I can't let you do that.'

'Why?'

'So many reasons.' She wanted to cry. This man was in love with her and wanted to see her again, and all she'd done was lie to him. 'Please, Roger.'

He kissed her hand. 'Rose, I've never felt this way about anyone before and I've never believed in love at first sight. But with you it's different. You're fun and so innocent and I love you. And I want to see you again, soon.'

'I have your address. I can get in touch with you.'

'No.'

'What?'

'If you won't let me see your father, then I'll collect you tomorrow after you finish at the office and we'll have something to eat and talk about our future together.'

Rose was in a daze. This was like something out of a book. Things like this didn't happen to people like her in real life. She picked up her handbag and the bag holding her frock. 'Can we go?'

They were both very subdued as they drove along the deserted streets, and all the while Rose was wondering about the reception she would get when she arrived home. She knew she had done wrong in her father's eyes. Would Lily be around to back her up? What time was she going to Harry's? For all her bravado, Rose was frightened of the consequences. Not that her father would hit her, but he would be very angry, and she hated the atmosphere it was going to cause.

'You're very quiet,' said Roger.

'I'm just thinking about Poppy inviting us for a meal on Saturday.'

Roger was smiling. 'We can talk about that tomorrow night. It will only be the four of us.'

Rose smiled back. What could she say? This could be the turning point in her life, but would she be willing to upset her family for him? There was so much going round in her head that she hadn't realised they were turning in to the church. What could she say? She began to panic. 'Roger, please drop me off here.'

'No. I can tell your father that I want to take you out again.'

'No. Please Roger. Stop here.'

Chapter 14

LILY LOOKED AT the wooden case clock sitting in the middle of the mantelpiece. It was twelve thirty. Where was her sister?

Her mother came into the kitchen and began to put knives and forks down on the table. She looked at Lily and said, 'I've done dinner for Rose, but if she don't come home your father will go mad.'

Lily knew they always had Sunday dinner at one sharp and the thought that was racing through her mind was, You've got half an hour so please Rose, hurry up and come home.

'Please Roger, stop here.'

'Well, if that's what you want.' They were moving very slowly and he was sitting forward looking through the windscreen. 'There seem to be rather a lot of people about.'

'It is Sunday.' For a moment or two as they sat in the car, Rose was relieved to see so many people coming from the church while others were walking into the cemetery with bunches of flowers. 'This is not a good day to come here,' she said.

'I can see that.'

'Would you mind if I got out now and went in?'

He smiled at her. 'No, of course not. But I will come and see you tomorrow outside the office, if that's what you want. And Rose, don't tell Nora too much about what happened this weekend, will you? Or about next Saturday. It might upset James if he doesn't get invited.'

'Of course I won't.'

Roger went to kiss her, but she moved away.

'I don't want anybody telling Dad what I was doing.'

'Sorry.' He took her hand and kissed it.

Rose quickly got out of the car and waved goodbye as Roger slowly drove away. When he was out of sight, she let out a sigh of relief and turned to make her way home. She knew she would be in trouble over last night and she was also too late for dinner, but she had got up late and it was hard to leave Roger.

In the scullery, Amy dished up the dinner in silence. Lily was helping. She wanted to scream and run away; the atmosphere was dreadful. Once the plates were on the table, she sat and waited for things to explode, but everybody was polite and passed the salt and pepper with the usual 'please' and 'thanks'. She knew Rose's dinner had been put back in the oven. If she was very late, it would be burnt.

'This is nice, Mum,' she said, just for something to say.

'Thanks. There's apple pie for afters.'

Lily looked at the clock and wished that it was two thirty, so that she could be on her way to meet Harry.

After dinner, they washed up and Lily went upstairs. In the bedroom, she sat on her bed, hoping that Rose would get there soon. When she was ready to go out, she went downstairs and poked her head round the kitchen door. 'I'll be off now, Mum, Dad. Bye.'

Her father just grunted.

Her mother stood up; she was going to come to the front door with her. Once she had closed the kitchen door behind her, she whispered, 'Don't be late, will you, love?'

'I won't. Tell Dad not to be too hard on Rose. He can't keep us locked up for ever.'

Her mother looked shocked. 'Is that what you think, that you're being locked up?'

'I'm sorry, Mum, but that's how it feels sometimes. We are eighteen and we would like a bit more freedom.'

'I'll have a word with your father.' She kissed her daughter's cheek. 'Bye, love.'

'Thanks, Mum. Bye.' When she heard the front door close, Lily walked away. What would have happened by the time she got home? Would Rose still be there? It wouldn't surprise her if her sister moved out if she couldn't get her own way. If she did that, it would break Lily's heart.

* * *

It was getting on for three o'clock, and Rose was very nervous as she pulled the key through the letter box. She knew there would an almighty row when she went into the kitchen. Should she go upstairs first and wait for her mother to come up, or should she face her father's fury? Her problem was solved when her mother opened the kitchen door.

'You're home, then,' she said.

Rose only smiled.

'You'd better come in here.'

As Rose walked into the kitchen, her father carefully folded his newspaper and placed it on the floor next to his armchair.

'Well, young lady, what have you got to say for yourself?'

'It was very late when we left the party and I couldn't get home.'

'Didn't one of the blokes have a car?'

'Yes.'

'Well then, he could have brought you home.'

'I couldn't ask. Besides, Nora said I could stay with her.'

'And where does this Nora live?'

Rose wanted to scream, but instead she said quietly, 'It's a place called Eagle Way.' There was no way she was going to give him Roger's address. 'It's very nice.'

'You do know I ain't had any sleep all night?'

'Why?'

'I was worried about you.'

'But I told Mum.'

'Yes, I know, but only as you left the house, and Lily said she didn't know much about it either.'

Rose felt guilty about her sister. Had she been getting the third degree?

'That's it. Every time you go out in the next month, I want you back here before nine o'clock.'

'What?'

'You heard.' Her father picked up his newspaper.

Rose was angry and feeling rebellious. 'And what if I'm not?' she asked.

'All the time you live under this roof, and until you're twenty-one, you'll do as I say. If not, you can just pack your bags and go and live with this Nora.'

Rose sat down at the table. 'You don't mean that.'

'Try me.'

She looked at her mother's shocked face, and Amy quickly looked away. Rose stood up.

'Your dinner's in the oven,' said her mother. 'Do you want it now?'

'No thanks,' said Rose. She picked up her bags and left the room.

'That was a bit harsh,' Amy said to her husband.

'It was meant to be. As long as they live here, they'll do as they're told.'

'But Ron, they're not children any more.'

'Then till they're twenty-one they should act like grown-ups and obey my rules.'

'I never thought I'd hear you talk like this.'

'I never thought that my girls would act like this.'

Amy sat at the table. 'Things are different today. The girls want more freedom.'

'And bring a load of trouble home.'

'They're good girls.'

There was no response from Ron. Amy wondered why he was being so unreasonable.

After a while she took Rose's dinner from the oven and carried it upstairs.

'Rose, it's me,' she said softly as she knocked on the bedroom door.

'What do you want?'

'I've got your dinner here.'

'I don't want it.'

Amy opened the door. 'Now don't be so silly,' she said. Rose was sitting on the bed with her back towards her. When she turned, Amy gasped. Rose's eyes and face were red with crying. She quickly put the plate on the dressing table and held her daughter close. 'Oh come now, it's not the end of the world.'

Rose couldn't say that it might be the end of her world if she couldn't go out with Roger again.

'I'm sure you can just make an effort to get home early for a few weeks, then everything will be forgotten.'

'Mum,' sobbed Rose, 'why is Dad so strict?'

'It's because he loves you and don't want anything to happen to you.'

Rose dabbed at her eyes with her handkerchief.

'He's got a funny way of showing it. I feel like a prisoner.'

Amy was taken aback. This was almost the same thing Lily had said earlier. 'I'll have a word with him,' she said softly. She left Rose's dinner on the dressing table and went back downstairs.

Lily knew she was very early when she arrived outside the shop, but she'd had to get away. When she saw Harry, she was relieved, as she'd been worried he might not turn up if his mother was poorly.

'Sorry I'm a bit late.' He quickly kissed her cheek.

'No, not really. I'm a bit early.'

Harry offered his arm and they began to stroll along the road.

'How is your mother today?' asked Lily.

'Very well, I'm pleased to say.'

'I'm really looking forward to meeting her.'

'And she's looking forward to meeting you.'

'Will your sister be there?'

'No, she don't bother coming on a Sunday as she knows I'm home.'

'I would have liked to have met her and the children.' Lily was thinking what a very uninteresting conversation this was. If only he was a bit more amusing, or they had more to talk about.

They lapsed into silence, and when they turned into Wood Street, Harry said, 'This is it,' and stopped at the gate to number thirty-eight.

It looked a very smart house, with bay windows

and a short path to the front door.

Harry took a key from his pocket and opened the door, calling out as he held it open for Lily, 'It's only me, Mother.'

The door at the end of the passage opened and a tall, well-dressed woman came out.

Lily was taken aback. She'd been expecting a bent-over old woman, but this one was upright and very smart, with her grey hair pulled back into a bun at the nape of her neck. She was wearing a navy blue frock that suited her fair colouring and slim body.

'Mum, this is Lily.'

Lily was speechless as she held out her hand. Mrs Thompson took it, smiling, and said, 'How do you do, my dear. Harry's told me so much about you. And I must thank you for the beautiful flowers. It must be lovely working with flowers all day.'

'Yes, it is.'

'Harry, take Lily's coat and we'll go into the front room.'

'Yes, of course.' He took her coat and Lily followed his mother into the front room, which was nicely furnished and looked very cosy.

'Please sit down.' Mrs Thompson gestured to the brown Rexine sofa.

Very tentatively Lily sat. 'Thank you.'

Mrs Thompson patted her grey hair and, smoothing down her frock, sat next to Lily.

'I understand that you've been a bit poorly,' said Lily.

'Yes, I had a fall, but I'm fine now. Would you like a cup of tea?'

'No thank you.'

Harry came in and sat down opposite.

'Right,' said Mrs Thompson. 'Now tell me all about yourself.'

'Not a lot to tell, really. I'm a twin.'

'A twin, how exciting. Are you identical?'

'Yes, but we have got our own styles.' Lily felt a bit like she was at an inquisition. She tried to look casually round the room. There were photos on the sideboard and a porcelain clock on the mantelpiece. 'This is a very nice room,' she said, for something to say.

Mrs Thompson stood up and took one of the photos and gave it to Lily. 'This is my late husband, Harold. He was a lovely man.'

'He looks very handsome.' Lily could see that he had been in the army, as he was wearing an officer's uniform.

'Yes, he was,' she said softly. Pointing to the other photos, she added, 'That's my daughter on her wedding day, and those are her children. Her daughter's very sweet, but her son can be a bit unruly.'

There was no mention of her son-in-law.

For the next hour or so, Lily seemed to be answering questions about herself and her family. It was only when his mother told Harry to bring in the tea that Lily could relax a little.

'Do you want any help?' she volunteered as Harry jumped up.

'No,' said Mrs Thompson. 'Harry can manage and everything is ready.'

In just a few moments the door was opened and Harry came into the room pushing a trolley laden with cakes and little sandwiches all nicely laid out on matching floral bone-china crockery.

Mrs Thompson sat and watched as he pushed the trolley towards her.

'Harry, give Lily a small table to rest her cup on and then sit down. Do you take sugar, my dear?'

'Yes please. Just one.'

'Would you like a sandwich or a cake?'

'Thank you.' Lily took a sandwich and Harry handed her a delicate cup and matching saucer. She felt so uncomfortable and wished the next hour or so away.

Later, as Harry walked her home, Lily felt very uneasy. She really didn't know what to say to him. Her thoughts were on her sister. Was she home, and what was the atmosphere like there?

'I'm sorry if it sounded like Mother was giving you the third degree, but there is something I've not told you about myself.'

Lily felt a shiver run down her spine. What was he about to tell her? 'You're not ill, are you?'

He smiled. 'No, nothing like that. It's more personal than that.'

'Do you think you should be telling me, then?'

'Yes. Yes, I do. So does Mother.'

Lily didn't know what to say. What was he going to tell her? What a weekend this was turning out to be.

Chapter 15

Rose was sitting in her bedroom waiting for her sister to come home. She had so much to tell her. She looked at their alarm clock. It was six thirty. Lily should be here soon. She glanced over at her dinner, which was still on the dressing table. It looked congealed and very unappetising, and she knew her father would be angry with her for wasting good food, but how could she eat when she was so upset at the thought of never seeing Roger again?

It was almost seven o'clock when Rose heard the key being pulled through the letter box, and she quickly went to the top of the stairs. She looked down at her sister and beckoned her up, but at the same time the kitchen door opened and Rose heard her mother's voice.

'Oh Lily, you're home. Come into the kitchen. Do you want a cup of tea?'

'No thanks.' Lily looked up at Rose and shook her

head; she would go up and see her sister as soon as she could. She had so much to tell her.

'Did you have a nice time?' asked Amy.

'Yes thanks.'

Her father gave her a nod from behind his newspaper.

'I'll go and take my hat and coat off,' said Lily.

'Yes, I expect you two have a lot to talk about. But come down for a drink before you go to bed.'

Lily quickly left the room.

She was very surprised when she saw her sister's face. It was red and blotchy. 'What's happened to you?'

'I've been crying.'

'I can see that. So Dad's been having a bit of a go, then?'

'For the next month I've got to be home by nine if I go out. That means I can't see Roger. Oh Lil, me life's in pieces.'

Lily wanted to laugh at the dramatics, but she could see how upset her sister was. 'I'm sure you'll be able to get round him in a week or two.'

'I don't think so. He was very cross.'

'So where did you stay?'

'At Roger's.'

'What?'

'He was in another bedroom.' Rose thought it was best she didn't say that she didn't remember being put to bed. 'He's got a fantastic house and the party we went to was at his boss's house. Lily, you should see it, it's like something out of a magazine. Huge rooms with big chandeliers and grandfather clocks. Poppy – that's his boss's wife – likes me and Roger is hoping to get promoted and we should be going to dinner there on Saturday and sometimes he goes to New York. Oh Lil, I could be part of his life. He's got a lovely house and he loves me.'

Lily sat with her back against the wall and looked at her sister. 'And you believe all that?'

'Yes. Why?'

'It sounds a bit far-fetched to me.'

'Well you would say that. I thought you'd be on my side.'

'I'm not taking sides.'

'Well I'm telling you. Roger is meeting me from work tomorrow, and if he wants me to go with him then I will.'

'Rose, you can't.'

'I will. By the way, what's Harry's mother like?'

'Tall, sophisticated and very nice. So different from what I was expecting.'

'Is he going to be Mr Right?'

'Don't know. I'll tell you all about it tomorrow. I think we've both had enough excitement for one day.' Lily wanted to go to bed. It was early, but she needed time to digest all that Harry had told her. 'I'm going down for a cuppa; do you want me to bring you up something?'

'I wouldn't mind a cup of tea. Can you take that plate down?'

Lily picked up the plate and took it downstairs.

She quickly walked through the kitchen into the scullery and scraped the food into the bin they kept at the side of the sink.

'Didn't Rose eat all her dinner?' asked her mother, coming into the scullery.

'No. She seems very upset.'

'Well that's her own fault. Your father was very annoyed with her.'

'I'm gonna make a pot of tea. Do you and Dad want one?'

Amy called out, 'D'you want a cuppa, Ron?'

'Yes please,' came back the answer.

When the kettle boiled, Lily made the tea and poured out two cups. She silently put them on the kitchen table, then went and collected two to take upstairs.

'Where you going with those?' asked her father as she walked through.

'Upstairs.'

'Tell that little madam to come down here if she wants tea. This ain't a hotel.'

'I don't mind taking—'

'Well I do.'

Lily was taken aback. Her father had never acted this way before. She put the two cups on the table and went to get Rose.

'I ain't going down there to be given another telling-off,' said Rose when Lily came back to the bedroom.

'Me and Mum's there.'

'I know, but that won't stop him from shouting at me.'

'I've never known you to be like this. Even when we were little, you never got as upset as this when Dad told you off.'

'This is different. I'm grown up now and I want to live my own life.'

'But Rose, what if this Roger doesn't want you after a couple of weeks?'

'He will. I know he will.'

'Is this all worth it?'

'Yes.'

'Look, come down for your tea.'

'S'pose I'll have to.' Rose slipped of the bed. 'Besides, I need a wee.'

Rose hurried through the kitchen and out to the lav. Lily sat at the table and began drinking her tea.

'So what is Harry's mother like?' asked her mother.

'Very nice.'

'Was his sister there?'

'No.' Lily had told them about his family.

Rose came back into the kitchen and sat at the table. The atmosphere was unbearable and Lily wanted to scream. This must be the worst day of her life, and her sister thought *she'd* had a bad day. What would next week bring?

Nothing was said as they all sat at the table and quietly drank their tea. As soon as it was finished, Lily jumped up and took the cups into the scullery and Rose quickly followed. As they were washing up, Lily wanted to tell Rose about Harry, but she thought her sister had had enough for one day. Besides, Lily didn't think she would be very interested.

* * *

On Monday morning Nora told Rose that they should have lunch together, so at one o'clock, Rose waited behind when the other girls went out.

'The weather has certainly changed,' said Nora as she locked the office door. It was late October and there was a definite chill. 'I hate the winter,' she added as she pulled the fur collar of her navy coat tighter round her neck. 'I didn't like to ask you in front of the others, but did you have a nice weekend?'

'Yes thank you.'

'As soon as we get in the café, you will have to tell me all about it.'

Rose knew she had to be very careful what she said.

After they had ordered some tea, Nora said, 'Well come on. Tell me about it.'

'We went to Roger's boss's house.'

'That would be Archie and Poppy's. It's very grand.'

'Yes, it is.'

'I've been to so many parties there. Was James there?'

'No.'

'That's good. I would have killed him if he had been.'

'Roger said it was mostly people from his and the American office.'

'I see. And where did you stay?'

This was the question Rose had been dreading. What could she say? They all knew each other. 'I stayed at Roger's.'

Nora raised one eyebrow. 'I see. Rose, a word of advice. I'm very broad-minded, but Roger has a reputation and he will tell you all sorts of things to get you into his bed.'

'I didn't sleep with him.'

Nora picked up her cup. 'Perhaps not this time. But believe me, he will.'

Rose didn't know what to think, and was pleased when it was time for them to go back to the office. She knew she would be seeing Roger at five thirty.

Although it was cold and blustery, when the shop closed Lily began walking home slowly, hoping that Harry might call out her name, but it wasn't to be. Perhaps he thought she might not want to see him again. She really didn't know how she felt. If only she had had a chance to talk to Rose about it, but Rose was too upset and concerned with her own problems to worry about her.

As she walked along, she went over and over the conversation they'd had yesterday when Harry took her home. Although it was a cold evening, they'd slowed their pace and Harry had given a nervous little cough.

'A few years ago,' he began, 'I was engaged to be married. Everything was arranged, and it was going to be a very grand affair. The day before the wedding, Emily told me she didn't love me and wasn't going to marry me. I was devastated.'

Lily took hold of his hand. 'I am so sorry, Harry.'

'It was a terrible shock. I had given her everything she'd ever wanted – I had furnished a flat with expensive furniture, just as she had asked – but it wasn't to be. I had a nervous breakdown and had to go away. Thank goodness Mother was there to help me through it. Since then I have avoided girls till I saw you. You looked so kind and understanding, and it gave me the courage to ask you out. Mother always said Emily was out for all she could get.'

Lily wanted to ask what had happened to the flat and its contents, but thought that might be a bit insensitive.

'You made a very good impression on Mother when you sent the flowers home, and she wanted to meet you.'

To Lily, Harry seemed such a sad, lost man. Perhaps Rose had been right when she'd asked if he was a mummy's boy. Was that why Lily had been asked to tea, to get his mother's approval? And did she like him enough to overlook all that? Was he stable? Was it his own fault that Emily had dropped him? At the moment, Lily didn't know what to think. And what if she refused to go out with him if he asked her? Would he be ill again? If so, she would blame herself. After all, Harry was kind, but not the most exciting person she had ever known.

Chapter 16

'GOOD NIGHT, MISS Evans,' said Rose as she left the office.

'Good night, Miss Flower,' replied Nora.

Rose knew Nora was being frosty with her because she hadn't let on too much about the weekend. She was desperately hoping that Roger hadn't arrived yet, as she hadn't told Nora that she was meeting him.

It was cold and blustery as she headed towards the corner. She stood in a doorway out of the wind and rain and watched Nora making her way to the bus stop. She hoped Roger wouldn't come along before Nora was on the bus, as she was bound to recognise his car.

Ten minutes went by and there wasn't any sign of him. Rose was cold and her spirits were getting low. Had she made a big mistake? Had he only been teasing her when he said he loved her? Tears began to well up. She would have to go home and live as she always had done. She'd have to face her father and his anger. Why was he so angry with her? All she wanted to do was lead her own life. Rose knew her dreams of an exciting future were slowing fading away. With a heavy heart, she began to walk towards the bus stop. A bus came in sight and she was just about to get on board when she saw Roger's car come round the corner. She hurried towards him; suddenly the sun seemed to be shining and life was wonderful.

'I'm so sorry I'm late,' he said as soon as he was out of the car. He held her close and kissed her, and all her fears about him disappeared. 'I'm sorry I made you wait in the cold. Quick, get into the car.'

Once in the car, Rose let her tears fall.

'My darling, what's wrong?'

She tried to speak, but the words didn't come.

Roger put his arms round her and kissed her cheek. 'Please tell me what's wrong.' He gently wiped her tears with a spotless white handkerchief. This made Rose sob harder.

Gradually the tears subsided and she began to feel calmer.

'Would you like to go somewhere for a coffee, or maybe something stronger?'

'A cup of tea would be nice. But I must be all red and blotchy.'

'You still look beautiful to me. Would you like me to take you home?'

Rose shook her head. 'I can't.'

'Why not?'

'It's a long story. Could we go to your house?'

'Yes, of course.' He looked at her lovely strained face and started the car.

Lily was always home after Rose, so she was surprised when her mother, looking very worried, said that her sister wasn't home yet.

'I wonder where she's gone?' said Amy.

'I don't know.' Lily was also beginning to be concerned.

'Your father will be very annoyed if she's not here by the time he gets home.'

Lily didn't know what to say or think.

Amy went into the scullery and Lily went upstairs. In the bedroom she looked for any clues that might give her some idea where her sister was. There wasn't a note and all her clothes were still here. Surely she wouldn't do anything silly? Would she?

Lily went downstairs when she heard her father come in. What was going to happen if Rose didn't come home? She couldn't even begin to think about such a thing; surely it would never happen. She walked into the kitchen. 'Hello, Dad,' she said cheerfully. 'Everything all right?'

She could see by his face that it wasn't.

Rose stood near Roger as he made a pot of tea in his small kitchen. 'Would you like something to eat?' he asked.

She shook her head, and followed him as he took the tea into the sitting room. They sat together on the sofa.

133

'Now, what's the trouble?'

Once again Rose began to cry.

'Oh my darling. Please tell me what's wrong.'

Rose knew she had to tell him. But would he still feel the same towards her if she told him the whole truth?

'Roger,' she sobbed, 'there's something I haven't told you.'

He visibly straightened.

'You see, I'm not an only child. I have a twin sister.'

He grinned. 'Is that all? That's nothing to cry over. So there's two of you?'

She nodded and gave him a weak smile.

'Is she as lovely as you?'

Rose didn't answer.

'So when do I meet . . .'

'Lily,' she said. 'I don't know. You see, my father was very angry with me for staying out all night, and I don't think I will be able to go back home.'

'That sounds a bit drastic.'

'My father is very possessive.'

'What are you going to do?'

'I don't know.'

'Look, I'll come and talk to him and try to make him see sense. He can't keep you locked away.'

Rose began to cry again.

'Rose, does he beat you?'

She shook her head.

'I know that some church people can be a bit funny at times.'

Rose wanted to tell him the whole truth, but she just couldn't. 'Please. Can I stay here?'

'Do you think that's very wise?'

'I don't know. I don't know what to think.'

'Come on. Let me take you home, and we can get this thing sorted out.'

'Don't you want me to stay?'

'Oh my darling, nothing would give me more pleasure than you being here with me. But I want to do the right thing by your family.'

'I think you want me to go.' Rose gathered up her handbag and stood up.

'Please, Rose, sit down. Let me get you a drink to calm you down.'

Dinner was a very quiet affair in the Flower household and Lily wanted to scream. She knew she had to say something.

'Dad. If Rose don't come home tonight . . .'

His head shot up. 'What? What do you know about all this?'

Lily was terrified at the expression on his face. She had never seen him look so angry. 'I don't know anything.'

He jumped up and his chair fell backwards. He walked round the table and stood over his daughter. 'Where is she?'

'I don't know.' Lily was shaking.

'Ron, sit down, you're frightening the daylights out of the poor girl.'

'I want to get to the bottom of this.' He went back to his place and picked up the chair.

'Lily, if you do know something, then please tell us.'

'Honestly, Mum, I don't.'

Lily knew that when she did set eyes on her sister, she'd have a lot to answer for.

Roger carefully removed his arm from round Rose's shoulders. All evening they had sat and talked, and eventually she had fallen asleep. Why was her father so against her going out? he wondered. He'd been prepared to go and talk to him, but this had upset her even more. Perhaps tomorrow he'd go to the church and try to find some answers – her sister Lily might even be able to help him – but for tonight Rose would have to stay here. He stood up and lit a cigarette. She looked so peaceful, and even with her blotchy red face she was still beautiful. He had never felt this way about anyone else before; she was so refreshingly different to the brash girls he usually took out. And despite his reputation, he knew he had fallen head over heels in love with her.

Rose moved but didn't wake. He waited a moment or two, then gathered her in his arms and carried her upstairs.

The following morning when Lily woke, she could see that her sister's bed was still empty. Tears began to trickle slowly down her cheeks. Where was Rose? Had she gone home with this Roger? Lily was worried. He sounded like a right rogue. Not the sort she should be mixing with. He was way out of her league. 'Please, Rose,' she said out loud. 'Come home and let's get back to how we used to be.'

When she went downstairs, she could see that her mother had had another sleepless night.

'Where is she, Lily?'

'I don't know. I'll ask Miss Tucker if I can have some time off and go to her office to talk to her.'

'Will you?'

Lily nodded.

'Bless you.' Her mother held her tight.

'I'll take her some clean stockings and underwear.'

'Thank you, darling.' Amy dabbed at her eyes.

Lily hated to see her mother like this. Rose certainly had a lot of apologising to do when she finally came home.

Chapter 17

ROSE OPENED HER eyes, and for a moment or two she was disorientated. When she looked around, she knew she was in Roger's bed again, and this time she was relieved to see she was fully clothed. She sat up just as Roger knocked on the door.

'Are you awake?'

'Yes.'

He walked in with a cup of tea.

'I must look a sight.'

He laughed. 'Well let's say I've seen you look better.'

She ran her hands through her hair. 'What time is it?'

'Nine thirty.'

'What!' She jumped out of bed. 'I'm late for work.'

'Don't worry. I'll phone Nora and tell her you won't be in today.'

'You can't.'

'Why?'

'I'll lose my job.'

Roger didn't answer.

'Shouldn't *you* be at work?' Rose asked.

'I'll go to the office later and explain the situation to Archie.'

Rose lay back on the bed. 'Now everybody will know where I spent the night. That's my reputation gone.'

'Are you worried?'

Rose nodded. 'And I seem to be messing everyone else's life up as well as my own.' She let her tears fall.

Roger sat next to her. 'Now come on, let's have no more crying.'

She looked up at him, and her heart was full of love. She put her arms round his neck and kissed him. 'Thank you.'

'What for?'

'Giving me a bed and being so understanding.'

'How do you know I don't have an ulterior motive?'

'I don't care.'

He laughed. 'You hussy.'

When Lily got to work that morning, Miss Tucker gave her a long look. 'Are you feeling all right? You don't look very well to me.'

'I'm sorry. Yes, I am well, but we're having a bit of trouble at home.'

'I'm sorry to hear that.'

'You see, my sister is missing.'

'Oh my dear girl. How long?'

'Last night. She didn't come home from work. Miss

Tucker, could I possibly have my lunch break a bit earlier and go to the office where she works and see if she's there?'

'Of course, my dear. Look, why don't you go now? We don't seem to be very busy.'

'Thank you.' Lily put her hat and coat back on and left. As she got to the bus stop, she wondered what Rose would say to her turning up like this. She didn't care what Rose thought; she just wanted to know that she was all right. And what would she do if Rose didn't want to come home? Well she would certainly give this Nora a piece of her mind.

'What shall we do today?' asked Roger.

'I don't know. I'm so worried about my sister. I hope Dad doesn't take it out on her.'

'Is he likely to?'

'I don't know. I've never left home before.'

'Look, let's go and have a word with him.'

'We can't.' Rose was beginning to get worried. Should she tell Roger that she didn't live at the vicarage? Would he still be interested in her if he knew she came from a very ordinary house in an ordinary street?

'Why can't we?'

'It's a long story. I'll tell you one day.'

He held up his hands. 'Fine, if that's how you want it.'

'It is for now.' Rose knew that if she wanted to be with Roger, she was going to have to explain everything to him eventually.

'Look. I'll tell you what we'll do. You need toilet things and some clothes, so how about I take you to the shops and you can get whatever you want.'

Rose looked at him bewildered. 'What are you saying?'

'Well, if you're going to be a frequent visitor, you don't want to have to bring all the stuff that you girls take around with you; you can just leave it here.'

'You want me to stay here sometimes?'

'More than just sometimes, I hope. Look, here's twenty pounds.' Roger opened his wallet and took out four crisp white five-pound notes.

Rose looked at the money in amazement. This was a king's ransom. She had never even held a five-pound note before.

'I'll go along to the office then I'll wait for you in Selfridges restaurant and we can come home and you can show me all you've bought.'

He said it like this was her home. Rose wanted to pinch herself. This was all a dream. Things like this didn't happen to girls like her.

'Are you all right?' Roger took her hand. 'You look very pale.'

'I'm fine, thank you. Roger, why are you being so kind to me?'

He smiled. He was so good-looking, she felt her knees buckle.

'I think I've told you before that I love you. You're lovely, and I will be proud to take you about and show you off.'

Although she loved him too, she wasn't sure she wanted to be a sort of trophy, and how long would it last? Her mind was turning over. Did he have a secret as well? She looked at him and smiled with the thought that at the moment, she didn't care.

When Lily walked into the office, the girls sitting at the typewriters stopped and looked up. She looked around and couldn't see Rose. Panic filled her. Where was she?

'Can I help you?' asked Betty James.

'I'm looking for Rose Flower.'

'She didn't come to work today.'

'Are you Rose's sister?' said Molly Parker.

'Yes, I am.'

'You're ever so much alike.'

Lily didn't comment on that. Where was Rose?

'Could I see Miss Evans, please?' she asked.

The girl gave her a puzzled look. 'I'll get her for you.'

It was only a moment or two before Miss Evans came in. 'You had better come into my office,' she said to Lily.

Lily followed the well-dressed woman into a small room. As soon as Miss Evans shut the door, she said, 'I expect you want to know where your sister is.'

'You know?'

'Yes.'

'Thank goodness. We are very worried about her.'

'So you should be.'

'What! Is she in hospital or something?'

'No, nothing like that.'

142

'Where is she then?'

'She spent the night with Roger Walker.'

'Alone?'

'I expect so.'

'Is that the bloke she went out with?'

'Yes.'

'How do you know she was there?'

Nora lit a cigarette. 'He phoned me a short while ago and said that Rose wouldn't be in today as she was going shopping.'

'Going shopping? Where does this bloke live?'

'I'm not sure. I think it's a mews somewhere, but I've never been there.'

Lily wanted to sit down, but there was only one chair and Nora was sitting on that. 'How can I get in touch with her?'

'I don't know.'

'Have you got his phone number?'

'No. But I do have a friend who works in the same building as Roger.' She looked in a pad and wrote a number down. 'Here you are.'

'Thank you.' Lily was beginning to feel physically sick. What had her sister done? 'Did this Roger say if she will be coming to work tomorrow?' she asked.

'No.'

'Our father will go mad. He might even call the police.'

Nora ground her cigarette out in the ashtray on her desk. 'That might not be a bad idea. Roger is known for being a bit of a rogue. Now if you'll excuse me, I have work to do.'

Lily left Nora's office and made her way down the stairs. Out in the cold, she began to cry. Where was her sister? And was she safe? If only she had someone to talk to. She just hoped that Harry would be waiting for her tonight. He normally met her on a Tuesday evening, and tonight she needed a shoulder to cry on, but would he be willing to listen to her troubles?

When Lily got back to the shop, she tried to put on a brave face.

'Did you see your sister?' asked Miss Tucker.

'No, she isn't at work.'

'Oh my dear. So you don't know where she is?'

'Her boss did say that she'd had a phone call from her telling her she wouldn't be in today.'

'How strange, not letting the family know.'

'We don't have a phone.'

'No, of course not.'

Lily didn't want Miss Tucker to know that the phone call was from Rose's boyfriend.

'I can see how much this has upset you. Would you like to go home?'

'No thank you. I'm better off keeping busy.'

'Yes, I can understand that.'

Lily went and put her hat and coat in the cloakroom. She took her apron from the peg and went back into the shop.

'We had a young man in while you were out, ordering flowers for his mother's funeral.' She opened the order book.

'When is it for?'

'Next Friday, so we've plenty of time.'

Lily picked up the book and read the address. 'What time will he be collecting them?'

'He said just after two. It seems the funeral is at three. It's quite local.'

Lily looked at the instructions. 'He wants roses for one and carnations for the other.'

'He did say he didn't mind, but it seems his sister told him what to order.'

'It's nice when people have some idea what they want,' said Lily. She was pleased that she had something to take her mind off her missing sister.

'He wants one of the cards to say "From your loving son" and the other "From your loving daughter".'

'No names?' asked Lily.

'Oh yes,' said Miss Tucker. 'It's over the page. The son's William Perry and the daughter's name is June.'

Lily looked at the page. 'William and June Perry. They used to live in our road.'

'Did you know them well?'

Lily smiled and nodded. 'We all liked Will. He was very good-looking.' She stood looking at the booking form. 'June was about the same age as us; she was very pretty. I'm sorry Mrs Perry's died. My mum knew her very well,' she said softly, feeling sad.

Chapter 18

ROSE HAD NEVER been so excited. Roger took her to Oxford Street and said he would meet her in the restaurant when she'd finished. She had been in this store before, but to go in and buy clothes and then go to the restaurant was beyond her wildest dreams. She wandered round trying to decide what to get first. She had twenty whole pounds to spend, and even though he'd told her not to bring any money back, she knew she had to be frugal and not buy anything too extravagant. First she bought some underwear, thrilled by the soft fabric, and then it was on to the make-up and perfume department. When she went along to look at the frocks, she was amazed at the variety, so different to Pecrys, where she normally bought her clothes. The attention she got from the assistants was amazing; they couldn't do enough for her. Roger had told her to get something for evenings as well as daywear. Next it was shoes. Rose felt dizzy with joy. It was like being a child left in a sweet shop. Loaded with parcels, she made her way to the restaurant.

Roger jumped up and kissed her cheek when he saw her. 'You look as if you've bought up the store,' he said, taking some of the parcels.

'I tried,' she said. Her face was glowing. 'This has been the best day of my life. Thank you.'

'I've ordered tea and cakes. Will that do for now? I thought we could go out to dinner later.'

Rose nodded. She just wanted to show Roger what she'd bought and see if it pleased him. She wanted to ask him about staying the night again, but thought she would wait to see if he said anything first. All she knew was that she didn't want to go back home.

'You look very thoughtful.' He reached across the table and held her hand. 'Is something on your mind?'

'Not really.'

'Can't you tell me?'

Rose looked around. 'No, not here. I'll wait till we're alone.'

'That sounds intriguing. I can't wait.'

That evening when Lily left the shop, she was pleased to see Harry waiting for her.

He took her hand and kissed her cheek lightly. 'Is everything all right?'

'No. Not really.'

'What's wrong? Don't you want to see me any more?' He looked sad.

'No.' She smiled and tucked her arm through his. 'It's nothing to do with you. It's Rose.'

'Oh my dear, what's happened?'

'She didn't come home last night and she's not been to work today, and I'm so worried about her.'

'Have you told the police?'

'No. You see, she's with her boyfriend and I only know he lives in a mews somewhere but I've no idea where. Harry, I'm so worried about her.'

'Would you like me to help you find her?'

Lily wanted to cry. Here was someone she knew she could rely on for help. 'I do have the phone number of a friend of this Roger. It seems they work in the same place.'

'I can help you there. I can always use the office phone.'

'I would be so grateful if you could. I need an address. I need to find her. You see, I daren't tell my parents where she might be, as Dad would get the police to bring her back home and I don't think that would be a good idea.'

'No, perhaps not. Look, you sound like you need company. Would you like to go for a coffee or something later tonight?'

'Yes please. I don't think the atmosphere will be very good at home.'

'I'll be round about eight, would that be all right?'

'It would be better for me to meet you here.'

'Yes, perhaps you're right.'

Harry quickly kissed her cheek and turned away.

As Lily began to walk home, tears ran down her face. She wondered if she would ever see her sister again.

Perhaps after Harry had made that phone call tomorrow, they might have some idea where they could start looking.

When they got back to Roger's house, Mrs B was there.

'Good afternoon, Mr Roger, ma'am,' she said, giving Rose a nod when they walked into the kitchen.

Rose, who had been laughing, suddenly stopped.

'Mrs B, this is Rose,' said Roger.

Mrs B looked down her nose at Rose but said politely, 'Hello.' She turned to Roger and asked, 'Is the young lady staying long? If so, would you want me to make up the bed in the spare room?'

'Yes please.' Roger put all the parcels on the table. 'Now, a cup of tea would go down well, Mrs B.'

As she went and put the kettle on, Roger turned to Rose.

'Right, my dear, let's take this lot into the other room.'

Rose quickly gathered up her goods and made her way into the sitting room.

'She doesn't like me,' she said as soon as the door was shut.

'She's not the one who lives here. I do. And I can bring who I like into my own home. Now come here and give me a nice thank-you kiss.'

Rose was in his arms and he was kissing her lips, cheek and neck so passionately that she began to wonder where this might lead. She had never been kissed like this before.

They parted when Mrs B knocked on the door. Roger jumped up and opened it. Rose felt embarrassed and looked away.

'Thank you. I'll take that.' He put the tray on the small table and waited for Mrs B to leave. 'Now, where were we?'

When Rose came up for air, she said breathlessly, 'Thank you so much for all my lovely things.'

'I'll pour the tea and you can start to show me what you've bought.'

One by one Rose undid the bags and brought out shoes, frocks, make-up, perfume and a nightdress. Roger seemed to approve of everything. When she got to the last one, she held the bag close to her.

'I don't know if I should show you these,' she said, smiling.

'I hope it's some very nice underwear.'

Rose blushed. 'I've never shown anything like this to a boyfriend before.'

'I should think not. I'm hoping I'm the first who's ever bought you underwear. Am I?'

She nodded.

'Good, now come on, show me.'

She held up a pair of frilly knickers.

'Wow.' He sat back. 'So when am I going to have the pleasure of seeing these on?'

Rose looked away. 'I don't know,' she whispered. 'It depends.'

'Depends on what?'

'If I stay here.'

'Do you want to?'

She nodded.

'What about your family?'

'I shall miss Lily, of course, but I don't think I shall miss my father.' Rose felt very guilty. She was almost branding her father as some kind of monster, which he wasn't. She just wanted her freedom.

Roger was sitting on the sofa. He patted the seat next to him. 'Come and sit down.'

She did as she was told.

'Now this could be a very big decision for you.'

'I know.'

'Are you ready to make it?'

Rose's heart was beating fast. 'What are you saying?'

'Rose, I would like you to move in with me, but I want you to be sure that this is what you want.'

That was it. There was no mention of getting engaged. She knew she would be breaking all the rules; living with Roger was a great step. Her heart said yes, she loved him, but her head said beware. What if after a few weeks he was tired of her? Where would she go then? She had to ask him. 'Roger, what if you get fed up with me after a few weeks?'

'The way I feel about you, I can't ever see that happening.' He lit a cigarette. 'I may have a bit of a reputation, but I can honestly say I've never felt this way about anyone before.'

Rose didn't know what to say, and the knock on the door made them sit apart. Rose quickly stuffed her new clothes back into the bags.

'Mr Roger, I'm just off.'

'Thank you.' Roger stood up and followed Mrs B from the room.

Rose sat back. What should she do? She loved Roger and desperately wanted to stay here with him, but what about her job? Nora wouldn't be too happy about it. And what about her mother and father? They would be very upset, and Lily, her wonderful sister, would be heart-broken. This could be a life-changing decision; did she want to take it?

When Lily arrived home, her mother opened the kitchen door. 'You alone?'

Lily nodded.

'Was she at work?'

'No.'

'I was hoping she would be with you. Where is she? Your father will go mad.'

'I don't know. I asked that Nora Evans, but she didn't know where this bloke Roger lives.' Lily wasn't going to build her mother's hopes up by telling her that she had a phone number, just in case it wasn't the right one.

'Did you believe her?'

'I don't know.'

The front door slammed and Lily waited for her father to walk in.

'Where is she?' he asked as he hung his cap on the nail behind the door.

'She's not here,' said Amy.

'That's it. I'm going to the police.'

'Ron, take your coat off and sit down and have a cup of tea. Then let's talk about this sensibly.'

'Sensibly!' he shouted. 'How can we talk about it sensibly? She's gone off with God knows who, and I bet in a couple of months' time she'll be back and in the club, bringing shame on all of us.'

Lily just sat quietly. She knew she had to find her sister.

'Lily went to her office this morning,' said Amy as she handed her husband a cup of tea.

'And?'

'She wasn't at work. Ron, you don't think anything could have happened to her?'

He put his tea on the floor and began to unlace his boots. He looked at Lily. 'What did Rose's boss have to say?'

Lily swallowed hard. She didn't want to get her sister into any more trouble, but what could she say? 'She said Rose hadn't been to work today.'

'That it?'

Lily nodded.

'Don't she know where she is?'

'No.'

Ron put his head in his hands. 'Why is she doing this to us?'

Lily wanted to cry. When she got hold of her sister, she'd murder her for what she was doing to her family.

Amy went and knelt in front of her husband. 'Ron, now come on. I know you're upset, but please don't take on so.'

He slowly lifted his head, and Lily was shocked to see

tears running down his face. She felt helpless and bewildered. She wanted to hug and comfort him. Her mother looked sad as she held him close. Why was Rose doing this? If Harry could find out where she was, Lily would be round there at once, and if need be, she'd drag her sister back home. This scene had upset her so much.

Chapter 19

I KNOW DAD loves us, but why has he got so upset?' asked Lily as she helped her mother dish up the dinner.

Her mother swiftly closed the door to the kitchen. 'Don't forget he lost his sister, and he's always been frightened of losing you girls to someone he disapproves of.'

'But surely the choice should be ours?'

'That's not the way he sees it.'

'And what if he doesn't like the blokes we choose?'

'I dread to think.'

They took the plates through to the kitchen, and dinner was eaten in silence. Not that her father ate very much, pushing his plate away after a few mouthfuls.

'Ron, please,' said Amy. 'This is not going to do you any good.'

'I'm sorry, love, but I just can't eat. I'm worried stiff about her.'

'We all are, Dad,' said Lily.

'How would we know if something really bad had happened to her?'

'I'm sure she's fine,' said Amy.

Although Lily knew her father thought the world of his girls, she'd never imagined she'd see him so upset at Rose going off. 'Dad, I'm going to meet Harry tonight, is that all right? I won't be late home.'

'All right.'

'You won't go to the police while I'm gone, will you?'

'Not tonight.'

Lily heaved a sigh of relief.

'I'll give her one more day to come to her senses and leave this bloke. If he's a decent sort, he'll come and see us and not keep her away. What's he got to hide?'

Lily just hoped that Harry would get an address tomorrow so she could go and find her sister. If he could bring it to the shop during his lunch hour, she would ask Miss Tucker if she could have the afternoon off; that way she might have some good news to bring home. With that thought she felt a little happier, and tackled the washing-up with gusto. While they were in the scullery, she told her mother about Mrs Perry.

'What a shame. She was such a lovely woman and she managed to bring her kids up on her own.' Tears filled her eyes. 'I was lucky your father came home, but her husband was killed just after her daughter was born.'

'I know, Mum.'

* * *

'I do have to go to the office tomorrow,' said Roger as they walked home from the restaurant where they'd had a lovely meal. All evening Rose had felt so sophisticated as she drank wine from beautiful glasses and the waiters, elegantly dressed in white shirts with black bow ties, hovered round them. She had felt very grand in one of her new dresses and matching shoes. Roger had his arm round her waist. This was the life she wanted to lead.

'I'd like to go to work as well. Can I get to the office from here?' she asked.

'Are you sure that's what you want?'

She nodded. 'I can't stay all day at your house with nothing to do.'

'Only if you're sure. You might find Nora will be a bit funny.'

'That's a chance I'll have to take.' Rose would wait till they got back to his house before she asked about moving in permanently. There was no way her father would let her go back home and still see Roger.

Roger touched her hand tenderly. 'I do love you, Rose.'

She blushed. Was this all a dream?

Back at the house, she went into the kitchen and began to make some tea.

'You seem to be at home in my kitchen.'

Rose was worried that she was taking liberties. 'I'm sorry. I just thought it would be nice for me to do something for you for a change.'

'No, that's fine. Although I'm going to have something stronger. Would you like one?'

'No thank you, tea will suit me fine.'

'You seem a little tense.'

'It's just that this is all so different to my way of life.'

'Do you have any regrets and want to go back home?'

Rose pulled out a chair from under the table and sat down. 'No. I want to be here with you, and I don't want to be pushy, but—'

Roger held up his hand, then he too pulled out a chair. 'I know. You want to know if my intentions are honourable.'

'Well, yes. In a way. I don't know what I would do if next week you dropped me for someone else.'

'My darling Rose, I love you.'

Rose began to worry. Was she trapping him into a corner? 'And I love you.'

'What would you say if I asked you to marry me?'

'What!'

'Would you?'

'I can't. I'm underage.'

'We can overcome that.'

'How?'

'Gretna Green.'

She laughed. 'Gretna Green. That's in Scotland.'

'Yes, and you can get married underage there and without your father's consent.'

Rose looked at him dumbfounded. 'You don't mean that?'

'I most certainly do.'

Rose sat with a look of amazement on her face. 'You really want to marry me?'

'Very much.'

'I don't know.'

'Don't you love me?'

'Yes, I do, but we hardly know each other.'

'I know it's a bit sudden, but if this is the only way I can have you, then marriage it is.'

'But I'm so young.'

'Well, we could live in sin, but I don't want that. I love you and want to make an honest woman of you. I want you to be my wife.'

Rose couldn't believe her luck. This good-looking, rich man wanted to marry her. This was something she had always dreamed of, and now it was going to happen. 'I would love to marry you, Roger.'

He came round the table and kissed her long and passionately.

When they broke away she asked, 'By the way, what will my surname be?'

Roger laughed. 'Yes, I suppose you should know. You will be Mrs Roger Walker. Does that suit?'

'Very much.'

'Tomorrow I'll tell Archie of my plans and arrange to have some time off. We have a lot of plans to make. We have to be in residence for three weeks.'

'We're really going to go to Scotland?'

'Yes. I'll give you some money to buy a wedding outfit.'

Rose just sat looking at him. This was happening too fast. She needed time to think about it. What about her family? What about Lily?

'Are you pleased?'

'Yes. Yes, of course.'

'So why the worried look?'

'Don't know. I suppose it's all happening so fast.'

'Well you said your father wouldn't let you stay with me, so I am offering you a way out.'

'Roger, are you sure this is what you want?'

'Are you having second thoughts?'

'No.'

'Good. Now, I think we should go to bed. We have a lot to sort out tomorrow.'

Although Rose was happy, she was worried that everything was being rushed along. She wanted to talk to Lily. She wanted her sister to be with her on her wedding day. They had always talked about being each other's bridesmaids, but it wasn't going to be.

When she came out of the bathroom, Roger was already sitting up in bed.

He patted the bed. 'Come on, my darling. This is what I've been longing for.'

Rose felt a little self-conscious as she got in beside him. He kissed her passionately. His hands were all over her body, and she shivered with excitement. This was what she wanted. To love and be loved.

Rose was finding sleep hard to come by. She couldn't believe what they had just done. When she said she was frightened of having a baby, Roger reassured her that it was fine, he had protection. She really didn't know what he was talking about. After the slight pain, she just lay and enjoyed the wonderful feeling that raced all over her. Roger was gentle, understanding and very loving. He also knew how to keep her satisfied. She looked at him lying next to her sleeping soundly, and when he stirred, a great tenderness came over her. She loved him so very much, and he wanted to marry her. Rose Flower, a girl from Rotherhithe, was going to run away to get married. If only she could tell her father that she was sorry, and that she really loved him and her mum and didn't want to hurt them. She would write to Lily and tell her her thoughts. If there was one regret, it was that she couldn't share all this with her sister. As children, they used to plan their weddings dressed in old lace curtains. Rose smiled to herself. She was always the bride and Lily had to walk behind. But Lily wouldn't be with her on her special day. That thought upset her, and with all this going round and round in her head, she finally fell into a fitful but satisfied sleep.

Chapter 20

ALL THE FOLLOWING morning Lily waited eagerly for Harry to appear. She had told Miss Tucker of her plan, and although she wasn't happy about letting Lily have time off from work, because of the circumstances she did reluctantly agree.

Just after one o'clock, Harry was outside and waving to her.

She put on her coat and hat and walked through the shop to meet him. As she opened the door, Miss Tucker wished her luck in her search.

'Did you manage to phone?' she asked Harry as soon as she saw him.

'Yes, I did.'

'Where is she?' Lily asked straight away.

'I'm afraid I don't know.'

Lily felt as if the bottom had fallen out of her world. 'You did phone that number I gave you?'

'Yes, but the girl on the switchboard wouldn't tell me

anything except that Roger, Mr Walker, wasn't in the office.'

'What am I going to do?'

'I did ask if he would be in later, but she didn't know. I've got the address of the office, though.'

Lily threw her arms round his neck and kissed him. When she broke away, she said self-consciously, 'I'm so sorry.'

Harry smiled. 'You don't have to be.'

Embarrassed, she asked, 'So where is this office?'

'In the City somewhere. Off Lombard Street. She said it was a funny little place, more like an alley than a street.'

'Do you know where Lombard Street is?'

'No.'

'Can we get a map?'

'Of course.'

'Can we go now?'

'I'm afraid I only have my lunch hour. I can't get away today as we're very busy.'

Lily looked devastated.

'I'm so sorry. I can ask for tomorrow off.'

'I need to see her today. Besides, Miss Tucker has given me the afternoon off.'

'I'm very sorry, Lily. I've let you down.'

She patted his hand. 'Don't worry, Harry. I'll go and see if I can find this place.' She looked at the piece of paper, Harry had given her.

'Can I see you tonight?' he asked.

'No. Just in case I'm with my sister.'

'I understand.' He kissed her cheek.

Lily began to walk to the bus stop. She knew she had to get to the other side of the river. When a bus came along, she turned and waved to Harry. She wished he was going with her to give her support.

After buying a map of London, she found that Lombard Street was near the Bank of England. So with a spring in her step and hope in her heart, she set off to find her sister.

'Right,' said Roger when he walked into the sitting room.

Rose had been keeping out of the way of Mrs B, who was busy in the kitchen. She didn't want to appear to be trying to take over.

'That's all settled. And what have you been doing with yourself this morning while I've been at the office?'

'Making myself pretty for you.'

'I'm sure that couldn't have taken you long.'

'Thank you, kind sir.' Rose went up to him and kissed him long and hard.

When they broke apart, Roger said, 'Miss Flower, I wish you would control yourself, otherwise I won't be responsible for my actions.'

'What? With Mrs B in the kitchen?'

'I don't care,' he said, laughing.

'Well I do. What did you tell Archie?'

'He couldn't believe it. He said we are to go to his house tonight and he and Poppy will give us a small engagement dinner. And now, my darling, I think we should go and buy you a ring.'

Rose couldn't believe this was happening.

'Is there anything you prefer? Cluster, solitaire?'

'No. No, I don't know.'

'Well let's see what the jeweller has, shall we?'

Smiling, Rose nodded.

Lily was looking at her map and making her way to Lombard Street. She shivered; it was very cold. As she wandered along, she looked for an alley of some sort. There were a lot of side shoots off, and Harry hadn't given her the name of the office.

As she walked past a group of men, one of them suddenly called out, 'Rose!'

She stopped, and he came up to her.

'Oh my God. I'm so sorry, I thought you were someone I knew.' He looked her up and down. 'You are so like her it's like looking at a twin. You haven't got a sister called Rose, have you, by any chance?'

Lily couldn't believe it. This must be Roger. 'Are you Roger?'

'No,' he laughed. 'Not that I'd mind being him. No, I'm James, a friend. And you are …'

'Lily. Rose's twin sister.'

'A twin sister, eh? Gosh, she certainly kept you quiet. You really are so alike.'

The way this man was looking at her, Lily knew he was probably wondering how they could look alike and yet be so different. She wasn't as fashionably dressed as her sister.

'So what are you doing round here? I'm sorry, I shouldn't be asking you questions.'

'No, that's all right. In fact, I'm looking for my sister. You see, she hasn't been home for a couple of days, and all I know is that she's with a man called Roger, and the family's so worried about her.' Tears began to spill from her eyes.

James glanced round. His friends had walked on. 'My dear, don't upset yourself.' He took a handkerchief from his top pocket and handed it to Lily, who took it without thinking.

'Thank you.'

'She's perfectly safe with Roger.'

'Then why don't she come home?' Lily wiped her eyes.

'Look, why don't we go and have a coffee and you can tell me all about it.'

'No. I must find Roger and make sure Rose is safe. Do you know where he works?'

'Yes, I do. Come along, I'll show you.' James was thinking that Roger must be such a seducer. He'd got Rose tucked away and had never mentioned a sister.

'Do you work with him?' asked Lily as they walked along.

'No. We're in the same block but different offices. Roger is more in the overseas department.'

Lily stopped. 'He wouldn't be taking her away, would he?'

'No, of course not. I know Roger is a bit of a Casanova, but he wouldn't want to be tied down for long.'

That statement worried Lily.

When they came to a stop and James pushed open a door, Lily didn't know what to expect. She was going to meet Roger.

They walked up to a desk and James said to the girl who was sitting behind it, 'Miss Ferguson, could you buzz Roger Walker's office and tell him there's someone here who wants to speak to him.'

'I'm sorry, Mr Flint, but Mr Walker only came in for a short while this morning and now he's gone.'

Lily felt her legs buckle. 'Do you know where he lives?' she asked quickly.

The girl shook her head. 'I'm not allowed to give out addresses.'

'I know where he lives,' said James.

'Is it far?' asked Lily.

'Too far for you to walk.' He edged Lily towards the door and said softly, 'Look, if you like, I can take you there now. My car's just round the corner.'

Lily glanced at Miss Ferguson, who raised her eyebrows.

'I don't know.' She wasn't sure if she should go with this man, but she didn't have a lot of choice if she wanted to see her sister. 'I don't want to put you out.'

'Don't worry about it, we can do more or less what we like here.' James was also wondering what it was that was keeping Roger hanging on to Rose. He had to find out more, and this bit of gossip was something Nora was going to enjoy.

Lily got into the car and James sped away. Lily had no idea where they were going, and just hoped she'd done the right thing.

After a while, they turned into a narrow cobbled street.

'This is it,' said James, stopping the car. He switched off the engine and got out, holding the door open for Lily, who she just stood and gazed at this lovely row of houses.

'Roger lives at number forty, over there.' James pointed to a house with pretty lace curtains at the bay window.

Lily felt so excited. She was here outside the house, and Rose could be inside.

James walked across the road and knocked on the door. Lily was right behind him. He knocked again, then peered through the letter box. 'There doesn't seem to be anyone home,' he said. He looked through the window, then turned and shrugged his shoulders.

Lily stood devastated. She didn't know what to do or say.

'I'm sorry. It looks as if he's out.'

'What shall I do?'

'You could come back later.'

'I don't know.'

'Look, I can pick you up and we could come back here tonight.'

'No. No thank you. I couldn't let you do that.'

James was thinking that that would be a turn-up, him arriving on Roger's doorstep with the sister in tow. He smiled. 'It wouldn't be any bother.'

Lily began to rummage in her handbag. As much as she wanted to see her sister, she didn't want this man to bring her back here. 'I'll leave her a note and she can get in touch with me and tell me what she wants to do.'

'Are you sure?'

'Yes. And thank you for being so helpful. I can find my way to the bus stop.'

'Only if you're sure.'

'Yes. I mustn't keep you from the office any longer.'

He took her hand and kissed it. 'It was a pleasure meeting you.'

Lily watched him get back in the car and breathed a sigh of relief. He was very charming, but if that Roger was anything like him, she could see why Rose had been carried away. She began to write a note to Rose telling her that she must come home. She also told her to come to the shop tomorrow lunchtime, and perhaps they could sort things out. She pushed it through the letter box and walked away.

Rose arrived back with Roger happy and laughing. She took her glove off again and looked at the lovely three-diamond ring on her finger.

Roger put the key in the lock. 'Now you must take it off until we are somewhere special where I can propose properly.'

She quickly kissed his cheek and said, 'I am so happy. Thank you.'

They walked into the hall, and as Roger shut the front

door he said, 'Someone's left a note.' He picked it up. 'It's for you.'

Rose felt the colour drain from her face. 'For me? Who knows I'm here? Who's it from?'

Roger glanced at it. 'It's from Lily.'

'Lily's been here? How did she know where I was?'

'She's obviously used her brain to find out. She could have been to see Nora.' He handed her the note.

Rose sat on the stairs and read it. 'What shall I do?'

'The choice is yours, my darling. Do you want to see your sister?'

She nodded.

'Well then, tomorrow we'll go to your house, and that way I might be able to persuade your father that my intentions are honourable.'

'No. No, we can't do that.'

'Why not?'

Rose had to think quickly. 'My father might call the police and they would stop me going away with you.'

'Perhaps you're right. So what do you want to do?'

'I can go to the shop where she works and talk to her.'

'If that's what you want. Don't look so sad. Tonight we're going to have a wonderful evening and celebrate, and with Poppy's help I'm sure it's going to be an evening to remember.'

Rose smiled. This was what she wanted, and tomorrow she'd face her sister and tell her everything.

Chapter 21

ALTHOUGH THE SHOP would still be open, Lily felt she couldn't go back to work, so she made her way home.

'Lily, what are you doing home so early? Do you feel all right?' asked her mother as soon as she walked into the kitchen.

Lily sat at the table and let the tears fall.

Amy raced round the table and held her daughter close. She gently patted Lily's head. 'There, there, love. What's upset you so much?'

Lily brushed away her tears with her hand. 'I'm so sorry, Mum.'

'You don't have to be. Now tell me what's bothering you. Has something happened at work?'

'No. Please sit down.'

Her mother did as she was told.

'Promise me that you won't tell Dad any of what I'm going to tell you.' Lily blew her nose.

'Whose is that?' Her mother pointed to the hand-kerchief James had given her.

Lily had to think quickly. 'It's Harry's.'

'I'll wash it and then you can give it back to him. Have you seen Rose?'

'No.' Lily shook her head. 'But I hope to tomorrow.'

Amy's face fell. 'Is she coming home?'

'I don't know. Mum, promise.'

Amy nodded her head.

Lily went on to tell her about Harry getting the address of Roger's office, and her going there and then to his house, and how she was so upset at not seeing her sister.

'But you've got his address?'

'Yes. Please don't tell Dad.'

'Why not?'

'I don't want him racing over there and Rose doing something silly. I left a note and I'm meeting her tomorrow.'

'Where? I'll come with you.'

'No, Mum. Let me do this my way.'

'Only if you're sure.'

'I think it's best.'

Amy sat for a while deep in thought. Although she had promised Lily that she would say nothing, never in all their married life had she and Ron had secrets from one another. What would Ron do if she told him?

All the while Rose was getting ready to go to Poppy's, she kept glancing across at the note from Lily sitting on the dressing table. Tonight should be the happiest time of her life, but now she had this hanging over her. Would Lily tell their father where she was living, and would he come here and start trouble? Should she go to the shop tomorrow and tell her sister everything, or should she wait till she came back from Scotland? She stood up and smoothed down the lovely pale blue dress that Roger had bought for her this afternoon. He was so generous. It shimmered with every movement she made. She thought about the one that was hanging in the wardrobe. Her first party frock, the one she had bought from Madam Tina's. That seemed a lifetime ago. This one came from Selfridges, and to her seemed very expensive. She carefully arranged her hairband with its matching feather, then took one last look in the long mirror and made her way downstairs.

'My God,' said Roger when she walked into the front room. 'You look absolutely gorgeous. I don't think we should go out, I think we should stay here and make love.'

Rose blushed. 'We can do that later.' She'd never thought she would say something like that to a man. But then she had never loved a man like she loved Roger.

'Perhaps you're right. Rose,' he suddenly sounded serious, 'what are you going to do about your sister?'

'I don't know. Can't we forget about it tonight and I'll worry about it in the morning?'

'Of course, my love.' He picked up her coat and helped her into it. 'Ready?'

She nodded and took his arm.

It was freezing outside, and she shivered and snuggled down in her fur collar.

Roger held the car door open for her. 'You'll have to get yourself a better coat than this one.'

'I know, but I haven't any money.' She thought about how thrilled she had been when she took this one home. At the time it had seemed very glamorous and she had saved hard for it. 'I must go back to work,' she said.

When they were settled and driving along, Roger said, 'I'll give you an allowance. That will tide you over till we're married. It should cover everything you need. That way you don't have to go back to work.'

'Roger, what can I say? You are so generous. Thank you.'

'That's because I love you and don't want to lose you.'

She leant over and kissed his cheek.

'Rose, please. I'm driving.'

She laughed. 'I'll never leave you and I do love you.'

'You can prove that later tonight.'

When Lily heard the front door shut, she was dreading her father walking in. She had tried to make herself look as if she hadn't been crying, and she and her mother were busy getting the dinner ready.

'Hello, love,' said Ron, coming into the kitchen and kissing Amy lightly on her cheek. 'Everything all right?'

'Yes thanks.'

'Lily, I don't suppose you've heard from you-know-who?' He had said he didn't want Rose's name mentioned till she had come to her senses.

Lily swallowed. She didn't want to lie to him, but she

didn't want to betray her sister either. 'Dad,' she said, 'I don't want to upset you, but I think I might be seeing her tomorrow.'

'She's got in touch with you?'

'No.' Lily looked at her mother, who was standing behind her husband, and she quickly shook her head. Lily went on, 'I went to her office again and told Nora that it was important that I contacted her. She said she would pass the message on.' Although she had crossed her fingers behind her back, she knew she was telling lies.

'So she's not at work, then?'

It was Lily's turn to shake her head.

'If she don't turn up tomorrow, then that's it. I'll go to the police and they'll bring her back. I'm not having her running about with any Tom, Dick or Harry.' He sat in his chair and put his head in his hands. 'Why is she doing this to us?'

Lily sat at the table. Whatever Rose was up to, she was making everybody else in this house very unhappy, and when Lily saw her she was going to give her a right piece of her mind.

Rose was greeted with open arms when Poppy opened the door. 'My darling, don't you just look absolutely fabulous?' She kissed Rose on both cheeks.

'Thank you. And so do you.'

'Oh this old thing, it's something I've worn before. If I'd had had more notice I would have got a new one.'

Rose looked at the wonderful gold cocktail frock Poppy

was wearing. She had seen one very similar in a magazine and it cost a fortune.

'Now come on, Archie is waiting with the champers.'

Archie kissed Rose on both cheeks and shook Roger's hand enthusiastically. 'You old dog. So you're going to marry this pretty little thing, then?'

'Yes, but we've got to go to Gretna Green to tie the knot, as Rose is underage and her father doesn't approve of me.'

'He's got more sense than his daughter, then.' Archie let out a loud laugh.

Poppy clapped her hands. 'I'm so excited for you both. It's so romantic. Can we go with them, Archie? They'll need witnesses.'

'When is this marriage going to take place?' asked her husband.

'As soon as. I need to talk to you about when I can have time off. I expect we'll be gone for about a month.'

Rose was standing next to Roger, and she felt tingles up and down her spine when he put his arm round her; she was smiling fit to bust. They were going to be away for a month. That would be almost till Christmas. She felt so excited.

'Now, show me your ring.' Poppy took Rose's hand.

'I haven't proposed properly yet,' said Roger. 'I've been waiting for a really romantic place.'

'Well how about in our garden room, that can be very romantic,' said Poppy.

'Sounds perfect.'

'I'll turn down some of the lights. That'll make it really special.'

Roger took hold of Rose's hand. 'Will that be all right for you, my love?'

'Yes.'

They moved to the garden room, the lights were turned down and Poppy and Archie left them alone.

When they'd been in here before, it had been full of people and smoke; now it was warm, and the scent from the flowers was lovely. Rose wondered if she would wake up from this wonderful dream world she was in.

Roger guided her to the chaise longue. 'Please sit down.' She did as she was told.

Roger got down on one knee. 'Rose Flower, I love you. Would you please make me very happy and agree to be my wife?' He took the ring from the box and held it up.

Rose wanted to cry she was so happy. Her thoughts went to her family. Why couldn't they see that Roger was everything a girl could want? 'I would love to be your wife.'

He slipped the ring on her finger and kissed her as only he knew how, long and passionately.

Although she was in Roger's arms, her thoughts were still on her family. She wanted to share this with them. How could they think that anything could go wrong? Tomorrow she would go and see Lily and talk to her, but she had to be careful. She wouldn't tell her she was going to Gretna Green to get married, just in case her father sent the police after them.

Chapter 22

ALL MORNING LILY was on tenterhooks. She desperately hoped that Rose would come to see her. She looked at the clock for the hundredth time. It was almost one. Rose knew that was the time she had her lunch hour. Perhaps she was waiting round the corner.

Lily went to the staff room and put on her hat, coat and gloves, then made her way through the shop. 'I'm just off, Miss Tucker.'

She got a nod as an acknowledgement, as her boss was busy finishing off a flower arrangement.

As Lily turned the corner, she almost bumped into Harry.

'Lily, how are you?' He kissed her cheek. 'Did you see your sister? I'm so sorry I had to leave you.'

'That's all right. I did understand. And no, I didn't see her. One of Roger's friends took me to where he lives, but unfortunately they were out. I left a note telling her to come here and see me today, but so far she hasn't turned up.'

'Oh Lily, I'm so sorry.'

'Shall we go and have a cup of tea?'

'I think that sounds a very good idea.' He pulled her arm through his, and with their heads bent against the cold wind they made their way round the corner to a café where they would be able to see Rose if she walked past.

They settled in a window seat and the waitress brought their tea.

'If you see Rose, I'll wait in here for you, or if you'd rather, I can make my way back to the office.'

'Thank you.' Lily was finding it hard to concentrate on any conversation.

Roger had gone to the office and Rose was getting ready to meet Lily. Mrs B was busy in the kitchen. She had just said a curt hello when Rose came downstairs. Roger had told her that Rose had moved in and they were going to get married but that she would still be wanted, but even that didn't bring a smile to her face.

The doorbell rang and Rose went cold. Had Lily come here? Was their father with her? She looked through the lace curtains, but Mrs B had already answered the door and invited whoever it was in. The sitting room door opened and Rose was surprised to see Poppy standing there.

'Poppy, what a pleasant surprise. Do come in.' They exchanged air kisses, then Rose said, 'Mrs B, could we have some coffee, please.'

Mrs B tutted and walked away.

'Whoops,' said Poppy. 'I don't think she approves of you.'

'I know. But hopefully after we're married she'll realise that I'm not just a good-time girl who is after Roger for the wrong reasons. So, what can I do for you? Not that it's not nice to see you, and thank you for the dinner last night.' Rose knew she was rambling, but she was worried that Poppy was going to tell her something awful about Roger. She looked at the clock, and was also worried about not getting to see her sister. 'Please let me take your coat.'

Poppy began to remove her beautiful soft brown fur coat.

'This is lovely.' Rose took the coat, secretly stroking it as she placed it gently on the sofa. 'Have a seat.'

'Thank you.' Poppy looked around. 'This is a lovely little house, and Mrs B has always kept it very nice for Roger.'

Rose was wondering what Poppy wanted. She sensed that this wasn't just a social visit.

Mrs B knocked on the door and Rose quickly called for her to come in. The coffee was put on the small table and Rose sat down and tried to relax.

Harry looked at his watch. 'I am sorry, Lily, but I have to go.'

'That's all right, I understand. So do I.' It was almost two o'clock and Lily knew her sister wasn't going to turn up. Reluctantly she went back to work.

The two wreaths for the Perry family were waiting for Will and his sister to collect. They looked beautiful, and their perfume was filling the shop. Miss Tucker had found it a little difficult to locate the flowers out of season, but as usual she came up trumps, and Lily was pleased that she had helped to make the arrangements as lovely as they were.

'I hope they like them,' said Miss Tucker when she saw Lily admiring them. 'After all the trouble I had getting the flowers.'

'I expect they will.'

When the shop door opened, Lily saw Will standing there. June was with him, and there was also another man and woman.

'Lily. Lily Flower,' said Will. He sounded very surprised.

'I was so sorry to hear about your mother. My mum sends her condolences,' said Lily.

'Thank you. Fancy you working here,' said Will.

Lily only smiled.

'How's Rose?' he asked.

'She's fine.'

'How are you, Lily?' said June, who was dressed in black. Her coat had a beautiful fur collar and she was wearing a cloche hat with a heavy veil.

'Fine, thank you.'

'This is my husband Neil, and Will's friend Sally,' said June.

Sally, a petite blonde who looked stunning in black, nodded her acknowledgment. Lily handed the wreath of carnations to June, who passed them on to her husband. Will picked up the other one.

'These are very nice,' he said.

'Thank you,' replied Lily. When the bereaved collected the flowers for their loved ones, it was always a solemn time.

After their quick goodbyes, they left and Lily closed the door after them. It was strange seeing Will again after all these years, but he was as friendly and kind as he always had been.

Rose and Poppy were still drinking coffee half an hour later and talking about nothing in particular. This was a very different Poppy to the one who was normally the life and soul of the party. That Poppy was full of life and giggly; this one was very serious and quite intimidating. Rose was still wondering what she really wanted, and as time went on, she knew that she was going to miss Lily's lunch hour at the shop.

'You keep looking at the clock, Rose. Am I in the way? Are you expecting someone?'

'No. I was going out, but it wasn't important.'

'Good. I expect you're wondering why I'm here.'

'Yes, I am. Is it to talk about the wedding?'

'In a way. You see, I want to warn you.'

'What about?'

'I am very fond of Roger. I have known him for many years and I don't want to see him hurt.'

Rose laughed. 'I have no intention of hurting him. I love him very much.'

Poppy sat back. 'I was like you once. I too came from

nowhere, and when I worked at the office where Archie had his business, I made a play for him. He was rich, successful and fun.' She took a cigarette from a gold case, then offered Rose one.

Rose shook her head and watched while Poppy placed her cigarette in a tortoiseshell holder and lit it. She blew smoke into the air before she continued. 'It wasn't long before we were married.'

'Why are you telling me all this?'

'I saw the way you looked at my house. I could tell that that was something you wanted.'

'I don't want your husband.'

'No, not my husband. You want to get your hands on Roger and have nice things. I don't blame you, but as I said, I don't want to see him hurt.'

'I'm no gold-digger.'

'You're not the first to try and get Roger up the aisle. He's always been one for pretty ladies.'

'I told you I love him.'

'I hope you do. But you see, we know nothing about you, and I'm concerned that you have something to hide. Why do you have to go to Gretna to get married?'

'Roger told you that my father doesn't approve.'

'Why is that? Will he do something about it when you get back?'

'I don't think so.' That worried Rose. Could her father have Roger arrested?

Poppy took the cigarette from the holder and stubbed it out in the ashtray. 'That's all right then.' She stood up.

'I hope you didn't mind me coming to talk to you.'

'No. It's nice that you have Roger's welfare at heart. But I will make him very happy.'

'I hope so. As I said, you're not the first to try and get him to the altar. He has a very good position in the firm and I would hate to see him upset.' She picked up her coat.

'I love Roger very much,' said Rose.

'That's good, because he is absolutely besotted with you. But remember; don't ever hurt him. Bye for now.'

She walked out, and Rose quickly followed her and closed the front door behind her. What was Poppy trying to tell her?

Rose stood by the door for a while, then she collected the coffee cups and took them into the kitchen. When she went back into the sitting room, she sat down. In some ways she felt guilty. She had set her sights on Roger when she first met him, but she'd never thought she would fall in love with him. She looked at the clock. She had to see Lily. If she left now, she could wait for her to finish work and then they could talk. She was beginning to get worried. Could Roger be arrested for marrying a minor?

When Mrs B knocked on the door, it made Rose jump.

'Was there anything else, miss?'

'No thank you.'

'Well I'll be off then, miss. I've done all the veg for dinner.'

'Thank you.' Rose noted how she emphasised the 'miss'.

This was the most the cleaner had ever said to Rose, and Rose dearly wanted to ask her how many other women had shared Roger's bed, but she knew she wouldn't get an answer.

Rose was still in the sitting room when Roger walked in.

'Rose. I thought you were going to see your sister.'

She stood up. 'I was, but Poppy came to see me.'

'So you had a chat instead. All about me, I hope?'

She gave him a slight smile.

'What is it? You look upset. What did Poppy have to say?'

'Roger, I do love you and I am not after your money.'

'I should hope not.' He sat on the sofa. 'Now come here and tell me what's wrong.' He patted the seat next to him.

When Rose had finished telling him what Poppy had said, he began to laugh.

'I'm glad you find it funny. I was very hurt.'

'Let me tell you something. Everybody in the office, including Archie, knew that Poppy was making a play for him, and he loved it that such a pretty young thing had fallen for him.'

'Did she love him?'

'We think she did. Anyway, they've been married for almost six years now, so something must be going right.'

Rose had her doubts.

'And as for the bit about me and other women, I'm a red-blooded man and I must admit I've had my share, but honestly, I've never loved anyone like I love you. Now give me a welcome-home kiss and then we'll think about your sister. By the way, I saw James today, and he thinks I'm a bit of a dark horse keeping her a secret.'

Now Rose had another worry. Would James ask Nora where Lily worked? If he went to talk to her, he might find out that they didn't live at the vicarage. Rose knew that Lily wouldn't pretend about anything. Perhaps now she should tell Roger her real address, but if she did, would he go and see her father?

Her life had been going so well; now everything was going wrong. This was her own fault for trying to be something she wasn't.

'You're very quiet,' said Roger. 'Poppy has really upset you, hasn't she?'

Rose shook her head and threw her arms round his neck. 'Roger, I do love you so very much and I want to be with you for the rest of my life.'

He looked at her, bewildered.

She wiped away the tears that had slipped down her cheeks. 'I don't want you to think badly of me when I tell you something.'

He laughed. 'I know, you've got six kids hidden away.'

'Promise me that you love me for myself?'

'I promise.' He began to look serious and took her hand. 'Now come on, tell me what's bothering you.'

Chapter 23

IT HAD BEEN raining for most of the afternoon, and as Lily walked home, she thought about Will and his family, who had been standing around in a graveyard in this weather.

Her thoughts were interrupted when Rose called out her name. Lily turned, and Rose rushed over to her and held her close. They both had tears running down their cheeks.

'Where have you been? We're all so worried about you.' Lily was holding her umbrella over her sister when she suddenly realised that a man with his trilby pulled down and his coat collar up was coming towards them.

'Lily, this is Roger,' said Rose, holding on to his arm.

He held out his hand. 'I've heard a lot about you.'

'I've heard nothing about you,' said Lily, ignoring his outstretched hand. 'Where have you been keeping my sister?' She knew her voice was rising.

'Lily.' Rose looked round. 'Keep your voice down.'

'What? After all the upset you've brought us? Rose, I'm so angry with you. You are so selfish.' Lily stepped back. 'But then that's you all over. If and when you decide to come home, you had better be prepared for Dad. He's very angry.' With that, she turned and stormed off. She wanted so much to talk to her sister, but why had she brought her bloke along? She was so cross, and as the tears streamed down her face she couldn't even think straight.

Rose just stood and stared at her sister's back. This wasn't like Lily at all.

'Lily. Lily!' called Roger.

She didn't slow down but he quickly caught up with her. 'Please listen to your sister.'

She tossed her head in the air. 'Why should I?'

He held on to her arm, causing her to stop. 'She loves you and your parents.'

Lily brushed his hand away. 'She's got a funny way of showing it.'

'I know all about your family and that you don't live behind the vicarage.'

Lily would have laughed if she hadn't been so angry. 'Is that all she's told you?'

'I also know your father is very possessive.'

'That's because he loves us and don't want us to mix with the likes of you, with and all your money and flash ways.' She walked on.

'Is that what you think?'

Lily walked on.

'Lily. I want to marry Rose.'

Lily stopped again. This time Rose was at Roger's side. 'We're going home to ask Dad if he'll give his consent,' she said.

'What?'

'I'm going to marry Roger.'

'Why?'

'Because I love him.'

'And you know what Dad will say to that, don't you?'

'Just let me try.'

'Please yourself. It's not my problem.' Once again she walked on.

Lily thought they had given up, and was surprised when a little later a car pulled up beside her and Roger jumped out.

'Please, Lily, get in and we'll take you home.'

'No thank you. I prefer to walk.'

'Stop being silly, you're getting soaking wet,' shouted Rose from the car.

Lily didn't care about getting wet; all she was worried about was what would happen when she got home. 'Just leave me alone.' She put her head down and hurried away.

When Lily turned in to Enfield Road, she could see Roger's car just along from their house. So they didn't have the courage to go in without me, she thought when she saw them sitting inside.

Ignoring them, she went up to the front door and

pulled the key through the letter box. Rose and Roger were out of the car and right behind her.

'Lily, is that you?' shouted her mother from the kitchen. 'Hurry and get your wet things ...' Her voice trailed off when she came out of the kitchen and saw Rose and Roger standing behind Lily.

'Hello, Mum,' said Rose. Roger was shaking the rain off his trilby.

Amy couldn't move, and when Roger came forward, she ignored him and turned to Lily. 'What have you done bringing them here?' she said.

'I didn't bring them.'

'I just had to see you, Mum,' said Rose. 'Can we go into the kitchen?'

'No. I think you and your fancy man had better leave before your father gets home.'

'But I want to see Dad.'

'He'll be wet and cold and he won't want to see you.'

'How can you say that?'

'Because I know how he feels.'

'Please, Mum, just give me a chance to explain things.' Rose had tears running down her face.

'Please, Mrs Flower,' said Roger.

Lily stood back while this was going on. She didn't know what to say.

Amy turned and walked back into the kitchen, and Rose and Roger followed her.

'I'm just going to take my wet things off,' said Lily, and left them to it. Upstairs, as she sat on the bed and took off her shoes and stockings, she worried about what would happen when their father came in. She didn't have to wait long. She heard the front door slam shut and her father call out.

'It's raining cats and dogs out there. I hope Lily didn't—' He stopped abruptly.

Lily hurried down the stairs and burst into the kitchen. Everybody was standing up.

It was Rose who spoke first. 'Hello, Dad. How are you?'

'What you doing here?'

'I've come to see you.'

'Well it's taken you a bloody long while to find your way back. What d'you want, a medal?'

'This is Roger.'

Roger stepped forward and held out his hand, but Ron ignored it.

'Just leave my house.'

Roger looked amazed.

'Dad, please listen.'

'You heard me. Now get out before I chuck you out.' He sat down and began to unlace his boots.

'Rose, I think you'd better go,' said her mother. 'And next time come alone.'

'There might not be a next time.'

'And why's that?' asked her mother.

'Because we're going to get married.'

'What?' Ron jumped up. 'I knew it. I always said she'd finish up up the duff, didn't I?'

'I'm not having a baby. We just want to get married

and we'd like your—' Before Rose could finish, her father, who was a strong man, grabbed hold of Roger's arm and shoved him bodily down the passage and out of the front door.

Lily and her mother looked on, shocked.

He was red-faced with rage when he came back. Wagging his finger at Rose, he said, 'Now you listen to me. If you want to stay here, you stop seeing that ponce. If not, you can go, and don't you ever come snivelling back here.'

'Dad, you don't mean that.'

'Don't I? Try me.'

Rose looked at her mother and sister, then, with tears running down her cheeks, she picked up her bag and left without another word.

When the front door slammed, Lily and her mother looked at each other in silence. They couldn't believe what they had just seen.

It was Amy who spoke first. 'Ron, what are you thinking of? Lily, go and get Rose back here.'

'You move and you'll be next out that door.'

'What?' Lily was shocked.

'Ron, whatever is the matter with you? Why can't you listen to someone else for a change and stop being so pig-headed? That's our daughter, and the way you have just behaved, I don't think we will ever see her again. Is that what you want?' Tears were streaming down Amy's face.

Lily went and held her mother close. Her father didn't answer.

It was a while before anyone spoke, then Lily asked softly, 'Would you like a cup of tea?'

'Yes please,' said her mother.

Lily went into the scullery and put the kettle on the stove. As she stood looking at it, her mother joined her. 'Mum, why's Dad so angry? He could at least have listened to Rose.'

'I don't know what's got into him. I told him this would happen if he didn't give you two a little more freedom. He can't keep you here for ever.'

'But why is he behaving like this?'

'He's always been upset about what happened with his sister.'

'I know that, but that was years ago and things have changed since then.'

'He always said that if his father had been a bit stricter with her, it wouldn't have happened. I also think that this has gone too far and he can't back down. That would show a kind of weakness.'

'How daft is that?'

'I know. Through his stubbornness, we might never see Rose again.'

Lily put her arms around her mother. She would go and see Rose as soon as she could. She would make sure that she never lost touch with her sister.

Roger kept his thoughts to himself as he drove back to his house. He couldn't offer any comforting words to Rose, who was crying all the way.

Silently he helped her out of the car. Once inside, he took her damp coat and dropped it on the floor. Then he gently ushered her into the front room, sat her down and removed her wet shoes before pouring them both a stiff whisky.

'I'm so sorry, Roger,' sobbed Rose. 'I didn't want this to happen.'

He lit a cigarette. 'It wasn't your fault. What's wrong with your father?'

'I don't know.'

'He's like a raving idiot. Why can't he listen?'

'I don't know,' repeated Rose.

'I can well understand why you wanted to get away from him. Has he always been like this?'

'I've never left home before.'

'It's Lily I feel sorry for.'

Rose's head shot up. 'Why? You don't think he'll harm her, do you?'

'I don't know. You know him better than I do.'

'No. He wouldn't hurt Lily.'

'But he could get our address out of her, and then God help us if he came round here trying to smash the place up.'

Rose wiped her eyes. 'He wouldn't do that.'

'I don't know. He looked very angry to me.'

'I don't think Lily would give him this address.' Deep down Rose hoped she was right. The last thing she wanted was for Roger to feel compromised. 'I could always try and find somewhere else to live.'

'You'll do no such thing. Come here.'

He took her in his arms and kissed her.

Rose sighed. This was where she wanted to be, and she was going to stay here with or without her father's blessing. She just hoped and prayed that her sister would understand. Surely he wouldn't do anything to Lily? But would she tell him where Rose was living?

Chapter 24

As soon as Lily walked back into the kitchen, her father was on his feet.

'Right, young lady, where do they live?' He grabbed her arm.

'What?' asked Lily.

'Ron, stop that!' screamed Amy.

Ignoring his wife and with his face close to Lily's, he shouted, 'You heard me.'

'I don't know.' Lily was frightened and shook his hand off.

'I don't believe you.'

Lily looked at her mother, wide eyed with fear. She had never seen her father act like this before.

'Ron, whatever is the matter with you? You're scaring the life out of the poor girl. Now leave her alone. I'll start to dish up the dinner.'

'I don't want any.'

'Thanks,' said Amy, going back into the scullery.

Lily followed her and shut the door. 'Mum,' she said, still trembling. 'What's wrong with him?'

'I don't know, love.'

Lily began to cry, and her mother held her close.

'I'll try and talk to him when he's calmed down.'

'I can't give him Rose's address. What if he sends the police after her?'

'I don't know, love.'

'She'll only run off again, and then we'll never see her. Is that what he wants?'

Lily's sobs were breaking Amy's heart.

They sat quietly at the table but nobody ate the dinner that Amy had so lovingly prepared. When she and Lily were in the scullery washing up afterwards, her daughter asked:

'Would he be like this if we were boys?'

'I don't think so.'

'So boys can do what they like and girls can't?'

'Well your father thinks that girls bring trouble home and boys would just be sowing their wild oats.'

'That's a bit unfair.'

'That's the way it is, I'm afraid.'

'It's very old-fashioned.'

'Your father is an old-fashioned man.'

'Mum, would he be like this if I wanted to get married?'

'What?' Amy quickly turned away from the sink. 'Oh no, Lily, you're not thinking . . .'

'No, Mum. I was just thinking out loud really.'

'Please, I can't stand much more of this.' Amy wiped

her hands on the towel hanging behind the door and went back into the kitchen.

Lily stood and looked at the rain running in little droplets down the window. It looked like the whole world was crying tonight.

'Roger, what if he sends the police after me?' asked Rose after she had changed out of her damp clothes into a lovely blue winter frock with long sleeves and a dropped waist. It was very elegant, and another gift from Roger.

Roger stood by the window watching the rain bounce off the cobbles outside. With a drink in one hand and a cigarette in the other, he went and sat next to Rose. 'I know a flat we can borrow. Tomorrow when I finish work we will move there, then as soon as I settle the time off with Archie, we can go to Scotland. When we come back you'll be my wife, and he can't do anything about that.'

Once again Rose's tears fell.

Roger put his drink down and stubbed out his cigarette, then held her close. 'Now come on. No more tears.'

'Thank you,' she said between sobs.

'What for?'

'For loving me like you do.'

He kissed her tear-stained face. 'Now wipe these away.' He ran his thumb over her cheeks. 'Tomorrow we start a new life.'

It took Rose a while to collect her thoughts. 'What about this house?' she suddenly asked.

'Don't worry about that. Mrs B will still come and look after things here. She's used to me hopping off somewhere. I can afford to rent a flat for a few weeks.'

'You'd really do all this for me?'

'Yes, of course. I do love you, Rose, and I never want to lose you.'

Once again Rose was reduced to tears. How could her father be so against this man when he didn't even know him?

The atmosphere was unbearable, and Lily went to bed as soon as she could. As she lay on the bed, her thoughts were full of the evening. Why did Rose have to bring Roger with her? And why had Dad reacted that way? Would she ever know the answer?

The following morning, after a troubled night's sleep, she heard the front door slam and knew that her father had left for work. She got up and went downstairs. She wasn't surprised to see her mother's pale face and red-rimmed eyes.

'Are you all right?' she asked.

Her mother only nodded and busied herself pouring out tea.

Lily sat at the table and picked up the cup her mother had silently pushed towards her. 'What we gonna do, Mum?'

'I don't know, love. All I know is that we can't go on like this.'

'I'll write to Rose and see if I can make her see sense.'

Amy sat at the table. 'I can't see what good that will do, not if she's that taken with this bloke. As I told your father last night, if he drags her back here, then he'll have to keep her locked up or she'll just up and go again.'

'What did he say to that?'

'Nothing. Lily, I'm really worried about him. Thank goodness it's Saturday and his half-day. At least he might be able to get some sleep this afternoon. I know he didn't get much last night, and if he's not wide awake with all that machinery, well, anything could happen.'

'Now come on, Mum. Don't worry about that. Dad's not stupid.'

'He is where his daughters are concerned.'

Lily couldn't argue with that. At least he didn't know Rose's address, so he couldn't go after her. She glanced at the clock. 'Look, I must get ready for work. Will you be all right on your own?'

'Yes. Course I will.'

'See you tonight, then.' Normally Lily didn't mind working on Saturday afternoon, but today she wished she didn't have to.

All the way to the shop, her mind was turning over and over. She had to see Rose. Perhaps she could go to Roger's house tomorrow afternoon. She wouldn't ask Harry to go with her; she would rather do this alone.

Harry always met her at lunchtime, and even though Saturday was his half-day, today was no exception. Once they were in the café, Lily told him all that had happened the evening before.

'My dear. What are you going to do?'

'I'm going to see her tomorrow.'

'Would you like me to come with you?'

'That's very kind of you, Harry, but I would prefer to do this on my own if you don't mind.'

He patted her hand. 'I understand.'

'Look, I must get back to the shop.'

'Can I see you tonight?'

'No, I'd rather not.'

'Well, the best of luck, and I'll see you Monday.' He kissed her cheek.

Lily went back to work, but her mind was on so many other things.

When Rose woke up, Roger's side of the bed was empty. She sat up, and Roger, fully dressed, came in carrying a cup of tea.

'I'm going to the office and to see about this flat. Now I don't want you opening the door to anyone. Understand?'

She nodded.

'While I'm gone, you pack your things. I'll sort out a suitcase for you.'

'What about your clothes?'

'I'll get Mrs B to see to that.'

'But she doesn't come in on Saturdays.'

'I know. I'll take what I want when I get back, then I'll leave the rest for her to sort out.' He kissed her cheek, and at the door, turned and blew her a kiss.

Rose was trying hard not to cry. How could she be so lucky? This man was so kind and he loved her.

When she got up, Rose went downstairs, where she tidied up and washed last night's crocks. The suitcases were in the kitchen, and she took them upstairs and began to pack her things. At the sound of a knock on the front door, she froze. Was it the police? She went to the window at the front and carefully looked down. She jumped back when she saw James standing there. He was looking up. Had he seen her? She sat on the bed.

The letter box rattled. 'Are you in there, you dirty dog. Roger, come on down.'

Standing back from the window, Rose saw him go towards his car. Why wasn't he at work? When she heard the car roar away, she relaxed and carried on with her packing. As she carefully put her lovely clothes in the case, she knew she was so lucky to have all these wonderful things that Roger had bought her. If only she could see Lily. If only she could take her to some of the restaurants she had been to with Roger. She knew Roger would love to take her sister out as well. They could all be so happy together. 'If only,' she said out loud.

Chapter 25

After Roger had collected Rose and the suitcases from the house, they drove to the flat, which he said was near his office.

'I'm sorry it's a bit small, but it'll do for now.'

'It's fine,' said Rose as she hung her clothes in the single wardrobe.

'At least we're together.' He kissed her cheek. 'Now tonight we're going to a club with Poppy and Archie. We'll make sure you enjoy yourself, so put your glad rags on and we'll paint the town red.'

'Thank you. What time are we going?'

'They're picking us about eight and we're going for a meal. You'll love this club, the music is fantastic.'

'Sounds wonderful.' Rose was a bit wary about seeing Poppy again after her visit. She was also worried about Lily. She would go to the shop next week and try and explain everything. She loved her sister and her parents and never wanted to lose touch.

* * *

Saturday evening had been very strained in the Flower household, and after dinner on Sunday afternoon Lily said she was going out. 'I don't know what time I'll be back, so don't bother leaving tea for me.' She was trying very hard to sound casual.

'Are you seeing your young man?' asked her mother.

Lily crossed her fingers behind her back. 'Yes.'

'It's a bit cold to be walking the streets. You going anywhere in particular?'

'I don't know, Mum. We may just go to a café or something.' Lily was getting cross with her mother. Why was she questioning her like this?

Her father began to fold his newspaper. 'You're not going to see *her*, are you?'

'If you mean my sister Rose, no, I'm not. I told you I don't know where she's living.'

'I'll come with you if you like.' He stood up.

'What?'

'I just want to make sure.'

'That's it. I'm not going anywhere if you come with me.'

'Ron, sit down and don't be so ridiculous. This is getting out of hand, you going for a walk with your daughter and her young man. By the way, in case you've forgotten, they'll be nineteen next year.'

Lily looked at her mother; she had never seen her look so angry. 'Thank you, Mum.'

'I honestly don't know what's got into you,' Amy continued. 'You used to be such a reasonable man.'

Ron Flower sat back down. Suddenly he looked very old and sad. 'I just want her home, that's all,' he said softly.

'Well this is not the way to go about it.'

Lily was shocked; she had never heard her mother speak to her father like this before.

'You go on out with your young man, love. Your father will stay here.'

Lily went to get ready. As she left the house, her thoughts were on Rose. She was really cross with her for causing all this upset.

Lily was cold as she waited at the bus stop, and when she arrived at her destination she was still feeling very upset. They used to be such a happy family. How could one man coming into her sister's life cause such grief? Lily just hoped she could talk some sense into Rose.

When she arrived at the mews house, she knocked on the door. There was no reply. She stood back and looked up at the bedroom window, then peered through the downstairs bay. From what she could see, it looked like a very elegant room, but there was no sign of life. She looked up and down the street, but there was nobody around she could ask. Everywhere looked dead. She had written another note for Rose in case she found no one at home, and now she pushed this through the letter box and with a heavy heart walked away.

After the disappointment of not seeing Rose, Lily took herself to the West End and looked in the shop windows.

Although it wasn't yet December, some of the big stores had already started their displays. What would Christmas be like in their household this year if Rose wasn't back? Every Christmas as far back as Lily could remember had been special. When they were little, Father Christmas always came and left a pillowcase full of toys and books. She and Rose would do their best to stay awake trying to see him, but they never did. Although they were upset when they were told he didn't really exist, they still left their stockings out, and there was always something in the bottom: nuts, chocolate, an orange and half a crown. Such little things, but they always brought a lot of joy. They were such happy times. The presents under the tree. The laughter and the games they played in the evening. Would Christmas ever be like that again? 'Rose, please come home,' she said softly. She brushed away the tears that had trickled down her cheeks and made her way to Lyon's Corner House for a warm, welcoming cup of tea.

It had been the early hours of Sunday morning when Rose and Roger had finally made their way back to the flat. Rose helped Roger inside and up the stairs. She had kept her head even though there was plenty of champagne; she had been very careful, as she didn't want to get drunk. Roger had fallen asleep almost at once, but Rose was still thinking about the lovely evening they'd had. She had never been to such a wonderful place in her life. When they walked in, the atmosphere almost took her breath away. Everybody was immaculately dressed, from the cigarette girls to the waiters. They were shown to a round table with a small light in the middle, and the band played softly while people were eating. When the meals were finished, the dancing girls came out and did a high-kicking routine that Rose thought was fantastic. Roger had looked so handsome in his evening suit. When they danced, he held her close and gently kissed her ear. She had never felt like this, and she loved him so much. She had looked around at the beautiful women in their fashionable low-backed shimmering sheath dresses – Poppy had told her to say dresses, as frocks sounded so common. Their jewellery had sparkled in the soft lights.

When she went to the powder room with Poppy, Rose had been on her guard.

'You look as if you're enjoying yourself,' Poppy said as she peered into the beautiful ornate mirror.

'I am. This is such a wonderful place.'

'How are you finding the flat?'

'It's fine.'

'It's a bit small, I know, but we keep it for when anybody comes from America for business. It's convenient for the London office.'

'So it belongs to the business?' Rose had been intrigued at that.

'Yes, but when you're married, you can go home, as your father can't touch you once you're Mrs Walker. You do love Roger, don't you?'

'Very much,' she had replied.

Later, Rose was still going over the evening when

Roger turned over. I shall be Mrs Walker, she said silently to herself. She was filled with joy. Her thoughts went to Lily. If only her sister could come to her wedding. She so desperately wanted to see her and to tell her how much she loved her.

She looked down at Roger and gently kissed the back of his head.

On Monday morning, after Roger had left for the office, Rose decided to go and see Lily.

She tidied the room and washed up the breakfast dishes. She was just getting herself ready to go out when she heard the front door open and shut.

She came out of the bedroom and was surprised to see Roger standing there.

'What is it? What's wrong?'

'Nothing.'

'But why are you home?'

He picked her up and spun her round and round. 'Business is very slow this time of year, so Archie has given me a month off. Which means, my darling, that we can go to Scotland tonight.'

When he put her down, Rose was stunned.

'But first we have to go shopping for a wedding ring, and of course you'll need a new outfit. Do you know what you'd like?'

'No. Oh Roger, are you sure this is what you want?'

He stopped smiling. 'Rose, you've not had second thoughts, have you?'

'No, of course not, but what about you?'

'I would be very honoured to be your husband.' Roger kissed her. 'That's settled, then. I would like to stay here, but I think we had better start things rolling if I'm to make an honest woman of you.'

Rose couldn't believe that this was happening to her. Soon she would be off to Scotland to get married. She knew she had to write to Lily. She would send the letter to the shop; that way Lily wouldn't have to open it in front of their mum and dad. This should be the happiest day of Rose's life, but it wasn't. She missed her sister and she wanted her to be there on her wedding day. Why did her father have to act this way?

All Monday morning Lily was hoping that Rose would come to the shop. At lunchtime, though, it was Harry who was waiting for her outside.

'Did you see your sister?' he asked straight away, as they made their way to the café. These outings were beginning to become a regular thing.

'No.' Lily felt relaxed with Harry and knew she could talk to him. 'Unfortunately she was out, but I left a note. I'm hoping she'll come to the shop sometime today.'

'Perhaps she'll be here when you close, like she was before.'

'I hope so. But I also hope she comes alone. I don't think I could stand another scene like that.'

They drank their tea and Lily told Harry about the shops with their Christmas displays.

'Already? It's not even December yet.'

'I know. But it will be next week. I think they want us to start spending our money early.'

'What are you doing over Christmas?' asked Harry.

'We shall be very busy in the shop. So many people like to give their loved ones flowers, and that's without all the holly wreaths we will be making. Will you be going to your sister's?'

'I expect so. She normally does a lovely dinner, and Mother likes to see the children.'

'You're very lucky.'

'Yes, I suppose I am.'

Lily knew her Christmas would be sad if Rose didn't come home. She looked at Harry; he seemed so bland. She couldn't explain it. Was she finding him dull and uninspiring?

It was almost closing time when the bell above the door tinkled, but when Lily quickly looked up, hoping to see Rose, she was surprised to see Will Perry standing there.

'Hello, Lily,' he said, turning his trilby round and round nervously. 'Can I talk to you?'

'Can you wait outside till we close?'

'Yes, of course.' He went out.

Lily collected her hat and coat, and calling good night to Miss Tucker, quickly left the shop. Outside, Will came up to her.

'I hope you don't mind me calling like this?'

'No,' said Lily, though she was not really paying much

attention, her thoughts still on her sister.

'You see, I've always liked you and Rose, and—'

'What?'

'I was wondering if I could take you out one evening.'

'What about your girlfriend?'

'Oh, Sally. She isn't really a girlfriend; she's more June's friend than mine.'

'But she went to your mother's funeral.'

'Yes, but that was really to please June. So would you like to come out with me?'

'I do have a boyfriend.'

'I'm sorry. Is it serious?'

'I beg your pardon?'

'Lily, I'm so sorry. I shouldn't ask such questions. But you see, I never thought I would see you again.'

'You knew where I lived.'

'Yes, I know, but I'm in the merchant navy and have been at sea for years. I came back home when Mum was so ill and I wanted to come and see you, but everything was happening at once.'

Lily stopped. 'So what do you want?'

'I was hoping I could take you out sometime. We always had fun together.'

'You mean you and Rose did.'

'You used to join in. Besides, Rose was a bit, well, bossy at times.'

'Yes, she was.'

'What's Rose up to these days?'

Lily smiled and tried to hide her tears. 'She's left home

and we don't know where she's gone.'

'Is she alone?'

Lily shook her head.

'I'm sorry to upset you by bringing it up, and I know this sounds a bit dramatic, but she's not been kidnapped or anything like that, has she?'

Lily wanted to laugh. 'No, she's gone off with some posh bloke.'

'That sounds like Rose all over. Always wanted to be better than anyone else. So, Lily, I'm back off to sea next week. Could I just see you one evening? I promise not to step on your boyfriend's toes.'

'I'm sorry, but I don't think so.' Lily held out her hand. 'It was nice seeing you again, Will. Look after yourself.'

'You too.' He kissed her cheek.

Lily watched him walk away. She touched her cheek. She knew she had been a bit curt with him, but she suspected it was Rose he'd wanted to see rather than her. What was it about Rose that made men fall at her feet?

Chapter 26

ROSE'S WEDDING RING was very plain, but expensive. There were times when she wondered about all the money Roger spent, but he certainly didn't seem to worry about it. He must earn a lot. After lunch, she bought a pale blue suit and black winklepicker shoes, and a silly little black hat with a veil. She didn't show Roger what she'd bought, and when she came out of the shop, he took her arm and propelled her into an elegant fur shop.

'Now, my darling, I want you to pick out your wedding present.'

The sales assistant came up to them, elegant in his black frock coat, pinstriped trousers and cravat.

'Good afternoon, sir and madam. Does madam know what she would like to look at?'

Rose shook her head. Everything looked so expensive.

'Can I suggest you take a look at the moleskin?' He clicked his fingers, and almost at once, a younger man who had been hovering close by came over with a beautiful dark fur coat over his arm.

Rose was trying to look at the price tag, but there wasn't one.

'Do you like it?' asked Roger.

She went up close to him and whispered in his ear, 'I think it's far too expensive for me.'

Roger laughed and turned to the assistant. 'Could you show us the mink?'

'Certainly, sir.' Once again he clicked his fingers.

Rose held on to his arm. 'No, Roger,' she said out loud.

He only smiled at her.

When the assistant brought out the lovely soft fur, Rose just looked at it in awe.

'Let me help you try it on for size,' said the salesman.

It was warm, yet light, and so soft that all she wanted to do was stroke it.

'Do you like it?' asked Roger.

'It's beautiful.'

Roger took out his wallet and walked over to the desk. 'Could you have it sent round to my address?'

'Certainly, sir.' The salesman was smiling. 'Thank you, sir,' he said, clutching a handful of five-pound notes.

When they were outside, Rose turned to Roger and said, 'What have you done?'

'I have bought you a practical wedding present.'

'Oh Roger, I haven't got you anything.'

'*You* are my present. It'll be freezing in Scotland and I have got to look after you.' He began to walk on.

'But a mink coat . . .'

'Don't you like it?' He stopped. 'I can always cancel it.'

'I think it's wonderful, but can you afford it?'

Roger laughed. 'My sweet innocent Rose. This is what I love about you. Only you would dream of asking a question like that.' He kissed her cheek. 'Now come on, let's get back to the flat and you can thank me properly.'

Rose couldn't believe it. She was going to have a mink coat. She had never seen one before, let alone tried one on. Her mother had a fox fur that smelled of mothballs, but Rose hated its beady eyes and fluffy tail, and the way Amy would clamp its tail firmly in its jaws when she wore it. Rose shuddered at the thought. Then she looked at Roger and knew she was the luckiest person alive. If only her father could see what a kind, generous man he was, then her life would be complete.

Lily was dreading going home, but she was determined to act as though everything was normal.

'Hello, Mum, Dad,' she said cheerfully as she walked into the kitchen.

There was no reply from her father.

'Hello, love,' said her mother. 'Been busy?'

'We've started to take orders for holly wreaths. It looks like I shall be working a few late nights later on, and even on Wednesday afternoons.' Lily knew this was a silly conversation; still, at least she was talking.

When she came back into the kitchen after going outside to the lav, her mother was waiting for her.

'I was hoping that Rose would come to see you in the shop today. She didn't, did she?'

Lily shook her head. She hadn't told her mother that she'd been to Roger's house yesterday; she didn't want to get her hopes up.

'Why won't she get in touch? Do you think she might have gone back to work?'

'I don't think so. She would have come to see me.'

'It looks like she's gone from our lives for ever.'

Lily held her mother close. 'Mum, please don't say that.' But deep down she knew her mother might be right.

Roger and Rose were on their way to Scotland. Rose was so excited, but also very upset that her sister wouldn't be with her. She had decided not to send Lily a letter till after she was married. They were travelling in the car, and Roger had told her they would be stopping at hotels along the way. The hotels were very luxurious and everything was wonderful. She smiled at Roger. She loved him so much and couldn't even think of life without him now.

'When we get to Scotland,' said Roger as they prepared for bed, 'we shall have to stay in a hotel near Gretna for three weeks to conform with the rules of residency. I hope you won't be bored?'

'No, of course not. I'm with you.'

'We can visit Edinburgh and one or two other interesting places. But it will be very cold.'

Rose smiled. 'I've got my wonderful coat.' She kissed him. 'Thank you. Thank you. Thank you.'

He laughed. 'I take it that you're pleased.'

She patted the bed. 'Come on. Let me show you how much.'

Three weeks later, on December the twenty-first, Rose and Roger were married. Rose wore her pale blue suit with her fur coat draped over her shoulders. Although she was happy, it wasn't the wedding she had always dreamed of. It should have been in a church, with her father giving her away and her sister walking behind her, but that wasn't to be. A tear rolled gently down her cheek when they were pronounced man and wife and Roger kissed her. After Roger had paid the two witnesses, the newlyweds made their way back to the hotel, ready for the start of the long journey home tomorrow.

As Christmas got closer, Lily was more and more upset that Rose hadn't contacted her. On Christmas Eve Miss Tucker let her go early, as all the orders were already out or waiting to be picked up. As Lily made her way home, she was constantly on the lookout for her sister. If only she would come to see them. At the market, children were wrapped up warm in their gloves and scarves, laughing at the organ grinder with his monkey. The smell of chestnuts roasting and the sweet sound of the carol singers gathered on the street corner made Lily cry. It was a happy, festive scene but not one that she could enjoy. She had bought her sister a pair of gloves, and she wondered if Rose had done the same.

The wind was making tears run down her cheeks, but they were tears of sadness. This year she wasn't looking forward to Christmas at all. She felt so alone; she wasn't even going to see Harry. The present he had given her at lunchtime was in her handbag. She had promised that she wouldn't open it till Christmas morning. All she wanted was for Christmas to be over so that she could go back to work.

The house looked sad when she walked in. There wasn't a tree this year, or any decorations, as her father had refused to put them up, and neither Lily nor Amy felt like celebrating.

'Dad not home yet?' she asked.

'No, not yet. There's two letters for you,' said her mother. 'I think they're Christmas cards. Who do you know in Scotland?'

Lily rushed over to the mantelpiece and picked up the envelopes, tearing open the one with the Scottish stamp. 'It's from Rose.'

'Rose? What's she doing in Scotland?' Amy let her voice drift off. 'Oh my God. You don't think she's gone there to get married, do you?'

'I don't know. All it says is "Merry Christmas from Rose and Roger".'

'What will your father say?'

'Do we have to tell him it was from Scotland?' asked Lily.

'I suppose not. He'll be upset enough that Roger's name's on it.'

Lily screwed up the envelope and threw it in the fire.

'Who's the other card from?' asked her mother.

'It's from Will Perry.'

'That's nice of him. He must have been very pleased with his mother's flowers to send you a card.'

'Yes, he must.' But Lily wondered whether he'd sent the card because he was hoping Rose had come back.

On the long, cold drive home, Rose thought about Christmas Day. This one would be so very different from all her other Christmases. It would be very quiet, but she was happy to be sharing it with Roger.

'When we get home, we'll go and see your family and tell them that we're married,' he said.

'Can we?'

'Rose, all I want to do is make you happy.'

'I just want to see Lily and tell her that I love them all so much. Why must Dad be like this?'

'I don't know, love. But you'll see, it will turn out all right.'

'Do you really think so?'

'I know so.'

When they finally arrived back in London and Roger opened the front door of the house in Puffin Mews, he swept Rose up into his arms. She was laughing as he carried her over the threshold.

'Merry Christmas and welcome home, Mrs Walker,' he said as he put her down and kissed her passionately. 'I'm sorry we don't have a tree or presents.'

'You're my present,' she said, taking his hand as they wandered into the sitting room.

On the small coffee table there was a huge bouquet of flowers. Mrs B had arranged them in a vase.

'Roger, thank you. These are lovely.'

'I didn't send them,' he said, going over and reading the card.

Rose's heart jumped. 'Are they from Lily?' she said excitedly.

'No. They're from Poppy and Archie. They want us to go over to them for the New Year.'

Rose slumped on the sofa. 'I was hoping they were from Lily.'

'I know, love. Tonight we're going out to wine and dine, but tomorrow, after we collect our things from the flat, we can go and see your sister.'

'Can we?'

'Why not? Even though Archie knows I'm home, I can still sneak another day off. We're not very busy this time of year.'

Rose kissed him. 'I do love you,' she said.

'And I love you, Mrs Walker. Now, how about a cup of tea?' He gently tapped her bottom as she left the room

Rose smiled. She really did feel at home and very happy, and tomorrow she was going to see her sister. She smiled to herself. Who knows, even her father might be pleased to see her when he knew she was married and wouldn't be bringing any disgrace on his house. That was her wish for 1929.

Chapter 27

ON WEDNESDAY LUNCHTIME, Harry came to see Lily, and over their usual cup of tea she told him all about how she thought Rose had got married and the sad time she'd had at Christmas. 'I'm so sorry to be burdening you with my troubles, but I need to talk to someone.'

He gently held her hand. 'I'm only too pleased to listen. I wish you could have spent Christmas with us. It was noisy, but you certainly don't have time to get bored.'

'It must be good fun with children around. Thank you for my scarf, by the way.'

'I'm glad to see you're wearing it. I hope you like it.'

'I do, and were the hankies all right?'

'They were lovely. I've never had my initial on them before. Now, we must do something on Monday evening. It's New Year's Eve.'

'I can't. I have to be at work on Tuesday, and I have only ever seen the New Year in with my family. It will be more important than ever this year, with Rose away.'

'I understand. How about Saturday? We could go to a film or the theatre. You choose.'

'Oh Harry, you are so kind. I would love that.'

'That's settled, then. We'll sort out the details later on in the week.'

Lily felt happier when she went back to work that afternoon. She knew she had to start to live her own life and not worry about her sister so much. After all, Rose didn't seem to care about her.

On Friday morning, Rose stood looking out of the bedroom window. It was raining, but that didn't bother her, as later today she was hoping to see her family. Next week would be 1929. What would the new year have in store for her? She turned and looked at Roger sleeping peacefully. Her life couldn't get any better. When they'd got home from Scotland, Roger had found the note from Lily. Rose was very upset that she had missed her sister before they left, but she knew that today she would be seeing her. She unconsciously turned her wedding ring round and round. She was excited at the thought of seeing Lily. Who knows, now she was married, perhaps she might be allowed back into her family. That would be the best New Year's present she could ever have.

Roger quickly sat up. 'There you are.'

'Were you expecting a cup of tea?'

'No, I was dreaming and I thought you'd left me.'

She went over to the bed. 'I would never do that. Now, I'm going to make some tea before Mrs B gets here.'

'Don't be too long.'

She stood at the door and smiled. Yesterday they had been shopping, and in the corner were the presents she would be taking home to the family.

When the bell over the shop door rang, Lily looked up quickly. She couldn't believe her eyes. Rose was standing there, beautifully dressed in a lovely fur coat. Lily wanted to go to her and hold her close, but before she could move, Rose was across the shop and holding her tight. They clung to each other and the tears fell. When Lily straightened up, she looked at the clock. It was almost closing time.

Miss Tucker was smiling. 'You can go off now,' she said.

'Thank you, Miss Tucker.' Lily wiped her eyes and turned to her sister. 'I'll only be a moment, I'll just get my hat and coat.'

'I'll wait outside,' said Rose.

As Lily collected her things, she wondered if Rose was alone. She soon had the answer to that when Roger came up and kissed her cheek. 'I'm allowed to do that now we're related.'

'What?'

'We're married,' said Rose, taking off her brown kid glove and showing Lily her wedding ring.

'Is that what you were doing in Scotland?' asked Lily, stepping back.

'Yes, and now we're taking you home and I'm going to make my peace with Dad.'

'Do you think it will be as easy as that?'

'I can only try.'

'And then you'll go off and leave me and Mum to live with the mess again?' Lily began to walk away.

'Lily,' called Rose. 'Please let me try.'

'I can't stop you from coming home, but I warn you, Mum won't be that pleased to see you. We have had the worst Christmas of our lives, and it looks as if 1929 isn't going to be any better.'

'Why, what's happened?'

'Dad's heartbroken, Rose.'

'Well let me come and see if I can't mend it.' She smiled.

'That's you all over. You just have to be flippant, don't you?'

'What else can I say?'

'I don't know.' Lily was beginning to feel very happy at seeing her sister again, but also very sad at the same time.

'Come on.' Rose took her arm. 'Let's go home.'

Roger opened the car door for them and Rose ushered Lily inside. Lily felt she couldn't argue any more.

'Now what have you been up to?' asked Rose when they were settled.

'Nothing much.'

'What about Harry? Is he still around?'

'I see him at lunchtimes.'

'Is that all? If you ask me, he seems to be missing a good thing.'

'He's just a friend,' Lily said, looking out of the window, not that there was a lot to see on this cold, dark evening.

'I have so much to tell you,' said Rose, patting her sister's hand.

Lily didn't answer. She was beginning to feel worried as they got closer to Enfield Road, but she knew it was pointless to argue with her sister. Rose had made up her mind that she was coming home to tell them her news.

'Is that you, Lily?' called her mother from the kitchen. 'Your father's not . . .' Her voice trailed off when she saw Rose, and behind her Roger. 'What do you two want?'

'We've come to see you and to bring your Christmas presents.'

Roger placed the bag of presents on the floor. 'I know it's a bit late, but we've been rather busy.'

Amy moved towards them. 'You can kindly take your presents and leave. Lily, I'll talk to you later.' She turned and went into the kitchen, shutting the door and leaving them standing in the passage.

Lily opened the door. 'Mum.'

'Get rid of them before your father gets home.'

'Mum, please. Just hear them out.'

'What?'

'Just let Rose tell you. Rose, come here.'

Rose came up to her mother. Tears were trickling down her cheeks. 'Mum, I'm so sorry for all the grief I've caused.' She went to hug her, but her mother backed away.

'You're a selfish little madam. Do you think you can come here in your fancy clothes and make your peace after all you've done to this family? Now get out and take your fancy man with you.'

Roger was standing behind Rose, nervously turning his trilby round and round in his hands.

'Mum, he's my husband.' She turned and took Roger's hand.

Amy looked at her. 'Your husband?'

'Yes, we were married in Scotland.'

Her mother's face turned ashen and she sat at the table. She turned to Lily. 'Did you know about this?'

Lily shook her head. 'I told you that I had my suspicions when we saw the Christmas card had been posted in Scotland.'

The front door slammed.

'Next door must have some fancy visitors. There's a lovely car out . . .' Ron ground to a halt as he walked into the kitchen. 'What the bloody hell are you doing here? I told you once before to get out; now I'm telling you again.'

'Ron, Rose is married.'

'Up the duff, are you? Well, serves you right. I expect he'll leave you for a younger bit before too long, and then you'll come running back here expecting us to look after you and your bastard.'

'Ron,' said Amy.

'Dad,' said Lily at the same time.

'I can assure you I will never do that, Mr Flower. I love

Rose and I shall make her very happy, but we would like your blessing.'

'Well you ain't getting it. Now go, before I take my belt to the both of you.'

'Dad, why are you being like this?' Rose went to go to him, but he pushed her forcefully away. 'Why can't you let me lead my own life?'

Her father began to unbuckle his belt.

'Dad,' screamed Lily. 'What are you doing?'

'I gave you a warning, now go.' He folded the belt and raised his hand.

'Rose, go on, get out,' shouted Amy, her voice filled with fear as she stepped forward.

In the scuffle that followed, Lily managed to get between her father and her sister just as he brought the strap down. The buckle end of the belt flew out of his hand and across his daughter's face. Lily's screams were loud and terrifying.

'Ron, what have you done?' screamed Amy. 'Rose, go. Go quickly. Now!'

'But Mum . . .'

'I said go.'

Roger looked stunned as Rose took his arm and, with tears running down her face, pushed him from the room.

'We can't leave Lily like this,' he protested.

'It's best,' said Rose.'

Blood was running down Lily's cheek and Amy was cradling her in her arms. She looked up at her husband. 'What have you done?'

He fell to his knees. 'I'm so sorry, Lily. I wouldn't hurt you for the world.'

'Go away,' Lily sobbed.

'What have I done?'

'You wanted to hurt Rose.'

'I was upset.'

'That's no excuse,' said Amy. 'Go and get me a bowl of warm water.'

He quickly did as he was told, and when he returned, Amy gently bathed her daughter's cheek.

'My poor darling.' Her father went to touch her.

'Go away. Don't touch me!' she screamed.

'Lily, I'm so very sorry. Please forgive me.'

'I'll never forgive you.'

Her father reeled back. It was said with such passion.

All the way outside, Roger was still protesting and trying to stand his ground. He held Rose's shoulders and said, 'We can't leave your sister like this.'

Rose brushed him away and got into the car. She was crying and shaking. 'What can I do?' she sobbed.

'I don't know what to say,' said Roger. 'I've never seen a man act like that to his daughter before.'

'It was me he was going to hit.'

'That would have been a very bad move.'

'I've never seen my dad behave like this.'

'He was almost like a madman. Rose, I've got to go back in there and see how Lily is.'

'But he might kill you.'

'I don't think so. Besides, she might need to go to the hospital. We can't just go off and leave her.' He got out of the car, and Rose quickly followed him.

Full of fear, she pulled the key through the letter box. What was going to happen now?

Chapter 28

WHEN ROSE WALKED into the kitchen, Lily was still sitting on the floor, being held and comforted by their mother.

Amy looked up. 'And what do you want? Get out of here, the pair of you. Don't you think you've caused enough damage?'

Ron was sitting in his chair with his head in his hands. Rose noticed that he didn't look up.

'We've come to see if Lily needs to go to the hospital.'

'If she does, we'll take her,' said her mother.

'We've got the car outside. It will be far quicker for her, rather than standing at the bus stop in this weather,' said Roger.

'I'll be all right,' said Lily softly. She was holding a cloth to her face, and the blood was slowly seeping through.

Rose dropped to the floor. 'I'm so sorry, Lil.' She held her sister's hand. 'Come on, let us take you to get this looked at.'

'We can be there in no time,' said Roger, looking at Ron, waiting for a comment, but the older man didn't take his head from his hands.

Amy didn't object when Rose and Roger helped Lily to her feet.

'You can come with us, Mrs Flower, if it will make you feel any happier,' said Roger.

'I'll just get me coat.'

Rose took off her own coat and put it round Lily's shoulders, not caring that blood might stain the fur.

'You can't do this,' said Lily, trying to shrug it off.

'Yes I can, you're shivering. Besides, I can wear yours.'

Tears rolled down Lily's cheeks and mingled with the blood. This was the saddest thing Rose had ever witnessed, and it was all her father's doing. They left without any comment from him.

When they arrived at the hospital, Roger sat and waited while Rose and her mother took Lily in to see the nurse. The journey had been very quiet. The only sound had been Lily softly sobbing. How could a bloke do that to his daughter? And what if it had been Rose? Roger knew that he would have hit Ron, and hit him hard. Nobody was going to hurt his wife. But what about Lily? Would she be scarred?

After the nurse had gently bathed Lily's cheek, the doctor came to look at it.

'I will have to put a few stitches in this. You say you fell over and caught your face on the edge of the table?

You were lucky you missed your eye. You should be more careful, young lady. I'm afraid this is very deep and will leave a scar.'

Rose and Amy both took a quick intake of breath.

'Now, if you two ladies don't mind waiting outside, I'll get on with the job.'

As soon as Roger saw them, he jumped to his feet. 'What's happened? Will she be all right?'

'The doctor's putting stitches in. He said she'll be scarred,' said Amy, sinking down on to the seat next to him.

'Very badly?'

'We don't know,' said Rose, who sat the other side of her mother and held her hand.

'How could her father do such a thing?' said Roger.

'It was meant for Rose.'

'I know. But whatever Rose has done, that's no excuse for violence.'

Rose squeezed her mother's hand and gave her a faint smile.

It was a while before Lily came out of the doctor's room. She had a large wad of dressings on her face and was being helped by a nurse.

'You can pay at the reception,' said the nurse.

Roger jumped up and made his way to the desk.

'I can pay,' said Amy, following him.

'Have you got your purse with you, Mum?' asked Rose. 'No.

'Well that's it. Roger can pay.'

'I'll give you the money.'

He just smiled and took out his wallet.

Lily was silent all the way back to Enfield Road. When they arrived, Rose helped her to the front door.

Amy took her daughter's arm. 'Rose, I don't want you and Roger to come in.'

'Why?'

'I don't want any more trouble.'

'You don't honestly think he'll do something else?'

'I don't know, but I'm not taking any chances.'

'Well I hope he's happy now he's let everybody know what he's really like.' Rose was burning with anger. She didn't want to leave her sister, and she wanted to tell her father just what she thought of him and his bullying ways.

'Please, Rose,' said Lily in a muffled tone. 'Just go.'

'Come on, love. We can come back another day.' Roger gently took her arm.

Silently her mother gave her her coat back

Rather than cause a fuss, Rose kissed Lily's cheek. 'I'll be in touch.'

Lily didn't answer.

'I'll make sure your husband gets his money,' said Amy as she opened the front door.

'You don't have to worry about that.'

Rose and Roger went back to the car.

'Will she be all right?' asked Roger.

Rose nodded. 'Mum will make sure she's safe.' This was one day Rose would remember forever, and for the rest of her life she would feel guilty. She knew it was all her fault.

Once inside, Lily went straight up to her room. There was no way she could face her father.

'I'll bring you up a cup of tea,' said Amy as Lily mounted the stairs.

'Thanks.' She was pleased her mother didn't want her to go into the kitchen.

She sat on her bed and began to cry. So many thoughts and fears were filling her mind. What had her father done to her? Why was he so angry with Rose and Roger? The two of them seemed so happy. Why didn't he just listen to them? What would this do to them? And what sort of scar would she have? Would Harry still like her? What about her job? Would she put customers off? With all these thoughts going round and round in her head, Lily threw herself down on the bed and wept uncontrollably.

All evening Rose was worried about Lily. Roger tried to comfort her, but no words would help the situation. She knew she had to go and see her sister.

'I'll go tomorrow,' she said, as they were getting ready for bed.

'Will you be all right?'

'Yes, Dad will be at work.'

'Only go in if he's not there. I'm sure I would do something to him if he ever hurt you.'

Rose kissed his cheek.

When she was settled in Roger's arms, she knew she

would always be safe with him. But what about Lily? Rose would never forgive her father or herself for what had happened to her lovely sister.

When Lily opened her eyes the following morning, she felt sick and her pillow was covered with blood.

She sat up when her mother knocked on the door. 'Lily, are you awake?'

'Yes.'

'I've brought you a cup of tea.'

'Look at the time. I must get up.'

'You can't go to work like this.'

Lily lay back down and began to cry.

Amy held her daughter close and kissed her hair. 'Come on now.'

'Mum, what am I going to do?'

'I'll go and see Miss Tucker and tell her you've had an accident.'

'It's our busiest day and I've got bouquets to do for a New Year's wedding.'

'You can't go looking like that.'

Lily was shocked. She had expected her mother to give her words of comfort. 'Will you tell her my father did it?'

'No, of course not.'

'So you'll just make out that I'm clumsy?'

'Oh Lily. What can I say?'

Lily turned her back on her mother. 'Has he gone to work?'

'Yes.'

'So life will go on just the same for him.'

'And so it will for you once the stitches come out.'

'Oh yes, but I shall have a long, ugly scar down my face.'

'It might not look so bad.'

'I've seen the soldiers who came back from the war, remember? Now leave me alone.'

Her mother left the room.

When she looked across at the mirror, Lily knew that things would never again be the same in this household. She would never forgive her father and she would never forgive Rose; as far as she was concerned, it was all her sister's fault. She also knew that she herself would never look the same. All she could see stretching in front of her was loneliness and sadness.

Chapter 29

'I'LL BE OFF now,' said Amy, poking her head round the door of her daughter's bedroom. 'Are you sure you don't want me to get you some breakfast?'

'No, I'll be all right.'

Amy gave her a smile. 'I'll be as quick as I can.'

'Don't hurry. I'm not going anywhere, so I'll still be here when you get back.'

When Lily heard the front door shut, she was relieved that she didn't have to pretend to be all right any more. She was alone, and this was how she wanted to be.

As Rose made her way down Enfield Road in her lovely fur coat, she felt proud when she saw some of the looks she got from people. She didn't care about all the stares, and the snide remarks, but she did feel bad about Lily. Her mind was going over and over what had happened. What if it had been her? Would Roger have hit her father? And if he had, what if he'd really injured him? Despite her lovely warm coat, Rose shuddered at that thought. But if it had been her, would Roger still want a wife who was scarred? What about Poppy? Would she still have wanted Rose to go with them to all those expensive places? And would she have been able to walk into them in one of her lovely frocks with an ugly scar down her face? Her life would have been over.

She went to pull the key through the letter box, but it wasn't there. She fumbled about. It had gone. She knocked. There wasn't any answer. Surely Lily hadn't gone off to work? Even if she had, her mother should be at home; she always went shopping early, so she should be back by now. She fished around for the key again, then called through the letter box. 'Mum. Lily. Can someone open the door?' Was Lily hiding? She banged hard with the knocker again. Still no reply. She stood back and looked up at the bedroom window. Small flurries of snow began to fall. That was all she needed. 'Will someone come and open this door!' she shouted.

Next door opened. 'I fink yer mum's gorn out,' said old Mrs Brown.

Rose knew that the old lady sat all day in the window, watching everybody go in and out their houses. Most families in the road didn't have a lot of time for her; she was a nosy old gossip.

'Thank you.'

'Nice coat.'

'Thank you,' said Rose again.

'Liked yer bloke's car.'

Rose wanted her to go away – all she wanted was to see her sister and hold her close – but decided that it was her that would have to leave.

As she turned to walk away, Mrs Brown said, 'What's wrong with young Lily? Saw yer come back yesterday and she had a dirty great bandage on her face.'

Rose felt a sudden pang of guilt. She had to think quickly. 'Toothache.'

'That all? Tell 'er she wanna 'ave 'em all out, ain't no trouble then.' She gave Rose a toothless grin.

'Thanks.

'I'll tell yer mum yer called.'

'Thanks,' said Rose again and quickly went on her way.

She looked back at the house before she got to the corner. Was someone in and they didn't want to see her? Was Lily in there? She would try again later when Roger came home from the office.

Lily had wound the string with the key round the door handle. She knew that Rose would be here today and she didn't want to see her. She didn't want to see anyone. While Rose was shouting through the letter box, she stayed in the kitchen with the door shut. She never wanted to see her sister or anybody else ever again.

Much later that morning, she heard her mother shouting through the letter box. As she went along the passage she called, 'Are you on your own?'

'Of course I am. Now come on, open this door.'

Lily stood for a moment or two listening for voices.

When she was sure her mother was on her own, she opened the door.

'What's the matter with you? Why have you put the key round the handle?'

'I thought you could see what the matter with me was.'

Her mother was holding a lovely bunch of flowers.

'And are those supposed to make me feel better?' said Lily as she walked into the kitchen.

'Miss Tucker sent them. She said you're not to worry about getting back to work, just go when you're ready. She said that now most of the orders are finished it's a quiet time of the year anyway. I'll just put these in water.'

'What did you tell her?'

'I just said that you've had an accident and cut your face.'

'But this wasn't an accident, was it?'

Amy couldn't answer that. 'I'd love a cup of tea. I was talking to next door; she said Rose had been here but couldn't get in. Is that right?'

'Yes,' said Lily.

'Why?'

Lily gave a hollow laugh. 'Do you honestly think I want to see the person who caused this? If she hadn't been so damn selfish and always wanted to do things her own way, this would never have happened. But that's Rose all over. Always has to have her own way.'

Amy was taken aback at her daughter's outburst. This wasn't like Lily at all.

Lily slammed the cup and saucer on the table. 'Here's your tea.'

'Thank you. Lily, sit down.'

'Why?'

'We need to talk.'

'What about?'

'Your future.'

'Do I have one?'

'Of course you do. It may not look too bad when the stitches come out.'

'For the rest of my life I will see it every time I look in the mirror, and be reminded of what my father did to me.'

'And he will regret it for the rest of his life.'

'Good.'

Amy had never known Lily to be so angry. 'What can I say?'

Lily walked out of the room.

When Rose returned, Mrs B was in the kitchen singing very off key.

'Oh, I'm so sorry. I didn't hear you come in,' she said when Rose opened the kitchen door. 'Is everything all right?'

Rose sat at the table and began to cry.

'Oh my dear. Whatever's the matter? I'm sorry, I shouldn't ask such questions. Would you like a cup of tea?'

Rose nodded.

Mrs B looked awkward as she smoothed down her overall and began to busy herself.

Rose thanked her when the tea was put in front of her. 'I'm sorry,' she said wiping her tears. 'Please, Mrs B, sit down.'

'But I've got the dinner to prepare.'

'I'll help you, but I just need someone to talk to.'

The older woman looked very uncomfortable. 'I really don't think it should be me.'

'I've no one else.'

'Are you in trouble?'

'My sister won't talk to me.' As she said it, Rose knew it sounded pathetic.

'I'm very sorry, Ma'am.'

'Please call me Rose.' Rose dabbed at her eyes and began to explain how her family didn't want to see her because she had run away to get married. She never mentioned that her father had hit Lily.

It was a while before she finished, and all the while Mrs B sat in silence. 'What can I do?' asked Rose.

'Now you shouldn't go getting yourself all upset. I'm sure they'll come round when they find out that Mr Roger is a very good man.'

'Thank you.'

Mrs B gently tapped the back of Rose's hand. 'Come on, wipe those tears away.'

Rose gave her a weak smile. 'I know you weren't very happy to have me here, but can we be friends? Can I talk to you?'

'Of course you can. Now come on, let me get on with preparing your dinner.'

'What can I do?'

'How about the tatties?'

Rose wanted to hug this woman. At last she had found a friend.

It was late afternoon when Ron Flower walked in. The first thing he said was 'Where's Lily?'

'She's upstairs. You're late.' Her husband normally finished at lunchtime on a Saturday.

He went to walk out of the kitchen, but Amy put her hand on his arm and said, 'Ron, don't. Just leave her alone.'

'I can't. I've been walking since I finished today and I can't stop thinking about what I did.'

She looked at her husband. He looked drawn and ill. She had never seen a man age so much in a day.

'Why am I so pig-headed?'

'What's done is done and you can't turn the clock back.'

'I know that, don't I? Why was Rose so damn difficult?'

'She's young and in love. He does seem a nice chap. I'll go up and see if Lily will come down.'

Amy knocked gently on Lily's door. 'You coming down for some dinner?'

'I'd rather not,' came the reply.

'Lily, you can't stay locked away for ever.'

'Why not?'

Amy opened the door. 'Now come on. You've got to eat.'

'I don't want to see him.'

'If you're talking about your father, I think you should come down. Please, Lily.'

Lily looked at her mother. She looked sad and drawn. This must be hurting her too. 'All right,' she said.

Amy hugged her, but Lily stood stiffly and didn't respond.

When Lily walked into the kitchen, she was shocked at the sight of her father. He was suddenly an old man. She wanted to go to him and hold him tight, but her pride wouldn't let her. In many ways she was glad that he too was suffering.

He stood up and went to hug her, but she quickly stood back.

'Lily, I'm so, so sorry. You know I wouldn't hurt you for the world.'

'But you were happy enough to hurt Rose.'

'I lost my temper in the heat of the moment.'

'That's no excuse to attack your own daughter.'

He didn't answer. He just sat in his chair and wept.

Amy went to him and held him close, and Lily left the room. She couldn't bear to see her father cry.

Chapter 30

'ARE YOU SURE you want to go and see your family?' asked Roger when he arrived home that afternoon. 'If Lily wouldn't open the door to you this morning, do you think she will want to see you now?'

'I've got to try and get to see her. I'll write a letter if she won't let me in. I must do something.' Rose looked sad.

'Please don't upset yourself. I'm sure this will all sort itself out. We'll go as soon as we've finished dinner. But what about your father? Will he be there?'

'I suppose so, but I don't care. Changing the subject,' she said, 'me and Mrs B had a long talk this morning. And I helped her prepare dinner.'

'That's even better. Just as long as you're not going to poison me,' said Roger jokingly. He knew he had to try and keep the conversation light-hearted.

'As if I would!'

'So what did you talk about?'

'I was very upset when I got back home, so I'm afraid I

just sat and told her about my family and how they have disowned me.'

'Oh my poor love. What did she say?'

'Not a lot, but she thought they might come round when they see what a nice, good man you are.'

'Always knew that woman had good taste. Now come on, as soon as we've finished, we can go and see if we can make amends.'

Dinner in the Flower household was very quiet. Lily didn't speak at all, and she wouldn't answer any of her father's questions.

'Your mum said that Miss Tucker was very understanding.'

Lily just looked at him.'

'Please, Lily, talk to me.'

Lily carried on eating her dinner, although every mouthful was sticking in her throat. It was hard to chew and swallow, as the stitches were painful when they pulled at her cheek. She could see that her mother was doing her best to try and bridge the gap, but it was an impossible task.

They were in the scullery when her mother said, 'I wish you would talk to your father.'

'Why?'

'This atmosphere is awful.'

'I don't care.'

'Lily, this isn't like you.'

'I've never been hit before.'

'Is this how we're going to be from now on?'

Lily shrugged and walked outside.

Although it was freezing cold in the lav, she just sat there. She had never been so unhappy in her life. She just wanted to die.

Lily was in her bedroom when she heard the front door shut. Someone had come in. Was it her father? He had said he needed to go for a walk. Amy had told Lily that he was very upset, and wanted to be alone. Lily opened her door and could hear her mother shouting.

'I told you before, now get out of here, the pair of you.'

'But Mum, I must see Lily.'

'Why?'

'To say I'm sorry.'

'And a fat lot of good that's gonna do.'

'Where is she?'

'She don't want to see you.'

Lily quickly shut her bedroom door and put the chair under the handle.

When Rose knocked on the door, Lily sat on the bed. The handle rattled.

'Lily, please let me in.'

'Go away.'

'No I won't, not till I've talked to you.'

'You can talk from there. Not that it'll do any good. I never want to see you again. Now go away and live your life of luxury and leave me alone.'

'Lily, please.'

Lily began singing very loudly.

Rose went slowly down the stairs. Her mother stood at the bottom with a grim look on her face. 'You've got your answer; now get out the pair of you. We never want to see you again.'

'But Mrs Flower . . .' said Roger.

'You heard me. I said get out. You've split this family and I shall never forgive you.'

'But it's Dad's fault,' said Rose tearfully.

'Yes, but you started it with your disobedience.'

Rose looked very dejected and tears ran down her face. 'I never thought you'd disown me.'

'Well things have changed. Now get out before your father gets back.' She gave Rose a push.

'Come on, love.' Roger took Rose's arm, and as they moved away, he looked over his shoulder and said, 'I hope you don't live to regret this.'

The only answer he got was the front door slamming.

Rose sat in the car crying.

'Come on, love. Give it a little time and then perhaps they will all come round and see that I love you and just want to make you happy.'

This made Rose cry even more.

Amy was standing at the front-room window. She could see how tenderly Roger was treating her daughter. Was she so wrong to act the way she had? But she knew that Lily would never forgive her sister or her father, and now she had to try and make the peace in this household, although at the moment she knew that could be an almost impossible task.

When they arrived home, Roger decided to remind Rose about the invitation to Poppy and Archie's New Year's Eve party, in the hope that it might cheer her up and take her mind off the present situation.

'I'm sorry,' said Rose. 'I don't want to go.'

'But we must.'

'How can I when my family are so unhappy?'

'Please believe me, darling, if I could make things better I would. But we have still got to live our lives. Besides, on Monday you must go and get yourself a new dress.'

Rose knew Roger was being kind and only trying to help her, but the days were very long without him around and her sister to talk to; what could she do with herself? She had suggested going back to work, but Roger wouldn't hear of such a thing.

Lily too was finding that time dragged. She longed to be at work surrounded by all those beautiful flowers. Should she swallow her pride and go back? She could always stay in the back room; she didn't have to meet the customers. She looked in the mirror. How could she? What would her face look like when the stitches came out? Once again tears ran down her cheeks and soaked her dressing.

On Sunday afternoon, Lily was horrified when she heard Harry's voice at the front door.

'I'm sorry,' said her mother. 'She doesn't want to see anyone.'

'Miss Tucker said Lily wasn't well. I hope she'll be better soon.'

'Thank you. I'll tell her you called.'

Harry walked slowly away. What was so wrong with Lily that she couldn't see him? Was she using this as an excuse not to go out with him again? Once more all his insecurities began to worry him. He looked up at the window. He did like her.

Lily waited till she heard the front door shut, then she went to the top of the stairs. 'What did you tell him?'

'Just that you weren't feeling very well. It was nice of him to come round.'

'We were supposed to be going out last night.'

'Well I'm sure he'll want to take you out again. He seems a very nice young man.'

'I don't think he'll want to take out a freak.' Lily went back into her bedroom and slammed the door.

'Ron, what are we going to do?'

Her husband looked up from his newspaper. 'I don't know, Amy. I would do anything to turn the clock back, but I can't.'

Amy sat on her chair. She had never seen her husband look so sad. 'Should we let Rose come and—'

He jumped to his feet. 'No.'

'But why not?'

'I can't give in. It would make me look weak.'

'Don't be so ridiculous. It would show that you're human.'

Ron went outside.

Amy knew that all this was going to take time to heal. She would try her best to make it happen, but she knew her husband was a very proud and at times a very stupid man.

On New Year's Eve, Rose was wearing the new dress that Roger had made her go and buy for herself. When she walked down the stairs, he quickly stubbed out his cigarette and just gazed at her.

'My God, you look so beautiful. I want to kiss you but I know you'll push me away in case I spoil your make-up.'

'You like the dress, then?'

'Turn round.'

Rose did as she was told. She knew that the figure-hugging pale blue satin with its very low back looked good.

'I am so lucky,' he said, going up to her and kissing her bare shoulder. He held up her fur coat and helped her into it. 'It's perfect, and I shall be the envy of every man in the room.'

Rose smiled. 'Thank you.'

Lily had gone to her room at nine o'clock.

'Don't you want to stay and see the new year in?' asked her father when she said good night to her mother.

She gave him a look that said it all. 'What have I got to look forward to? Only me stitches coming out.'

'Please, Lily. I can only say I'm very, very sorry so many times.'

She didn't reply, and left the room. Once she was safe in her sanctuary, as usual she felt very sorry for herself. She loved her father and wanted to forgive him, but she couldn't. In the last few days she had seen him go from an upright, proud man to a sad, bowed figure, and it upset her to see him so unhappy. If only she could bring herself to forgive him, but she knew that at the moment that could never be.

Poppy looked at Rose and then held her tight. 'Darling, you look absolutely fantastic. Married life has certainly given you a glow.'

'Thank you. You look wonderful as well, and I love your dress. That colour really suits you.' Poppy was wearing a very pale pink satin sheath dress tonight.

Poppy kissed Roger's cheek. 'You look lovely as well, my darling.'

'Thank you. I was worried you might not notice me now I have a wife.'

Rose was looking round the room. 'Nora,' she said, going up to her old boss. 'What a surprise. And as usual you look wonderful. I love your dress.'

'I did mention we sometimes came to Poppy's parties. I must say you look very different from the little office girl I knew. And I hear that you are now married.'

Rose only smiled, and Nora came up close and said softly, 'So you got your man, then?'

'How's everything at the office?' Rose tried to sound casual and polite.

'We're managing without you.'

Roger came over to them. 'Excuse me, ladies, but Rose, Poppy's looking for you.'

'We'll catch up later,' said Nora.

'I hope so,' said Rose.

'Where's Poppy?' Rose asked Roger as they moved away.

He looked guilty. 'She's not really looking for you, but I could see Nora was making you feel uneasy. Was she asking personal questions?'

'No, not really.' Rose smiled. She remembered that it wasn't that long ago when she had envied Nora. 'I do have a lot to thank her for. I would never have met you if it wasn't for her. But thank you for rescuing me.'

'That's me. A knight in shining armour.'

Rose took his arm and they walked off laughing. They didn't notice Nora go up to James and the pair of them begin talking and looking towards Rose and Roger.

At midnight, while Rose and Roger were toasting 1929 in with champagne, Lily sat on her bed and cried. Both girls were thinking about each other. Rose was wishing that soon they could be together, while Lily was wishing she could forgive her sister. She missed her and wanted to be able to talk and laugh together as they had done all their lives.

'A penny for them?' said Roger after 'Auld Lang Syne' had been sung and all the kissing had finished.

'I was thinking about Lily and how much I miss her, and how we used to laugh and talk together.' A tear trickled slowly down Rose's cheek. 'Will I ever see her again?'

Roger took her in his arms and held her tight. 'Of course you will.' He kissed her lips. 'Happy New Year, my darling, and I hope this is the first of many many new years to come for us.'

Rose smiled. She knew she was the luckiest woman alive to be married to someone like Roger. When she was taken back into her family, then her life really would be complete.

Chapter 31

1929

Rose sent a letter to Lily, begging her to reply. When Lily had read it, she waited until the evening, when her father and mother were sitting in front of the fire, then, without a word, she slowly tore it up and threw it into the coals in front of them.

'Was that from Rose?' asked her mother.

Lily nodded as she watched paper curl in the flames then disappear.

'What did you do that for?' her mother enquired.

'I shan't be answering it.'

Her father looked up from his newspaper and Lily could see the hurt look on his face. In many ways she wanted to talk to him, but her pride still wouldn't let her give in. She wanted everyone to suffer the same as she was.

'I'll come with you tomorrow to have your stitches out,' said her mother.

'You don't have to.'

'Don't be silly, Lily, of course your mother will go with you.'

She just looked at her father and went out to the scullery. 'I'm going to make a cup of tea.'

She stood looking out of the window. All day it had been dark and gloomy, and it was cold too. It had been trying to snow on and off ever since she got up, and she was fed up with being home all day. If after tomorrow her face didn't look too bad, perhaps she could go back to work. She needed to get out again. But what would she look like? If only she had Rose to talk to, but that was her own fault: she kept turning her away. Lily felt very sorry for herself, and although she desperately wanted to make things better between everybody, she knew every time she looked in the mirror that that could never be.

On the bus people were looking at her, and the conductor gave her a pitying smile. Lily, feeling very self-conscious, sat and looked out of the window. If only she'd taken up her sister's offer to let Roger take her to the hospital in his car.

When they arrived, she was surprised to see Rose waiting outside. Rose rushed up to her and Lily quickly stepped back. 'What you doing here?' she asked.

'I knew you were having your stitches out today and I wanted to be with you.'

Lily wanted to scream at her to leave her alone, but she knew she couldn't make a fuss outside the hospital.

Amy looked on. She felt guilty at abandoning her

wayward daughter. Like Lily, she too wanted them all to be a happy family again, but things had gone too far and nobody was prepared to give in and forgive Rose.

Lily went inside and Rose and their mother followed.

'Well, young lady, how are you today?' asked the doctor.

Lily didn't answer.

'Now let's get these nasty things out, then you can start feeling like your old self.'

Lily looked at him. 'I shall never be my old self ever again.'

He smiled. 'That's what a lot of the young men said when they came back from the war with some terrible injuries, but give it time and you will heal.'

Lily felt like screaming at him to just get on with it, but she knew he was only trying to put her at her ease, so she kept quiet.

There was no mirror in the doctor's room, and when she walked out to her mother and sister she looked very carefully at their reactions. They both smiled and she knew they were just putting on an act.

'Are you all right?' asked her mother.

'No,' she said sharply.

'We will have to get you some make-up,' said Rose.

Lily scowled. 'Will that make it go away?'

Rose looked uncomfortable. 'No, but it will help to hide it.'

Lily walked out of the hospital and made her way to the bus stop.

Amy said to Rose, 'You had better be on your way.'

'Please, Mum,' Rose said softly. 'Can I come home?'

'No. And don't start making a fuss here,' Amy hissed. 'You know you're not welcome at home. Goodbye.'

Rose looked very sad as she called out, 'Bye, Lil.'

Lily walked on. She guessed what her mother had been saying. She didn't turn round and say goodbye.

When they arrived home, Lily ran upstairs to look in the mirror. She gasped. There was an ugly deep red weal down her cheek. The skin round it was puckered. Tears sprang to her eyes and she threw herself on the bed and cried.

'Lily.' Amy knocked on her bedroom door. 'I've brought you a cup of tea.'

'Go away.'

'Please, love. Open the door.'

'No.'

'Lily, this won't help.'

She didn't reply.

'It will fade in time. Please let me come in.'

Lily sat up as her mother opened the door. Amy put the cup and saucer on the dressing table and sat next to her daughter.

'Come on, love. I know how you must feel, but please try to be the nice loving person you have always been. Don't let this make you sad and bitter. People love you for what you are not for what you look like.' She went to put her arm round her, but Lily moved away.

'I'm going to the lav.'

Amy watched her daughter leave the room. She picked up the untouched tea and took it downstairs.

That evening when her father came home, he said, 'Hello, love. It must be better for you now the stitches are out.'

'Yes, of course it is. Look how lovely I look.'

'Lily, please.'

'You did this to me.' She pointed angrily at her face. 'Who wants to look at me now?'

'Lily, if I could turn the clock back I would. I will never forgive myself.'

'Good, that makes two of us.'

Her father winced.

Amy watched this scene from the doorway. It hurt her so much to see such anger in her daughter. And so much sorrow and guilt in her husband.

'How was Lily?' asked Roger as soon as he walked in.

'She's had her stitches out. Oh Roger, it looks horrible.'

'It will fade in time.'

'I don't think so. It was very deep. Dad must have used an awful lot of force.'

'He was very angry.'

'I know, but he shouldn't have done that. They don't want to see me ever again.'

Roger took Rose in his arms. 'But I do. Now come on. We're starting our new life together. I don't want to tell you to forget your family; I would never say that. When my mother died, I was devastated.'

'Is that the photo you have?'

'Yes. I should have told you who it was before, but so much has happened.'

'I don't really know that much about you.'

He lit a cigarette and puffed the smoke high in the air. 'There's not a lot to tell really. I was an only child and my parents were rich enough to give me a very good education. When I started in the bank I quickly went up the ladder. Then Archie, who I knew at college, asked me to join his team dealing with stocks and shares. My father was a gambler, and over the years, unbeknown to my mother, he went through his money. My mother was the wise one.' He stopped and took another long drag at his cigarette. 'It must have been a great worry to him, as he then had a massive heart attack,' he said sadly.

'Oh Roger, I'm so very sorry. Your poor mother. Was she left penniless?'

'No. As I said, she was clever. She kept a very nice nest egg, and after she got over the shame of it, she lived very comfortably.'

'How old were you when all this happened?'

'It was just after I started at the bank.'

'So when did she die?'

'Three years ago.'

'But you don't visit her grave?'

'Not very often.'

'Why not?'

'Life has been very hectic since I met you, but I do sometimes go on my way home from the office.'

'I wish I'd known all this before we were married.'

'Why?'

'Don't look so shocked. It's just that I would have loved to put some flowers on her grave. So please, can we go together?'

'Yes. Of course.'

She kissed him. 'Both of us seem to have parent problems.'

'But mine are finished.'

'I know. Roger?'

'That sounds ominous.'

'What are your feelings about having a family?'

'I would love it.'

'Would you really?'

He kissed her long and hard. 'How about we start trying now?'

Rose giggled.

'D'you know, my darling, this is the happiest I've seen you look since we got married.'

'I do love you so much and I want to make you happy and have a wonderful life with you and our children.'

'More than one, then?'

Rose nodded.

'In that case, we had better get started.'

Rose knew that her sister would never turn her away if she knew she was going to be an auntie. Lily loved babies, and hopefully when it happened, it would bring them all together again.

Chapter 32

O N SUNDAY NIGHT, Lily knew that tomorrow she had to go to work. She was going mad staying indoors with nothing to do day after day.

'Are you sure you're ready for this?' asked her mother the following morning as Lily stood in front of the mirror adjusting her hat.

'No.'

'So why put yourself through the agony?'

'Because I need to do something. Miss Tucker will let me stay in the back room, and at least I'll have a purpose in life.'

'Well only if you're sure.'

Lily moved closer to the mirror and dabbed some powder on her scar. Amy felt like crying. Her daughter's beautiful face was so disfigured. Would that scar ever fade away?

'At least I don't have to get on the bus,' said Lily as she picked up her handbag and left the room.

Once she was outside, she pulled her scarf up round her face. The wind was biting cold and the snow was beginning to settle.

'Lily,' said Miss Tucker, her face lighting up when Lily walked in. 'I'm so pleased to see you.'

Slowly Lily unwound her scarf. Miss Tucker tried hard not to show her reaction. 'My dear, how are you?'

'Do you mind me coming back to work looking like this? I can stay in the back room. I don't have to meet the customers.'

'I must admit I have missed you, and it would be nice to have you around, but only if you're sure.'

'I can't stay shut away for ever.'

'No, I suppose not.'

'I'll just put my overall on. Is there anything for me to do?'

'Yes, I have a wreath to make up. In fact there are a few; this cold weather is taking its toll on the elderly. So you can see I'm really happy to have you back.'

'Thank you.' For the first time in weeks, Lily felt she was wanted and useful.

'Your young man has been here a few times hoping that you were back at work,' said Miss Tucker as they began to sort out the flowers.

'If he comes in today, please tell him I'm not here.'

'Of course, if that's what you want.'

'Just till I get used to being out again.' But Lily knew it was because she didn't want Harry to see her. She didn't want to see anyone who might be sympathetic.

At one o'clock, Lily could hear Harry in the shop talking to Miss Tucker. She wanted to see him but knew she had to wait a few more days, till she was ready to cope with his reaction. She knew what a sensitive person he was, and that her looks would upset him, and she had to be strong for that.

The following week Lily heard raised voices in the shop and knew that one was her sister's.

'I'm sorry, Lily,' said Miss Tucker when Rose barged into the back room with the older woman behind her.

'That's all right,' said Lily. 'Rose, what are you doing here? How did you know I was back and what do you want?'

'I've come to see if you're all right. I've been a few times, but Miss Tucker looked at this door when I came today, so I guessed you were here.'

Miss Tucker left them, and Lily ignored her sister and continued with her work.

'Please go. I don't want to make a fuss in here. As you can see, I'm rather busy.'

'Lucky you.' Rose sat on a chair. 'I wish I was.'

Lily looked anxiously at the door. She didn't want to upset Miss Tucker. 'I thought your life was one long round of shopping and going to parties.'

'I have been shopping and I've brought you some make-up.'

'I don't want your gifts, thank you. Please go and leave me alone.'

Rose could see her sister was getting agitated. 'All right. But I will be back sometime, and I'll make you want to see me.'

'I don't think so. Not after all you've done to split this family.'

'I'll never forgive myself for that.'

'Good. Now go.'

At the door, Rose turned round. 'They say that time is a great healer, and I've got plenty of time. Goodbye.'

After Rose left, Lily felt like crying. She did so want to talk to her sister. She could see that Rose wasn't happy at being cast out. But she knew she couldn't give in, not at the moment, when she still felt hurt and upset at all that had gone on.

Lily picked up the bag her sister had left behind. It was from a very expensive store in the West End. Inside was foundation cream, some face powder and a card. The card said, 'With love from me to you.'

Lily held the bag close. She loved Rose and knew that she had to see her sister sometime, but when would she be ready?

Weeks went by, and gradually Lily was getting used to wearing the make-up Rose had given her. It certainly helped to cover the scar, which had now lost a lot of its angry redness. But was she ready to face Harry yet?

That decision was taken away from her on her half-day.

Lily thought the shop was empty and closed. She walked in from the back room with an order she had just finished, and at the same time Harry came in through the shop door.

Miss Tucker, who was in the window, moved away as Harry and Lily stood looking at each other.

'Lily! I knew you were back at work and didn't want to see me.'

For a moment or two Lily stood still.

'I didn't realise you . . .' He stopped.

Lily turned and went into the back room. Tears were stinging her eyes. Harry followed her.

'Lily, I'm sorry.'

'I know, you didn't realise I looked this ugly.'

'You're not . . .' He couldn't say the word.

'Please, Harry, go.'

'Can't we talk?'

'I don't think so.'

'Why not?'

'What's the point? You don't want to be seen out with a freak.'

'How can you say such a thing? You're not a freak.'

'In my eyes I am, and I don't want people looking at you and feeling sorry that you've got yourself landed with someone like me.'

'I think you're being very hard on yourself.'

'Please go.' Tears began to fill her eyes.

He left the room and Lily began to cry.

A moment later Miss Tucker walked in. 'I'm so sorry,

Lily. I should have locked the door.'

'It's all right,' she sniffed. 'I suppose I had to see him sooner or later.' She wiped her eyes.

'He seemed genuinely upset. Are you sure you want to cut yourself off from the rest of the world?'

Lily nodded. 'It's going to take me a while before I get my confidence back. Just as long as you're happy with me working in the back room.'

'Of course I am.'

'Harry came into the shop today,' said Lily as she was sitting drinking a cup of tea with her mother.

Amy put her cup down and looked at her daughter. 'Did you see him?'

'Yes.'

Although Amy was dreading the answer, she had to ask. 'Did you talk to him?'

'Yes, and I told him I didn't want to see him any more.'

'What did he say to that?'

'Not a lot. He just left.'

'Is that it. He just left? What else did you say to him?'

'Just what I told you. That I didn't want to see him.'

'Why not?'

'Oh Mum, can't you see?' She pointed at her face.

'It's not going to last for ever.' Amy collected the cups.

'No. It'll be gone when I'm dead.'

Amy was beginning to lose patience with her daughter. 'I never thought you would get so down about this and let it alter your personality. You used to be kind and respect other people's feelings, but now . . .' How could she tell her daughter that she was a becoming a sad, boring person who only thought of herself? Amy looked at Lily, all she wanted was for her to be happy.

Lily got up and walked away. She did so want to be liked and not turn into a miserable old maid. But what could she do? Should she go out with Harry? Her feelings were mixed. There had been many times when she had needed a shoulder to cry on, but deep down she worried that Harry wouldn't be strong enough for her.

At the end of February, Lily was surprised to receive a letter from Will Perry. She smiled when she saw that he was in Canada. In his letter he told her about how cold but lovely it was there and asked if she minded him writing to her. He said he would be away for a long time and liked to know what went on back in England. His sister was too busy with her children to write that often. Lily was more than pleased to have someone to write to, and she sat down and answered his letter almost at once. She knew she was safe from seeing him and it gave her something else to think about, as well as something to do in the evening.

Over the following weeks Will and Lily exchanged several letters. Hers were light-hearted and his were very funny; he told her some of the things people got up to in the various countries he visited, and painted word pictures of the wonderful landscapes. Sometimes he sent her postcards, and Lily really looked forward to every letter.

She also wrote to Harry and told him she was sorry for being so hard on him, but he didn't reply. This upset her very much.

She still couldn't bring herself to talk to her father, though she noticed that over the months he had gone from being a tall, upright man to looking very old.

'I'm worried about your father,' said Amy one afternoon when Lily was home and sitting at the table reading Will's latest letter.

'Why? What's wrong with him?'

'His leg is playing him up. Lily, is there any chance you could talk to him? This has been going on for a long while now.'

'I know.' Lily put down her letter. Suddenly, she wanted all the fighting to stop. 'If he lets Rose come back, I might.'

Amy gave her a wide smile. 'I'll talk to him tonight.' She went and kissed her daughter's forehead. 'I have prayed that this feud would end and now it looks as if my prayers will be answered.'

Lily just picked up her letter again. Would her father give in? Why were they all so stubborn? Even Rose had stopped coming to the shop. Had she too given up on the family ever being united again?

In April, when it was the girls' birthday, Lily sent a card to Rose. She couldn't let it go without some form of contact. When she got home from work, she was surprised to see that Rose had sent her a beautiful handbag. It looked very expensive.

'Did you send Rose a card?' asked her mother when they were alone in the scullery.

'Yes, but not a present.'

'Were the cards the same?'

Lily shook her head. 'No. The one I bought wasn't as expensive as hers.'

'Still, it's the thought that counts.'

Lily put down the plate she was wiping up and brushed away a tear that had trickled down her cheek. A couple of weeks ago her mother had asked her father to let Rose come back, and he had refused. Lily knew now that she would go and visit her sister soon. This had gone on for too long and somebody had to give in. She gently touched her cheek. The scar didn't look so angry, and the make-up Rose had given her had helped to cover it. There was another lot of make-up inside the new handbag, along with a letter from Rose saying that she wished she could be with Lily on their birthday.

Her mother broke into her thoughts. 'There's a cake outside in the larder.'

Lily smiled. 'You been baking?'

'It's not very big, but I thought we needed something extra this year.'

Lily hugged her mother. 'You feel the same way as I do, don't you?'

'Yes I do. I wish we could all be together again.'

'So do I. Why can't Dad see it as well?'

'I don't know. Perhaps I'll have another word with him.'

'It didn't work the last time you asked.'

'I know, but he might be coming round a bit more.'

'Let's hope so.'

Chapter 33

'HAVE YOU HEARD anything from your sister lately?' asked Mrs B one afternoon in June as they were busy making a pie.

Rose mopped her brow. The weather was very hot, but she enjoyed being in the kitchen with Mrs B. Over these past months they had got on very well as Mrs B had given her lessons in cooking and taking care of the house. Rose also enjoyed having someone to talk to.

'I won't be here for ever,' the older woman had told her when Rose had asked her if she was worried that she might be taking her job. 'Besides, you never know what's going to happen,' she had added.

Rose reassured her that she would always be wanted; she also knew now that her name was Mrs Brook, but she was happy just being Mrs B.

'No,' she said in answer to Mrs B's question. 'I've given up trying to make her see sense. I'm afraid she can be very stubborn.'

'Give her time.'

Rose sighed. Her life would be complete if only Lily would talk to her. She had so much to tell her. She also knew that before the year was out, she would need Mrs B around more than ever.

It was last week that the doctor had confirmed what Rose had suspected weeks ago: that she was going to have a baby early in December. When she told Roger, he had been beside himself. He had leapt round the room whooping and grinning fit to bust, causing Rose to say, 'I gather you're rather pleased with the news.'

'Pleased? Come here, my beautiful, clever wife.' He had taken her in his arms and kissed her. 'So it could be a Christmas baby. Don't worry, he or she won't miss out on presents.'

'Now I don't want you spoiling our baby.'

'As if love is spoiling.'

Although Rose was very pleased at the idea of being a mum, she had also felt sad. How would her father feel towards his grandchild?

The following day, Roger came home with a silver charm bracelet. 'This is going to be a family keepsake. Every time something wonderful happens, I will buy a charm to go on it. As you can see, there is already a silver bell – that's for when we got married – and next to it is a tiny ring. With every baby I will buy another ring, and something appropriate when they arrive.'

Rose had cried.

'Don't you like that idea?'

'I think it's wonderful. I am so very lucky. I love you so much.'

'And I love you.'

When he took her in his arms and kissed her, her thoughts went to her sister. If only she could share their happiness.

When Poppy heard the news, she was round to see Rose straight away.

'You are so lucky,' she said.

'I know.'

'Archie and I have always wanted a baby, but so far it hasn't happened. Let's hope it's my turn next.'

Rose was really surprised at that statement; she'd never thought that a baby would be part of Poppy's plan.

She decided to write to Lily and tell her the good news. If anything would make everything all right, it must be a baby.

When Lily got the letter, she sat at the table grinning. 'Mum,' she said. 'You'll never guess. You're gonna be a granny.'

'What?'

'Rose is having a baby.'

Amy sat next to her daughter, smiling. 'When?'

'December sometime.'

'How wonderful – a baby. Surely your father has got to come round now; he loves babies. And I'll need to be with Rose, to help her.'

'When will you tell him?'

'I'll wait till we've finished dinner.'

That evening, once again, dinner was eaten in silence. Lily wanted to shout at her father, but she knew that a lot of this was her fault as well. She wondered what he would say at the news.

'Lily had a letter from Rose today,' said Amy as she began to clear the dishes away.

As usual he looked angry at Rose's name. 'Who?'

'She's got some very good news.'

'What's that, her bloke's left her?'

'No. You are going to be a grandfather.'

He looked at Amy, and Lily was worried that he was going to burst a blood vessel he looked so angry. 'So what does she want, a handout?'

'No. She just told us, that's all.'

'Good for her. Now don't mention that trollop's name ever again.'

'Ron, when are you gonna stop this stupid nonsense and let her come and see us?'

'Have you looked at her?' He pointed at Lily.

Lily took a sharp intake of breath. 'Rose didn't do this.'

'It was you,' added Amy.

'But she made me do it.'

'How did she?'

'She went against my wishes.' He stood up.

'Do you know, you can be such a stubborn sod at times.'

Lily looked at her mother. She was shocked. She had never heard her swear before.

Her father stood still and glared at his wife. 'What did you just call me?'

'You heard.' Amy went into the kitchen and Lily quickly followed her. She could see that her mother was shaking.

'Mum. Mum, are you all right?'

'No I ain't, and I'm sick to death of the atmosphere in this house.' She slammed the dishes down on the draining board. 'I'm going out.' With that, she stormed through the scullery and past Ron, who was still standing in the kitchen looking bewildered. She slammed the kitchen door, then they heard the front door shut.

'Now look at what you've done,' said Lily as she ran through to the hallway. She collected her coat from the peg, quickly noting that her mother had taken hers, and left the house.

Although it was still light outside, Lily didn't know which way her mother had gone. She stood at the gate for a moment or two, looking up and down the road. When next door opened, she knew that Mrs Brown would tell her.

'Yer looking fer yer mum?'

Lily nodded. 'Yes. Which way did she go?'

'Had a row, then?'

Lily ignored that question and the woman went on.

'Fought I 'eard a lot of door-slamming. She went up that way.'

Lily quickly made her way in the direction Mrs Brown had pointed.

As she hurried along, Lily felt frantic. Where had her mother gone? As she passed the paper shop, she could see a figure standing back in the shadows of the doorway.

'Mum?'

Amy was crying.

'Mum.' Lily went to her and held her close. She was shaking. 'It's all right.'

'Lily. Oh Lily. What's happened to this family? We were always so happy.' Her sobs were loud, and Lily looked around hoping no one would ask them what was wrong.

'I don't know who to blame. Rose for being so selfish or your dad for being so stubborn.'

'But Rose wants to come back to see us.'

'I know. But we have to live with him and he won't give in. Look how he was with his sister. What makes him so possessive?'

'I don't know. Come on, Mum, let's go home.'

'I don't know if I want to.'

'We can't stay out all night.'

Amy surprised her by saying, 'I know. We could go to see Rose.'

'What? But I thought you would do as dad wanted and stop seeing her?'

'He don't have to know, does he?'

'Well, no.'

'You know where she lives.'

'I know, but I ain't got any money for bus fares. Look, if you want to go and see Rose, we'll go another time.'

'Yes we will, and sod him.' Amy turned round and had a defiant stride as they made their way back home.

The kitchen door opened when they walked through the front door.

'So you've come back, then,' said Ron.

'Yes,' said Amy. 'Lily make us a cuppa, there's a love.'

Lily looked at her mother in amazement. She looked so relaxed and calm. There was no sign of the trauma they had just been through. Lily took off her coat and went into the scullery to make the tea, leaving the door open.

She couldn't make out what her father was saying and when she took the tea in her mother looked happier. 'Everything all right?' asked Lily.

'Yes love,' said her mother. 'We've decided not to mention your sister's name again as it upsets your father.'

Lily tried to hide her anger at her mother's sudden change in attitude. 'Well that's a change of heart, but if that's what you want then I'll just have to obey the rules.'

'I wouldn't call them rules. It's just that we want this to be a happy household again,' said her mother, fussing with the tea things.

'I don't see how it can ever be that.'

'Give it time, love, give it time.'

Lily looked at her mother. What was going on in her mind? Was she putting on an act?

'So you're not even going to acknowledge your grandchild when it comes along?'

'If that's what your father wants.' There was a hint of sarcasm in her mother's voice.

'But why? This stupidity has gone on long enough.'

Her father hadn't said a word.

Lily turned on him. 'I thought you loved us,' she said, and stormed out of the room. She was angry and confused. Surely her mother wasn't giving in to her father, or was all this talk just to keep the peace for now? She would write to Rose and tell that all her letters must go to the shop. She would explain that although her father didn't want to keep in touch, she did, and would come and see her whenever she could. Despite everything that had happened, the bond between twins was very hard to break.

Chapter 34

I<small>T WAS THE</small> end of July when Lily's letter arrived. Rose was over the moon. On Wednesday, Lily's half-day, she was bringing their mother to see her, unbeknown to their father.

'My mother's coming here,' she told Roger as soon as he got in.

'That's wonderful news. Has your father come round?'

Rose shook her head. 'No. It seems that they mustn't mention my name at all in front of Dad. But Mum's more understanding. She's thrilled about the baby and wants to see me. Lily said that Mum's been very different since she told her she was going to be a granny. Who knows, this might be the beginning of everything turning out all right.'

'I do hope so, my darling. I know how much all this has upset you. So is Lily going out a bit more now?'

'I don't think so. From what I can gather, she just goes to work and that's all.'

'Has her boyfriend been around again?'

'She hasn't said anything about him.' Rose smiled. 'I shall know all the news on Wednesday.'

'I haven't seen you look this happy for a long while.'

'I haven't been this happy, but I'll be glad when this morning sickness stops.'

Roger squeezed her hand. 'I think you're being very brave.'

'I feel so wretched in the mornings, but Mrs B said that it shouldn't last for much longer.'

'I do worry about you, but it's all going to be worth it,' said Roger.

Roger was so attentive that sometimes she had to tell him to stop fussing; she wasn't the first woman to have a baby.

'I'm not going to break.'

'I know.' He kissed her cheek.

'What are you going to be like when he or she arrives?'

'Once I know that you're safe, then I'm afraid I shall be like putty in our baby's hands.'

Rose laughed. 'With your background, how do know what putty feels like?'

On Wednesday, Rose was being sick when Mrs B arrived. She walked into the bathroom to see Rose sitting on the floor next to the lavatory pan.

'My dear, are you all right?'

Rose wiped her face. 'I will be.'

'I'll make you a cup of tea. Have you had anything to eat this morning?'

Rose shook her head.

'Some toast will help settle your stomach. I expect you're getting excited at your mother coming to visit.'

Rose stood up. 'I am a bit worried that something might happen and they can't make it.'

'Now come on downstairs and I'll make that toast.'

Rose smiled. She was very fond of Mrs B.

When Rose was sitting at the table, Mrs B asked, 'What are you doing for lunch? Will your mother and sister be here?'

'No. Lily don't finish work till one. We'll just have tea and a few sandwiches. And can you make one of your delicious cakes for us?'

'Of course. Do you want me to stay a bit longer today?'

'Thanks all the same, but I can manage. I am so excited.'

'Mrs Rose, you must calm down.'

Rose had insisted she call her Rose, but Mrs B said it wasn't proper, so they settled for Mrs Rose, which always made Rose smile.

All morning while Lily was working she kept thinking about taking her mother to see Rose. She knew Amy was really getting excited about it and had been trying hard to keep calm in front of her husband. Lily knew that her mother hadn't even mentioned that she would be coming to the shop.

Lily was also getting excited. She had bought the baby a teething ring, which her mother said was a bit premature, but Lily said she had to buy something. Her mother had bought a small dress, which had been carefully hidden away at the bottom of Lily's wardrobe.

At half past twelve, Amy arrived at the shop. 'I'm sorry I'm early,' she said to Lily when Miss Tucker ushered her into the back room, 'but I couldn't wait around indoors any longer. I didn't think Miss Tucker would mind.' She turned to Lily's employer.

'Of course I don't. Have a seat till Lily's finished. I know how much this visit means to you both.'

Lily had told Miss Tucker some of what had happened at home, but she did leave out the bit about her father being responsible for her scar. Miss Tucker only knew that Rose had run away to get married and that had upset the family.

'Sit yourself down, Mum, while I finish these button-holes.'

'They look nice,' said Amy as she perched herself on the chair. 'By the way, this letter arrived with the lunchtime post. It must be from Will, it's got a foreign stamp on it.'

Lily smiled. She loved getting his letters. She took it from her mother and put it in her overall pocket. 'Thanks. I'll read it on the bus.'

When they left the shop with the bunch of flowers Lily had bought her sister, she felt very underhand about deceiving her father, but if it was the only way her mother could see Rose without more scenes, then so be it. Lily had been sad and angry about the whole affair, which had been going on for far too long, and she knew that this rift had to be healed.

In the excitement of going to see Rose, Lily had left Will's letter at work. 'I can read it tomorrow,' she said when her mother asked her about it.

'She lives here? In this posh road?' asked Amy when Lily knocked on the door. She was looking all around her at the elegant houses in the mews where her daughter lived.

The door was thrown open and Rose stood there wearing a very elegant loose-fitting frock. She flung her arms round her mother. 'I've waited so long for this day,' she cried. 'I can't believe you're here.'

Amy had tears in her eyes. 'I must say, you look very well.'

'Come on in.'

They moved into the hall.

'This is very nice,' said Amy.

Lily handed Rose her flowers and kissed her sister's cheek. 'How are you keeping?'

'Getting over the morning sickness soon, I hope. Come into the kitchen. I expect you're dying for a cup of tea.'

'That'll be very nice,' said Amy.

Amy was taken a back once again by the small but well-laid-out kitchen and the beautiful crockery that was set out for tea.

'Mrs B did the sandwiches and she made us a cake.'

'Mrs B?' asked Amy.

'She's the lady that comes in a few days a week to help out.'

'You have a maid?'

'She's not really a maid; she's become more of an acquaintance. She's teaching me to cook. And I shall need her when the baby arrives.'

Amy felt a pang of jealousy. This should be her job. She should be here for her daughter and grandchild.

After Amy and Lily had been given a tour of the house, they all sat and talked and laughed. It was like old times. Rose heard about Will writing to Lily.

'So with Harry out of the picture, could there be romance in the air?'

Lily ignored the reference to Harry. 'Of course not. Besides, I think it was you Will was hoping to see.'

'I don't believe that. I reckon when he gets back home he'll be banging on the door with flowers.'

'I don't think so. Besides, I won't want to see him.'

'Why?' asked Rose.

'Have you looked at my face?'

The atmosphere suddenly went cold.

'I'm so sorry, Lil, I didn't mean to upset you, but I don't see that when I look at you; I only see my lovely sister.'

'I think it's about time we left,' said Amy. 'I don't want your father getting home before us.'

They all stood up.

'Mum, you will come again, won't you?'

'Of course.'

'Promise.'

'I promise.'

Rose held her mother close. 'Thanks for the little dress. I'm sure the baby will look lovely in it.'

She went to her sister. 'Please, Lil, forgive me for being so insensitive, but it's true what I said. People won't look at your scar, they only see you. And thank you for the flowers and the teething ring. I do love you so very much, and please come again any time you want.'

'By the way, thanks for the make-up,' said Lily.

'Does it help?'

Lily didn't answer.

When they were on the bus, Amy said, 'What Rose said is true, you know. We don't look at your face, we only see you, and I'm sure that's how young Will will feel as well. Have you told him?'

'No need to, he's still halfway round the world. And anyway, I won't be seeing him if and when he gets home.'

'Please yourself. But I still think you're being very silly.'

Lily didn't reply. What would happen when Will got home? Would he want to see her? It was Rose he'd wanted to see when he first got in touch, and Lily was only second best, someone who would write and keep him informed of all that was happening back home.

'I didn't realise what a lovely place Rose has got,' said her mother, breaking into her thoughts and trying to change the subject.

'She is very lucky.'

'If only your father would come round. If only he could see how happy she is.'

'As I said, she is very lucky.' Lily was suddenly feeling very low. She looked out of the window. She knew she would never be as lucky as Rose. She would never have a husband, a nice house and children. Harry hadn't been around since that day when he'd first seen her scar. It had upset her and she was angry. Her father had a lot to answer for.

Chapter 35

WHEN THEY ARRIVED home, Lily went straight up to her bedroom. The visit had upset her. She knew she was jealous of her sister. Rose had everything. A lovely house, a husband who adored her and she was going to have a baby. Lily sat on the bed and cried. What did she have? A face that to her was hideous.

She wiped the tears from her eyes when her mother knocked on the door.

'Lily, I've made a cup of tea.'

'I don't want one.'

Amy walked in and sat next to her daughter. 'Now come on. Don't get so upset.'

'It's not fair, Mum. Rose has got everything.'

Amy put her arm round her daughter's shoulders. 'It's not like you to be jealous.'

'I'm never gonna have a husband or a family.'

'Of course you will.'

'Who'd want to look at me like this? Who'd want to kiss me and ...' She began to cry. Her body was racked with sobs as she buried her head in her mother's shoulder and cried bitter, heartfelt tears.

Amy felt useless. What had her husband done to this poor girl? Lily had now lost all the confidence she'd just started to get back. If Rose was around she would help her sister through all of this. Lily needed Rose to talk to. Amy was angry and knew that when her husband came home she was going to let him know her feelings. She really didn't care if it upset him. She had had enough of all this.

Amy looked at the clock when she heard the front door shut. She was trembling with anger. She loved Ron, but enough was enough. This house was being torn apart and she knew that the time had come to make a stand. She wanted to be able to help her daughter with this baby. She wanted Rose to confide in her and for poor Lily to have her sister around, to share the joy and to be loved. She knew she had to be strong and stand up to her husband.

'Hello, love. All right?'

'No it ain't bloody well all right.'

Ron stopped smiling and looked shocked. 'Why? What's happened?'

'I've been to see Rose today, and I want her to be able to come here to see us whenever she wants.'

'What?' His face went red and he threw his cap on the floor in rage. 'You've been to see her?' he yelled.

Amy nodded. 'Lily took me.'

'What?'

'You heard.'

Lily was surprised at all the shouting that was coming from downstairs. The kitchen door was wide open, and going to the top of the stairs, she could hear her mother and father shouting. What was happening? She heard Rose's name mentioned and went down to see what this was all about.

When she walked into the room, her father shouted, 'What the bloody hell have you been up to?'

'What d'you mean?' She wiped away the tears that were still wet on her cheeks.

'You've been to see her?'

'If you mean my sister, your daughter Rose, then yes. Mum wanted to see her.'

He turned to Amy. 'You know my feeling about that. I forbid you to see her ever again.'

'What?'

'You heard.'

Amy went towards him, wagging her finger in his face. 'I'm your wife, not your slave. And I will do what I like when I like.'

'Not while you live in this house you won't.'

Lily stood open-mouthed. What had got into her mother?

'It's about time I stood up to you,' Amy said defiantly.

'So who feeds you and gives you a roof over your head?' Ron sat in his chair and started to undo his boot-laces.

'I'm sure me and Lily could make do, and I know Rose and her husband would help.'

'Mum,' said Lily, wide-eyed. 'What you saying?'

'We're gonna leave him. See how he gets on without us.'

Lily looked at her father, and when he stood up with his fist raised, she got between him and her mother.

'Lily, get out of the way,' said Amy grimly, and pushed her aside.

Ron lowered his arm and sat down in his chair.

Amy turned on him. 'I never thought you would ever raise your hand to me, but I can see now I was wrong. All the time I did as I was told we were a happy household. Now look at us, we've been torn apart. And it's all your fault.'

Lily stood looking at her mother, who was bustling around and tidying up unnecessarily. Her father was slumped in the chair. Neither of them looked at him till they heard unfamiliar noises.

'Dad. Dad! What's wrong?'

Amy rushed to his side. 'I'm so sorry, Ron. I didn't mean it.'

Lily was shocked to see her father with his head buried in his hands, crying. What had this family done to deserve all these problems?

'I'm so sorry,' said Ron, raising his head. 'Please believe me, Amy, I'm so so sorry. I would never hurt you.'

Amy glanced at Lily. 'I know, and I think all this has gone far enough. We should all sit down and talk quietly, and perhaps these problems can be sorted once and for all.'

Lily looked at her mother. How could her problem ever be sorted?

'Lily love. Make us a cuppa.'

Lily went into the scullery. In her eyes, nothing could ever be said to make things better.

'So did everything go all right today?' asked Roger after he'd kissed Rose.

'It was wonderful. Mum said she wanted to come round again, and do you know, Lily was looking a lot better. I'm sure the make-up is helping to give her her confidence back.'

'That's good.'

'And look what they bought baby.' She opened the bag. 'This little dress from Mum, and a teething ring from Lily.'

Roger laughed. 'All we've got to do now is wait till it gets some teeth. I'm so pleased to see you looking so happy. How about we go out for a meal tonight? You deserve a night out.'

Rose kissed him. 'I'd like that.' She was so happy. She knew that all her problems could be disappearing and she might even be going back to see her family again.

Lily sat at the table with her mother and father. Her mother seemed to have grown in stature while her father had shrunk. He looked sad and dejected.

'Ron, can you please tell us why you have this hatred towards Rose?'

He looked shocked. 'It ain't hatred. I don't hate her. I love my girls.'

'You've got a bloody funny way of showing it, keeping them under lock and key.'

He looked at his wife. 'Is that what you think?'

'It's the way they think.'

'Perhaps I've been wrong.'

'Wrong.' Amy gave a hollow laugh. 'Well I'm glad that at last you've admitted it.'

'Mum, give Dad a chance to explain.'

'Well come on, then.'

Lily couldn't believe how her mother was behaving; it was so out of character.

'You know how upset I was over me sister. Well I didn't want my girls to go down the same road and I thought that if I kept a tight rein on them they would always behave. You see, I just wanted them to find nice boys and settle down.'

Lily stood up. She was trembling with anger. 'So you thought that by throwing Rose out and disfiguring me for life, it would keep us under your control?'

'No. No, of course not. Lily, please forgive me.'

'I don't think I ever will. I shall never have a nice husband or children like Rose. I shall be an old maid for ever.'

'I'm sure you'll find someone. What about that nice lad you went out with?'

'Harry? He took one look at me and hasn't been seen since.'

'Lily, please sit down,' said her mother.

'So what about my sister? Are you going to let her back into this family?'

Ron sat up and very carefully began to roll a cigarette. After what seemed to Lily a painfully long time, he lit it and then spoke.

'I'm not sure. I don't want her to feel as if she's won.'

'What!' screamed Amy. 'Ron, this ain't a game; this is our daughter. There's no winners or losers. I want her to be able to come back here with her husband and child whenever they want, and if you make a fuss, then I shall go to the police about you hitting Lily.'

Lily sat with her mouth open.

'You know they won't do anything. A man is the master of his house.'

'That's it. Lily, get your coat, we're going to look for rooms. We can come back later for our things.' Her mother marched up the hall with Lily close behind.

Rose felt so very happy. They had been quietly enjoying their meal. Roger leaned across and held her hand.

'You look positively radiant tonight.'

'Thank you. I don't know for how long, though. I already feel the size of a whale.'

He smiled. 'I shall love you whatever your size.'

'I don't believe that for one moment. Roger, do you mind if we go? I feel very tired.'

'No, of course not. It must be all the excitement of the day.'

'I think so. I still can't believe that I shall be seeing Mum again, and hopefully she can talk Dad round too.'

Roger helped her with her coat and gently kissed her cheek. 'I hope so as well, my darling.'

Chapter 36

AFTER YESTERDAY'S TRAUMA when her mother had threatened to leave home, and her father had finally given in about Rose and Roger, Lily was still feeling on edge. That morning as she walked to work she couldn't believe what might have happened if her father hadn't given in. Did he mean it, though? Would Rose and Roger be allowed in the house? Only time would tell.

It had been a very tense evening, but Amy had finally got her way. Last night Lily had written to Rose on her mother's instructions to ask her and Roger if they would like to come over to tea on Sunday. She could see that her father wasn't pleased about it, but he didn't comment on the arrangement and anyway Lily didn't care what he thought. Rose was hopefully coming home again.

When Lily arrived at the shop, she remembered Will's letter. She smiled when she read that he was on his way to New York and would send her a picture of the Statue of Liberty. Since he'd started writing to her, she had been reading about all the lovely places he'd been to, and she did so look forward to his letters.

Amy was over the moon when on Saturday morning Rose's letter arrived saying they would be happy to come to tea.

'What shall we have?' she asked Lily, as her daughter was getting ready to go to work.

'I don't know, Mum. But don't go mad, let's see how Dad reacts first.'

Amy smiled. 'He knows how *I'll* react if he don't behave.'

Lily couldn't believe this new Mum. Suddenly she was full of confidence and so sure that things would go her way. Lily just hoped that it would turn out all right; she felt she couldn't take any more traumas in her life.

On Sunday morning, Lily, like her mother, could hardly contain her excitement. All morning Amy had been buzzing about making a fruit cake. As soon as dinner was finished, the plates were whisked away and the apple and custard was put in front of them. Lily wanted to laugh. Wait till she told Rose about this. The washing-up was soon done and then they began laying the table up for tea. The tablecloth that was only used at Christmas came out, as did the cake stand that had become almost a family heirloom. Bread was sliced thinly, and the ham, cheese and salmon sandwiches were cut into neat squares and placed daintily on a floral plate.

'Mum, don't go mad,' said Lily, who had been given

the task of arranging the table decorations. She had brought home some flowers and they stood in an elegant vase in the middle of the table. 'It's only Rose coming to tea. Remember, she did live here once.'

'I know, but she's going to be with her husband, and from what we know of him, he has been very well brought up.' Amy stood back and admired her work. 'I can't believe that after all this time we will all be sitting at the table together. Oh Lily, I do hope your father behaves himself.'

'So do I.' Lily had been watching her father through the scullery window. He had been sitting on the bench under the window reading his newspaper all morning. He had hardly said a word. What was he thinking? Would there be any trouble? She prayed that there wouldn't be. She began to dread what her mother would do if things didn't go well today.

At three o' clock, Amy was in the front room waiting for her daughter to arrive.

'They're here,' she screamed out when she caught sight of the car coming along Enfield Road.

Lily went along the passage as her mother came out of the front room.

Amy patted her hair. 'Do I look all right?' she asked Lily as she smoothed down her pretty pinny that was only worn on special occasions.

Lily smiled. 'You look lovely, Mum.' Her mother had also changed into one of the few frocks she possessed.

Amy opened the front door. 'Hello,' she said sheepishly, before hugging Rose. She turned to Roger and held out her hand. 'It's so nice to meet you under much nicer circumstances.'

Lily stood back, laughing. She was almost expecting her mother to curtsy.

After all the greetings and kisses, they went into the kitchen, where Ron was sitting in his chair reading his newspaper. Lily thought that by now he must have read every single line.

'Hello, Dad. How are you?' asked Rose. He just gave a nod.

'Hello, Mr Flower,' said Roger.

That was ignored.

Rose went to him and kissed his forehead.

There was no response.

Lily looked at her mother and gave a quick shake of her head. She didn't want any trouble today. 'Tea, everyone?' she asked.

'Yes please,' said Rose. 'I'll give you a hand.'

Together they went into the scullery.

'This is just like old times,' said Rose. 'God, I've missed you.'

'And I've missed you.'

They held each other close and Rose could feel a tear running down her cheek. When she looked at her sister, she could see the same was happening to her.

They both laughed and brushed the tears away.

'Anyway, how are you?' asked Rose.

'Just the same as I was when you last saw me. But look at you, you're positively blooming, and getting fat.'

'Thanks. I feel like I'm the size of a house and I've got

another few months to go yet. Lil, I can see that Dad's not happy about us coming here.'

'Mum has changed so much. I think he's just going along with it to keep the peace.'

'Oh dear. What happened?'

'I'll tell you when we have more time.'

'Is it that bad?'

'We can cope.'

Roger was sitting at the table, and although Amy was chatting and doing her best to put him at ease, he still felt very uncomfortable. What should he do if the old man decided to throw them out? If he laid a finger on Rose, Roger wouldn't be responsible for his actions. He almost sighed with relief when Rose and Lily came back into the kitchen. The joy on his wife's face was wonderful. If only things could be like this all the time.

They sat through tea telling each other what had happened since they were last together.

'Do you still hear from Will?' asked Rose.

Before Lily could answer, her mother said proudly, 'Lily's young man is going to New York.'

'Mum, he's not my young man, we just write to each other. Will's in the merchant navy and he goes all over the world,' Lily explained to Roger.

'And he's going to New York? It's a wonderful place.'

'You've been there?' asked Lily, wide-eyed.

'Just a couple of times. My company has offices there.'

'He's going to send me a postcard of the Statue of Liberty.'

'That is very impressive.'

'Roger brought back some records from New York,' said Rose.

'You've got one of those new gramophones. I've seen them in the department stores. They're ever so expensive,' said Lily.

'I should have shown you when you came over.'

'We had so much talking to do, we didn't have time, but you can show us the next time we come to see you,' said Lily.

Rose looked at her father, who hadn't said a word all through tea.

After a while Rose asked, 'Mum, do you mind if we go? I'm beginning to feel a bit tired.' She smiled. 'It must be all the excitement of seeing you all again.'

Her mother jumped up. 'No, of course not. Do you feel all right?'

'Yes thanks.'

Roger collected Rose's lightweight jacket and helped her into it.

Amy was beaming. 'I'm so happy to see you both. Do you want a girl or a boy, Roger?'

'I don't mind, just as long as Rose and the baby are all right.'

'Don't forget you could be carrying twins.'

Rose sat down quickly. 'My God, I hadn't thought of that.'

'Well you could be; after all, you are one.'

Lily grinned. 'That'd be a laugh.'

'Mum, how on earth did you manage?' asked Rose.

'I must admit it was difficult at times, especially when your father was away in the army.'

Lily looked at her father. Was that a slight smile on his face? Was he secretly enjoying this talk about babies?

After the hugging and the goodbye kisses, Lily and her mother stood at the gate and waved the visitors away.

Amy dabbed at her eyes. 'Oh Lily, I never thought this day would come.'

'Mum, would you really have left Dad if he hadn't given in?'

'I don't know. I was very angry.'

'I could see that, but to leave home . . .'

'I know. Let's go and see if he's mellowed a bit now.'

When they walked into the passage, Ron came out of the front room.

'You been looking out of the window?' said Amy, surprised.

'Yes.'

'Why?'

'I wanted to have another look at his car.'

'You could have asked him. I'm sure he'd have taken you for a drive if you were that interested.'

'I was curious, that's all.'

He led the way to the kitchen and Amy squeezed Lily's arm.

Lily smiled. It looked as if things were going to get better. Could Roger's car help? She really hoped so.

* * *

Rose was waving frantically at her mother and sister.

'I'm pleased that it turned out all right,' said Roger. 'Mind you, I was on tenterhooks watching your father for any sign that he might suddenly start something.'

Rose began laughing.

'What's so funny?'

'When I was waving goodbye just now, I saw the front-room curtain twitch.'

'Do you think he was just making sure we'd left?' asked Roger.

'No. I think he was looking at the car.'

'Why didn't he say he was interested? I would have let him have a proper look. We could even have gone for a drive.'

'Give it time, my love. Give *him* time.' Rose laid her head back against the lovely leather seat and smiled. 'This is something I've waited a long while for.'

Roger gently patted her knee. 'Let's hope it's the first of many visits.'

'Can we invite them to tea one Sunday?'

'Whenever you want.'

'I am so lucky.' Her thoughts went to Lily and she felt guilty. If there was only some way she could help her. 'Roger, could we take Lily to a nightclub one evening?'

'Do you think she would come?'

'I can try and persuade her. It's always dark in those places and she shouldn't feel out of place.'

'If you think she might like that, then go ahead and ask her.'

'She might take a lot of persuading.'

'You can only try.'

Rose began working it all out. She would give her sister one of her lovely evening dresses that she herself couldn't get into. She would also help her to do her hair and make-up. They could have a wonderful evening together. 'I'll write to her tomorrow and tell her that she can come and stay with us whenever she wants.'

Chapter 37

THAT EVENING, LILY wrote and told her sister all that had happened between their mother and father. She also said how pleased she was that everything had gone off well when they came to tea, and that they would like them to come again soon.

At the end of the week Rose replied.

'Everything all right?' asked her mother as Lily was reading the letter.

'She wants me to go and spend a Saturday night with them.'

'That's nice. Does she say when?'

'No. She wants to take me to a nightclub. Here, you read it.' She passed the letter to her mother.

'It sounds wonderful,' said Amy, smiling. 'It'll do you good to go somewhere nice.'

'She's trying ter get you married off to one of his posh mates,' said her father, who was sitting in the chair dozing.

'Ron, don't you start.'

'Just making a comment, that's all.'

'Well you can keep your comments to yourself.'

'I don't know if I want to go,' said Lily.

'Why not? You don't have to worry about getting a new frock. Rose says she'll lend you one of hers.'

'It's not that. I'm frightened.'

'What about?'

'Going somewhere where people will look at me.'

'But she says you've nothing to worry about as those places aren't very well lit and with the dancing girls it's always dark.'

Her father got up and went outside. Amy could see that he was still hurting.

'Why don't you go?'

'I'll have to think about it.' Although over these past months things had sometimes been fraught and at times Lily had almost disliked her sister, she was still her sister and twin and there would always be that bond between them.

Amy smiled. She knew Rose would come up with something to help get her sister's confidence back, and this could be a start.

For almost a week Lily toyed with the idea of going out with Rose. On Saturday evening as she was leaving the shop, she saw Roger's car waiting for her. There was no sign of Rose. Lily hurried over.

'Roger, where's Rose? Is she all right?'

'She fine, but she wants to see you. Can you come now?'

'I'll have to let Mum know. This is not so you can take me out tonight, is it?'

'No. I'll take you home first and then to our place, and then I'll bring you back later. Would that be all right?'

'Just as long as it's only for the evening. Promise.'

He laughed. 'Come on, get in and I promise.'

Lily climbed in the car and sat back and enjoyed the ride.

When they arrived in Enfield Road, Roger remained in the car when Lily got out.

'I'll stay here till you're ready.'

'No. Mum will be most upset. You must come in.'

'What about your father?'

'That's been taken care of.'

Reluctantly Roger followed Lily to the front door.

'Hello, Mum. It's only me,' she called out.

The kitchen door opened. 'You're early, love. Roger,' she added, very surprised to see him standing there. 'Is everything all right? Is it Rose?'

'Rose is fine, thank you.'

He followed Lily into the kitchen. 'I'm just here on an errand. You see, Rose wants Lily to come over for the evening.'

'I see. Are you going, love?' she asked her daughter.

'I'm not going out with them tonight, if that's what she wants.'

'What about your dinner? It's all ready.'

Lily knew that she had to have her dinner after her

mother had prepared it; to waste food was almost a sin. 'Roger, can you wait?' she asked.

'Of course, but Rose has got something for your dinner.' Roger was turning his smart grey trilby round and round in his hands

Lily was getting angry. 'That's typical of her. Everybody has to jump when she says so. She should have told me first before sending you over.'

'Lily, mind your manners,' said her mother, shocked at her daughter's outburst.

'I'm sorry, Roger,' said Lily. 'It's bit inconvenient. Tell her I'll see her next Saturday.'

'Lily, please come, she'll be very upset. What about tomorrow?'

'All right. I'll come and see you both tomorrow afternoon.'

He smiled. 'That's good. I'll pick you up about three, will that suit?'

'You don't have to come all this way. I can go on the bus.'

'I insist. It's no trouble.'

'Well only if you're sure.'

Roger began to walk out of the kitchen. 'Goodbye, Mr Flower, Mrs Flower. I'll see you tomorrow, Lily.'

'Goodbye, Roger,' said Amy.

There was no acknowledgement from Ron.

Lily walked up the passage with Roger. 'I'm sorry for that little outburst. But I know my sister.'

He opened the front door. 'Don't worry about it. I'll see you tomorrow. Goodbye.'

Lily waited till he drove away, then closed the door behind him. Rose was so very lucky.

'Where's Lily?' asked Rose as soon as Roger was through the door.

'I told you it was a bad idea. She's coming over tomorrow. I'm picking her up at three.'

'I would have thought she would have wanted to come here.'

'It was because she wanted to have her dinner first.'

Rose laughed. 'That's typical of Lily, always worried that she might upset Mum.'

Roger looked at her. 'Be fair, it was rather short notice.' This was a side of Rose he hadn't seen before. Was Lily right? Did she always want her own way?

'You know I was hoping we could go out tonight,' said Rose, pouting.

'Yes, but I don't think Lily's ready for that just yet. Have you noticed that she always turns her head away when anyone speaks to her?'

'Yes, but she was always the shy one.'

'Anyway, she's coming here tomorrow.'

'I'll see about making her face up. That way she might feel a bit more comfortable about coming out with us.'

Roger smiled. 'It looks like I could be taking two beautiful ladies out.'

'Just as long as it's me you have in your bed.'

'Mrs Walker, you say the naughtiest things. Come here.'

Rose went to him and kissed him. 'I love you so much.'

'I know. And I love you. Always remember that.'

'I will.'

The next day Lily was wearing a light summer frock, as it was very warm.

Her mother mopped her forehead. 'I feel sorry for Rose in this weather.' They were in the front room looking out of the window for Roger's car.

'Do you think I should say anything about Dad being interested in his car?'

'I suppose you could, but I can't see your father talking to him just yet.'

'He might be different when the baby comes.'

'I hope so. Right, madam, it looks like your carriage has arrived. Have a nice time,' said Amy as Lily went out.

'Thanks. I'll try.'

The ride to see Rose was wonderful, and so much nicer than waiting at bus stops.

'How's Rose coping in this heat?' Lily asked.

'She gets very tired.'

'She shouldn't be having me over then to wear her out.'

'Seeing you again has made her so very happy. And she wants to help you as much as she can.'

'I know.'

When they turned in to Puffin Mews, Rose was at the door. She rushed to the car, and after helping her sister out she held her very close. 'I'm so pleased to see you.'

'You only saw me last week.'

'I know. I want to see you every day. I miss you so much.'

She led the way inside. 'How about a glass of ginger beer?'

'Sounds lovely. But sit down and let me do it. You just tell me where everything is.'

'Lily's right. You go and put you feet up and I'll bring it in,' said Roger.

All afternoon the sisters laughed and chatted. Roger showed Lily how to dance, and she just loved the music.

'You wait till we take you to the nightclub, Lil,' said Rose. 'It's like something out of a film. You'll love it.'

'I'm not sure. I still don't know if I'm ready for that.'

'Roger, take Lily upstairs and show her my dresses. Just pick out whatever you fancy. I can't get into any of them now.'

When Roger opened the wardrobe door, Lily gasped at the wonderful array of evening dresses in lovely colours. 'Your sister has very good taste,' he said.

'She always did have.'

He held out a lovely blue one. 'This should suit you.'

Lily held it; it was beautiful and not too low at the back and front. She thought that some of them looked a little bit daring. She would never ever wear anything like that.

Roger put the dress on the bed. 'Look, why don't you try it on?'

'I suppose I could do.'

'I'll go and tell Rose.'

311

When he had left the room, Lily picked up the dress. It was so lovely, and the material felt so shiny. She held it against herself. What if she did wear it and they went to this nightclub? What if she spilled something down it? Would Rose forgive her? Lily remembered that when she lived at home she was very possessive about her clothes. But that was when she was buying them out of her own money. Were things different now? Money didn't seem to be any problem in this household. Lily looked at herself again and decided that she might not get another chance to try on something so lovely, so she took off her frock and put Rose's on.

For a few moments she just stood and gazed at herself. She looked and felt wonderful. She turned this way and that in front of the long mirror and felt almost like a princess. She said out loud, 'Cinders, you shall go to the ball.' She giggled.

'What are you doing up there?' shouted Rose. 'Come on down and let us see.'

Lily was still grinning when she opened the door and, carefully holding up her dress, made her way downstairs.

Rose and Roger were standing looking up.

'Lily, you look like a princess,' said Roger.

'My sister has just blossomed,' said Rose when Lily reached the bottom. 'Turn round.'

Lily did as she was told.

'What does it feel like?' asked Rose.

'Wonderful.'

'It fits you perfectly,' said Roger.

'I told you we were both the same size.'

Roger laughed.

'I'll be that slim again one day,' said Rose.

Roger kissed her cheek. 'I know you will, my love. But at the moment I love you just the way you are. Now come on, let's go and sit down and discuss when you're going to wear this lovely creation.'

Lily sat down very tentatively. She was terrified of creasing this dress.

'You just name the day,' said Rose. 'Roger will pick you up from the shop and bring you here, then you can get dressed and we can be off. We'll have dinner at the club and watch a show. You can stay here the night and Roger will take you home the next day. It'll do you good to get out.'

Lily sat listening to Rose making everything sound easy and wonderful.

'Dad won't make a fuss if he knows you're here with us.'

'I don't know.'

'Oh come on, Lil. Please. I won't be going out for much longer.'

'I still feel very self-conscious.'

'And I still feel very guilty. I can do your hair and make-up. Please, Lil, let me try and make it up to you.'

'You'll never do that.'

Roger was getting worried that the atmosphere was becoming decidedly chilly. 'Lily doesn't have to make her mind up right away. Give her a week or two to think about it. Believe me, Lily, you will enjoy yourself. It's a wonderful place.'

'I'll think about it.' She stood up. 'I'll just take this off.'

'I'll get the tea while you're upstairs,' said Rose.

In the bedroom, Lily sat on the bed for a moment or two. She desperately wanted to go out with Rose and Roger, but would she enjoy herself? What if someone made a comment about her face? She would want to die on the spot. Should she risk it? She would give them an answer when she was good and ready and not be bullied into it. She knew what her sister was like.

Chapter 38

THE FOLLOWING MORNING while Lily and Miss Tucker were sorting out some blooms, Lily told her about her visiting her sister.

'I'm so pleased that things are a lot happier at home. And you said that she wants to take you to a nightclub? Lucky you. I've heard that they are very glamorous. And the ladies wear some wonderful gowns.'

'That's what Rose said.'

'So when are you going? You'll have to wear a corsage, and you must make one up for your sister.'

'I'm not going.'

'My dear, whyever not? Is it that you've nothing to wear?'

'No, my sister said I could borrow one of her dresses. She's having a job to get into them these days. She really does have some beautiful clothes.'

'So what's stopping you?'

'I'm afraid.'

'Of what?'

'Somebody making a comment about my face. I'm still very self-conscious about it.'

'My dear, to be truthful I don't notice it at all now. It was a bit of a shock at first, but now the scar's beginning to fade, and with your make-up, people don't notice it. I think you're worrying unnecessarily.'

'Do you really think so?'

'I wouldn't be saying it if I didn't believe it.'

Lily had a lot of faith in what Miss Tucker said, as she'd always found her to be a very truthful person, but perhaps this time she was just being kind.

Lily was still pondering on what to do. In the end she asked her mother. 'Do you think I should go?'

'I'm sorry, love. I can't make up your mind for you. Would you like to go?'

'Yes.'

'Well then, make the most of the moment. Soon Rose won't want to be going out to places like that, and when the baby arrives she won't have time to go gadding about.'

'I expect that Mrs B will help her look after it, so that won't stop her.'

'I don't know about that. But as I said, I can't make up your mind for you.'

That night Lily went over and over the idea of going out with Rose and Roger. She did so dearly want to go, but ... When she remembered how she'd come to look like this, her anger returned.

The following morning a letter arrived from Rose. In it she begged Lily to go out with them, and said that this would probably be one of the last times she would be going to a place like that for a very long while.

At last Lily decided that she would take a chance and go.

That evening she told her mother, who was so very pleased. Then she wrote to Rose and told her.

When Lily got a reply from her sister, everything seemed to happen very fast, and soon it was Saturday and Roger was waiting outside the shop to take her to their house. Once again Rose was on the doorstep with open arms waiting for her to arrive.

Rose took charge of doing Lily's hair and make-up, and when she donned that dress again, even she had to admit she looked and felt a million dollars.

'Wow, Lily,' said Roger when she went downstairs. 'You look positively beautiful.'

'I told her that,' said Rose proudly.

Rose was wearing a long, loose dark blue dress with a wide gold belt just under her bust, and she too looked elegant and lovely. Roger was in evening dress, and Lily thought how grand they all looked. At that moment she knew she had made the right decision, but what would the evening bring forth? Only time would tell whether she finished up happy, or in tears.

'Right, my lovely ladies, may I escort you to the car?' Roger held out his arms, and with one sister on each side they made their way outside.

Lily was giggling as they sat in the car and made their way to the club.

Although she was very nervous when they walked in, the surroundings took Lily's breath away. It was everything Rose had told her, including the very low lighting. They were shown to a table, at which she was introduced to Roger's boss and his wife.

Archie stood up and held out his hand. 'Another beautiful young woman that Roger has kept hidden away.'

Lily smiled as she shook his hand.

Archie turned to Roger and said, 'I've ordered the champagne.'

Poppy also greeted Lily warmly, and soon they were seated and enjoying a lovely meal.

Lily just couldn't believe all this was happening to her. The surroundings, the conversations, everything. She was a little nervous when they went to the cloakroom, as it was very well lit, but nobody even looked at her, and Poppy just carried on talking. Lily watched her sister, who was very relaxed. No wonder she was so happy. She had everything.

As the evening wore on, Lily began to really enjoy herself. She loved the champagne. She danced with both Roger and Archie, and when the dancing girls came on, she sat back and clapped enthusiastically.

It was well past midnight when she noticed that Rose had begun to look tired. 'Are you all right?' she asked when the music was soft.

Rose smiled quickly. 'I'm fine.'

When Lily was dancing with Roger, she said, 'Is Rose all right?'

'She's fine.'

'Does she want to go?'

He glanced across at his wife, who was in conversation with Archie. 'I don't think so. Do you want to?'

Lily smiled. 'No, I am having a really wonderful time.' She didn't want this evening to end.

It was two o'clock when they finally left, after all the goodbyes and kisses. Archie and Poppy told Lily that she must come out with them again.

'I expect we'll meet up at the christening,' said Poppy.

'The champers will really be flowing that day,' said Archie. 'And you, young lady, must come and see us again.'

'I'd like that,' she said.

When they arrived home, Lily said good night to her sister and Roger and went upstairs. She knew as she took off her beautiful dress that the fairy tale had ended, but she still felt happier than she had done for a long while.

The knocking on the bedroom door woke Lily with a start. She was disorientated. Where was she? The door opened and Rose walked in, carrying a tray.

'Good morning. Your morning tea, madam.'

Lily grunted.

Rose put the tray on the dressing table. 'Did you enjoy yourself last night?'

'Rose, it was magical. You are so lucky to have all this.'

'I know.' She sat on the bed. 'If only Dad would come and see how happy I am and that Roger is a good man. Then my happiness would really be complete.'

Lily touched her hand. 'I'm sure when this baby comes along everything will work out just fine.'

'I hope so. I just want us to be a big happy family. Anyway, what did you think of Poppy and Archie?'

'She's nice and he's very well-mannered and a good dancer.'

'Well they certainly took to you, and I noticed quite a few young men looking at you. I reckon if you play your cards right, we could soon get you sorted out.'

'You forget it wasn't very well lit in that place.' Suddenly everything seemed different. Her dream bubble had burst.

'Oh, come on. I keep telling you, it hardly shows now.'

'I've got to go to the lav.' Lily got out of bed.

'I'll see you downstairs.' Rose left the room and Lily sat back down.

'Why do I always upset things?' she said out loud.

'I was so happy to see you and Rose together,' said Roger as he was driving Lily home. 'I don't think she'll be going out and about much more; she does get very tired.'

'I gathered that, but she tries to hide it.'

'I know. Anyway, you must come over and spend another Saturday night with us. We don't have to go out; we can always just play cards if you'd like that.'

'I'd love it.'

'And you and your mum must come over for tea one Sunday.'

'Mum will love that. She's so worried that she won't see much of the baby when it arrives.'

'She will, I promise. Right, here we are. Enfield Road.' Roger began laughing.

'What's so funny?'

'I was just thinking about when Rose said that you lived by the church.'

Lily laughed too. 'She was frightened of losing you.'

'I know. But thank goodness all's well that ends well.'

He stopped the car outside the house.

'You really do love my sister, don't you?'

'Very much. I never thought that anyone could make me so happy.'

'I'm so pleased for you both. I only wish our dad would come and see how happy you both are.'

'I'm sure he will one day. Now don't forget to tell him that I'll take him for a spin any time he wants. I might even let him drive.'

Lily was pleased that she had told Roger about how keen their father was on cars. 'Who knows, this could start something.'

'I hope so.'

'Do you want to come in?'

'Thanks all the same, but I'll be getting back.' He kissed her cheek. 'Thank you, Lily, for coming.'

'Thank you for taking me. It's something I'll never forget.'

'We'll do it again.' He got out of the car and opened her door. 'Bye.'

'Bye.' Lily could see her mother was looking through the net curtains. The front door was opened immediately she got to it.

'Why didn't you come out and talk to Roger?' Lily asked.

'I didn't like to. It would have looked as if I was waiting to pounce on you.'

Lily smiled as they walked into the kitchen. 'I think you were. Right. What do you want to know?'

'Did you have a nice time?'

'I had a wonderful time. That place was all and more than Rose said it would be. I danced with Roger and his boss Archie and sat and talked to Archie's wife Poppy.'

'That's a bloody silly name,' said her father.

'I didn't think you were listening.'

'Couldn't help it, could I.'

'Honestly, Mum, the frock I wore was wonderful. I felt like a princess.'

'I'm so pleased you enjoyed yourself. It's about time you went out and about.'

'Roger wants us to go to tea one Sunday.'

'I'd like that.' Amy glanced at her husband.

'By the way, Dad, he said he'd take you out in his car whenever you fancy it. He also said he could teach you to drive if you want.'

'Ron, that would be lovely.' Amy's face was wreathed in smiles.

'What do you say?'

'Nothing,' came back the answer.

Lily went to say something but her mother stopped her.

'Why don't you take your things upstairs?'

Lily knew that perhaps this wasn't the time to discuss it. He needed time to think about things, but perhaps the rift was slowly healing.

'Give him time, love. Give him time,' whispered her mother as she left the room.

Chapter 39

THE FOLLOWING DAY, Lily was telling Miss Tucker all about her night out.

'Sounds as if was very exciting.'

'It was. It was like something out of a film.' Lily laughed. 'I felt like a film star.'

'It's so nice to see you happy again.'

'I can honestly say it was the best night of my life.'

'So your sister was right. I'm so pleased for you. Will you be going there again?'

'Not before the baby's born.'

'When's it due?'

'About six weeks' time. Sometime in December.'

'So you'll have the new baby to buy Christmas presents for?'

'I'm really looking forward to it. Hopefully this Christmas will be a lot happier than last year.'

'I remember that. It must have been very hard for you

when Rose ran away to Gretna Green to get married. Has your father forgiven her now?'

'In a way.'

'I'm sorry, I shouldn't be asking you all these questions.'

'That's all right.'

'I'll just go and put this display in the window.' Miss Tucker went into the shop.

Lily thought about this past year and all the problems it had brought with it. Next year must be better.

'Everything all right, Mum?' asked Lily when she walked into the kitchen.

'Fine. Have you had a good day? There's a letter from Will on the mantelpiece for you,' said Amy.

Lily quickly opened it. She loved his letters. 'Look, here's a postcard of the Statue of Liberty.' She passed it to her mother.

'It looks wonderful.'

'Will says he's been all the way up to the top and looked out. And he says it's a wonderful view of Manhattan. It looks very tall.' Lily stopped suddenly.

'He's a very lucky lad to be travelling like this.' Amy looked at her daughter's sad face. 'What is it, love?'

'He said he's coming home and wants to take me out.'

'Does he say when?'

'Should be round about Christmas time. He said they'll be docking at Liverpool.'

'What's wrong with that?'

'I don't want to see him.'

'Whyever not?'

'I would have thought that was obvious.' Lily picked up her hat and handbag and went upstairs.

Amy was upset. Her daughter was just beginning to get her confidence back and now she'd had another setback. She knew Lily had never told Will about the accident, but surely he wasn't the kind of lad who would be upset by it.

When Lily came downstairs for her dinner, her father was standing next to the table. He pulled out her chair for her.

'I hear young Will's coming home. That should be nice for you. He must have a lot of exciting things to tell you.'

Lily looked at her father. This was the most he'd said to her for months. 'So you approve of Will. Is that it?'

'Lily, I don't want to stand in the way of your happiness.'

She laughed, but it was a bitter, hollow laugh.

Her mother walked in with the dinner. 'Now sit down, both of you,' she said.

'I'm so pleased we took Lily to the club. She really did enjoy herself.' Roger hung his trilby on the hat stand.

'And she did look lovely,' said Rose as he sat next to her on the sofa.

'Yes, she did. Do you think it helped her to get some of her confidence back?'

'I don't know. I hope so.' Rose smiled and touched her

stomach. 'This baby's certainly going to be a dancer.' She put Roger's hand on her bump.

He laughed. 'Well if she's anything like her mother, she'll have plenty of practice.'

'I only hope Dad comes round before the baby's born.'

'So do I.'

'I'm sure Mum and Lily will work on him.'

'I'm sure they will. Now, put your feet up while I make us a cup of tea.'

'Thank you.' When Rose was alone, she thought of the joy she hoped this baby would bring.

When Lily went to see Rose the following Wednesday afternoon, she told her about Will coming to see her. Rose was thrilled.

'Oh Lil, that will be wonderful.'

'Will it?'

'What d'you mean?'

'I don't want to see him.'

'Whyever not?'

'Do you think he'll want to see me?'

'Of course he will.'

'Harry didn't.'

'He's never been back since that first time?'

Lily slowly shook her head.

'Well that just goes to show what a shallow person he was, and certainly not good enough for you. And don't forget that was a long while ago, just after it happened. Believe me, Lily, it really doesn't look so bad now.'

'I think you're just saying that to keep me happy.'

Rose threw her arms round her sister. 'Lily, I love you, you are part of me and I just want you to be happy.'

Lily pushed her away. 'I don't want to see him.'

'Why? Look, if Will wants to see you, then I think you should. He was always a nice boy. Remember all the kids we played with? Some of them had horrendous scars and injuries that drunken parents had inflicted on them and no one turned a hair.'

'That was different.'

'Was it? We didn't look at them, not really. What about all the men who came back from the war? Do you think their wives didn't want to see them again?'

Lily looked at her sister. 'I do want to see him, and when you put it like that, perhaps I should.'

Once again Rose hugged her sister. She only hoped that she had said all the right things.

As the weeks went on, Lily would spend most Wednesday afternoons with her sister. Roger would always take her home afterwards, and some evenings Rose would go with them. The first time Rose went into the house, she was very nervous.

'Come on, Rose,' said Lily as she opened the kitchen door.

'Rose. How lovely to see you, and you as well, Roger. Sit yourselves down and I'll make a cup of tea,' said Amy, jumping up.

Rose looked at her father, who just gave them both a nod.

Rose followed her mother and sister into the scullery.

'How are you keeping, love?' asked Amy.

'Not too bad, but I do feel like an elephant.'

'I must say, you look very well. Lily, put the tea things on the table, there's a love.'

When Lily left the room, Rose said, 'Mum, what can I do to help her get her confidence back?'

'I don't honestly know. She should be looking forward to Will coming home, but somehow it's sent her back into her shell again.'

'I did try to talk some sense into her, and she said she'd think about seeing him. But I don't know. Should I write to him?'

'Lily would go mad if you did that.'

'Well I feel I should do something.'

'We've got a little while yet. I'll talk to her again. Now you go and sit down.'

As they were driving home, Rose mentioned to Roger about writing to Will.

'If you ask me, I don't think that would be a good idea.'

'Why not?'

'You would be interfering.'

'But she needs someone to push her.'

'I don't think so.'

At the same time as Rose was having this conversation with Roger, Ron and Amy were sitting quietly, he with the newspaper and she busy with her knitting for the baby. Lily was in her room.

'So when's this baby due?'

Amy quickly looked up. This was the first time he had even acknowledged that Rose was having a baby.

'The middle of December.'

'So she wasn't up the duff when she got married?'

'No.'

He went back to his reading. Amy sat looking at him. Was this the beginning of his daughter being allowed back into the fold? And would he make them feel properly welcome? She desperately hoped so. She wanted to be part of this new baby's life.

The following day, Lily, who was alone in the shop, was looking out of the window when she saw Harry walk past. He stopped and came in.

'Lily. You're looking very well.'

'Harry.' She tried to sound indifferent. 'It's a while since you've been here.' She quickly turned away from him. 'How's your mother?'

'She's very well, thank you.' There was an uncomfortable silence. 'Would you like to come out for a coffee or something?' he asked.

'No thank you.' Lily couldn't believe that her sister had only been asking about him a short while ago.

'I still feel bad about not calling in to see you before.'

'That's all right, I understand.' Lily wanted him to go. He was annoying her.

'Could we go out again?'

'I don't think so.'

He was looking embarrassed, and Lily could see that he didn't know what to say.

'Those flowers look very nice.'

She laughed. 'You don't have to stay, Harry. I can see that you're uncomfortable. So goodbye.' She went to go into the back room when he put his hand out to stop her.

'I have missed you and our talks and coffee, and I would like us to still be friends.'

'Harry, that's all we were, just friends. Now if you don't mind, I have work to do.'

'Yes, of course. I understand.' He turned and left the shop.

Lily watched him walk away. She would have liked to go out with him, but he had hurt her. If he had been a true friend, he would have stood by her and helped her. But was it her fault for being so defensive?

That evening, the more she thought about Harry, the more depressed she became. Should she have gone out with him? But would he have been embarrassed about being seen with her?

'Why don't you go over and see Rose on Sunday?' said her mother, who could see that her daughter was moping around and couldn't seem to concentrate on anything. She had even cast aside the baby matinee jacket that she was making.

'I'll write to her and ask if I can go for the day. You wouldn't have to get my dinner, as I'm sure Rose can feed me.'

'She's turning out to be quite a good cook. That Mrs B has certainly taken her under her wing.'

Lily smiled. They'd only ever been over a few times for tea, and then Mrs B had made the cake and all Rose had to do was put it on the plates. That evening she sent her sister a letter and waited eagerly for a reply. She loved going to Rose and Roger's house; they always seemed so happy.

Chapter 40

IT WAS A cold, drizzly October Sunday morning when Roger collected Lily. She quickly gave him a kiss on the cheek. 'I love this car and I'm glad I'm not waiting around for buses.'

Roger just gave her a smile. Somehow he didn't seem to be his normal smiling, chatty self. 'Is everything all right? Is it Rose?' she asked.

'No, she's fine.'

'Are you sure?'

'It's just a bit of a problem at the office, that's all. Nothing for you to worry your pretty little head about.'

Lily smiled. He was such a good-looking smooth operator, just like the heroes in the films, and she could see why Rose had fallen for him. She could also see that he wasn't in the mood for conversation, so decided to let the subject drop.

When they arrived at the house, Lily noted that Rose too looked concerned. 'Is everything all right?' she asked her sister as soon as they were alone in the kitchen.

'I don't honestly know, but all week something has been happening in New York and Roger said it could affect Archie.'

Lily wasn't any the wiser.

She was sad when it was time to leave, even though this hadn't been like the other Sundays she'd been here, which had been filled with music and laughter. This time everything seemed very quiet and subdued, and although Roger had been trying hard to lighten the mood, Lily could see that he had something on his mind.

'Are they all right?' asked her mother as soon as Lily walked in.

'I don't know. Roger didn't seemed his usual cheerful self.'

'Is Rose all right?'

'She seems fine, but I think she's worried about Roger.'

'Did she say what's wrong?'

'Something to do with New York.'

Her father suddenly spoke. 'What does he do for a living?'

'Not sure. He makes a lot of money and he's been to New York with his job. That's all I really know.'

'If he's in stocks and shares, then things could be bad for him.'

Amy looked worried. 'What d'you mean?'

'The stock market in America has crashed and people are losing thousands.'

'Oh my God,' said Amy. She looked at her daughter. 'Do you think that's what's happened?'

'I don't know. But would it affect Roger?'

'Only time will tell,' said her father.

Lily was surprised at her father's reaction and for him to talk about Rose and her husband without shouting was unusual. Was he concerned about his wayward daughter?

The next day in her lunchtime Lily bought a newspaper and was reading it in the back room.

'Don't often see you reading a paper,' Miss Tucker said.

'I'm worried about Rose.'

'My dear, why?'

'Her husband works in the City and his firm has offices in New York, and I'm worried that it could be caught up in this stock market collapse. Not that I know anything about it.'

'Neither do I, but I think it's very bad over there.'

'The last thing Rose wants at this stage is worry.'

Miss Tucker gently patted her arm. 'I'm sure it will all work out all right.'

'I hope so.'

That evening when Lily got home, she was surprised when her father asked, 'Rose's husband. Any more news on whether he will be affected by this trouble in America?'

'I don't know.'

'He could lose everything if he is.'

'He's a very sensible lad,' said Amy. 'I'm sure it'll be all right.'

Lily was concerned. 'It won't affect things over here, will it?' she asked her father.

'Don't know. Don't know much about that sort of thing.'

Amy sat listening to Ron and Lily. For the first time in months they were talking civilly to each other, and there wasn't any malice in Ron's voice when he mentioned Rose's husband. Could it be that he was really worried about them? She began thinking about Rose. If this crash did affect them, how would she react to losing her lifestyle?

'Lily, perhaps I could meet you outside the shop on Wednesday afternoon and we could go and see Rose, just to let her know we'll be here if they need help.' She looked at her husband, waiting for his reaction, but there wasn't any.

'That's a good idea, Mum. I'll try and finish this matinee jacket by then.'

Amy smiled at Ron. Even if it was something bad, she hoped that this might be the thing that could bring them all together again.

On Wednesday, when Rose opened the door, she didn't look at all well.

'Are you all right?' asked her mother anxiously.

'I'm fine.'

'Well you don't look it.'

'We've got a lot on our plate at the moment.'

'Is it about this New York thing?' asked Lily.

Rose looked surprised. 'What do you know about it?'

'Not a lot. But Dad tried to explain it to us.'

'I bet he's having a good laugh about this. He must enjoy telling you that we're heading for a fall.'

'No, he's not,' said Amy. 'In fact he's very worried about you.'

'Why? Does he think I'll come running home if Roger loses everything.'

Lily took a sharp intake of breath. 'He won't, will he?'

Rose shrugged her shoulders. 'I don't know. But if he does lose his job, he doesn't know anything other than banking. He does have some savings, but what with the baby and everything he doesn't know how long they'll last.' Rose began to cry.

Amy, who was sitting next to her daughter, held her hand. 'I'm sure it won't come to that.'

'Mum, I'm so worried.'

'Of course you are.'

Lily sat and watched her mother and sister. Despite all the sadness and uncertainty, it was lovely to see them together again, a mother comforting her daughter.

As the afternoon wore on, Rose became a little calmer, and when the time came for them to leave, Amy asked, 'Are you sure you don't want Lily to stay with you till Roger comes home?'

'No, I'll be fine.'

'He can always run me back in the car,' said Lily.

'No, honestly, I'll be all right. I'm so glad you came here today.'

'I'll be over on Sunday,' said Lily.

'I tell you what, why don't you and Roger come to us,' said her mother. 'You can have dinner and we can sit and chat. By then you might know how things are going.'

'I'd like that. But what about Dad?'

'He's really sorry for all the trouble he caused and he wants you to feel you can come back home.'

Lily was angry. He was sorry, was he? What about her? Would that make up for everything that had happened?

'Don't worry too much about things, Rose. I'm sure it will all work out fine in the end.'

'I hope so, Mum.' Rose held her mother close and kissed her cheek. Then she hugged her sister and tears began to trickle slowly down her cheeks. She quickly brushed them away.

When they left, Lily said, 'Did Dad really say that, you know, that he was sorry?'

'In a roundabout way.' Her mother quickly changed the subject by saying, 'D'you know, I think there's more to this than Rose is letting on.'

'So do I.' But Lily was still thinking about her father. Was her mother just hoping that he had said those things? She would know on Sunday.

Amy was looking anxiously at the clock. Where were Rose and Roger? Her daughter knew they always had dinner sharp at one; it was now a quarter past. 'I'll have to dish up soon,' she said to Lily. 'Otherwise it'll be spoilt.'

The sound of the front door being shut put a smile on her face. Lily opened the kitchen door.

'Everything all . . .' She didn't finish her question as she could see that Rose was crying. 'Rose, what is it?' Roger was behind her sister looking very drawn and sad. 'Come on in and sit down.'

Ron put down his paper and looked on as Amy put her arms round their daughter. 'What is it, love?'

Roger just stood looking very uncomfortable.

Ron stood up. 'What's the trouble, mate?' he asked him.

'I'm afraid I've lost my job.'

'Why?'

'This New York stock exchange collapse is unfortunately affecting the business I'm in.'

'But it's in America, not over here,' said Ron.

'My firm deals in stocks and shares and now they're worthless.'

'What you gonna do, son?'

Both Lily and her mother looked at Ron in astonishment. Even Rose stopped crying and looked up.

'I don't know.' Roger bowed his head.

'I'll get the dinner,' said Amy, trying to ease the situation.

In the scullery, Lily wanted to say something, but it was deathly quiet in the other room and she knew everybody would hear her.

They finished dinner in silence, although Roger and Rose didn't eat very much.

'I'm sorry, Mum, but I don't feel very hungry.'

'You should eat, you know. After all, you're eating for two.'

'I know.'

The table was cleared, and when Lily and her mother had finished the washing-up, they were surprised to see that Ron was still sitting at the table deep in conversation with Rose and Roger.

'Roger wants to know if there's any houses to rent round here,' Ron said as soon as they walked in.

Amy was almost speechless. This was what she'd prayed for, her husband talking as if his son-in-law was his best friend. What had got into him? 'I don't know,' she said.

'Have you got to give up your lovely home?' asked Lily.

'I think so. You see it's only rented, and if I don't get a salary I can't pay the rent.'

'And I can't go to work,' said Rose.

Roger tapped the back of Rose's hand. 'So we thought we'd better start looking as soon as we knew for certain that things were going to get bad.'

'Next week I'm taking my fur coat and a lot of my frocks to the pawn shop.' Rose gave a sob.

'That's such a shame,' said Lily.

'If there's anything you would really like, Lil, you can have it.'

'Do you have to?'

'I can't fit into any of them, and we shall need the money. Besides, it'll be a long while before we can go to those sort of places again, if ever.'

Roger looked at Ron. 'I'm so sorry, sir. I've let you and your daughter down. You can throw me out if you like. I know how much you hate me, but I love Rose and always will, and together we will get through this one way or another.'

You could have cut the silence with a knife. Lily and Amy were looking at Ron, waiting for him to say something. When he stood up, Lily went cold. What was he going to do?

'Rose. Roger. I know I've been a fool. And I can't tell you, and you Lily, how sorry I am about all this upset I've caused. For months now, Roger, I've seen how you've looked after Rose and made her very happy. As I said, I'm very sorry.'

Lily looked at her father. She was angry. Did this apology clear his conscience? What about her? Just because Rose was in difficulties, that didn't help her cause. She left the room. She knew that if she stayed there, she might say something she would regret.

It was a while before Rose came into her bedroom. 'Lily, what can I say?'

'Nothing. Him saying sorry to you makes everything fine, but what about me? For months I've had to put up with this hideous scar, and I'll have it for the rest of my days. You've got a husband and a baby on the way. And whatever happens, you'll be all right. What have I got? A bit of an apology from my father.'

'I'm sure Dad did mean—'

'I've stuck up for you for months. Now go. I want to be alone.'

'Now you listen to me, Lily. It's about time you stopped

feeling sorry for yourself. All right, I know I was to blame, but you can't go through life not enjoying yourself. Write to Will and tell him you've had an accident. I'm sure he'll understand. Then who knows, you could end up having a wonderful life.'

'I don't think so.'

Both Roger and Rose were very quiet as they drove home. At last Roger spoke.

'Rose, I'm going to see Archie in the morning and see if he can find a way out of this mess. I'm also going to try and sell the car.'

'Do you have to? I know how much it means to you.'

'Keeping a roof over yours and the baby's head is far more important. At least it will give us some money to be going on with, and if we can move near your parents, that would be good for you and them.'

'I can't believe that Dad seems to have forgiven me. But Lily is still very angry.'

'I think it will take years for her to really forgive your father.'

'I don't think deep down that she will ever forgive me.'

'Give her time, my love.'

Chapter 41

THE FOLLOWING MORNING, Rose watched Roger drive away. She would be sorry to see the car go. She had loved it, but Roger was far more practical and sensible than her.

They had also talked about Mrs B, and when she arrived later that morning, Rose had the sad task of telling her that she wouldn't be needed any more.

'I'm so sorry, but we will have to move.' Rose hugged her.

Mrs B held her close. 'I'm sorry as well. All the years I've been here, I've been so happy. I was hoping to be able to help you with this baby. You will let me know when it arrives, won't you?'

Rose only nodded.

'Would you like me to stay this morning?'

'No. Thanks all the same, but Roger will be home soon and we have got to start getting rid of some of our clothes.'

'This is a very sad time for you.'

343

'Yes, it is.'

Rose held Mrs B close again. 'I want to say how grateful and happy I am that I met you. You have been so kind to me?' Rose let her tears fall.

Mrs B broke away. 'It's been my pleasure.' She brushed aside a tear of her own and walked from the house for the last time.

Later that morning, Rose brought her lovely clothes down into the sitting room and laid them on the sofa. Tears ran down her face as she remembered the occasions for which she had bought each dress and the happy memories they brought back. She ran her fingers over her wonderful mink coat. It was so soft. She sat and thought about her wedding. It wasn't the wedding all little girls dreamed about, but she was happy, she had Roger. She was going to be very sad when they had to move, but they had each other and that was all that mattered.

When Roger walked in, she could see he was upset. She kissed him and said, 'I won't ask if everything is fine, as I know it isn't, but do you know any more about what's happening?'

'The good thing is that James is still in a job.'

'Does that mean he could get you into his office?'

'I'm afraid not. They're cutting their staff back as this has affected them as well, though not as badly. He said he will buy the car if he can sell his, so that's good news.'

'And what did Archie have to say?'

Roger looked uncomfortable.

'What's wrong?'

'I don't know. Nobody has seen him.'

Rose quickly put her hand to her mouth. 'Oh my God, you don't think he's done anything silly, do you?'

'I don't think so.'

'But a lot of people in America are . . .' She couldn't bring herself to say the words.

'No, I don't think Archie is that stupid. It's more than likely he's emptied the safe and done a runner.'

'Do you know that?'

'No. I couldn't get into his office as it's all locked up, and mine has been stripped of anything valuable. I tried the flat, but that too is locked. So my darling, it looks as if we are on our own.'

'But we've got each other.'

'Yes, we have.' He held her close and then kissed her. 'And we've got someone else to worry about.' He gently touched her stomach.

Rose knew that whatever happened in the future they had each other, and that was the most important thing.

When Lily arrived home that evening, she was still thinking about all that Rose had said to her. For a long while the previous night she couldn't sleep as she went over and over that conversation. She felt sad for Rose, about to lose everything, but life had to go on, and even she was beginning to see how senseless her feeling sorry for herself was. It didn't help anyone. She decided to take Rose's advice and tell Will that she'd had an accident and now had a scar down her cheek. She was going to tell him that if he didn't want to see her she would understand.

'I told the rent man about Rose and Roger when he came this morning,' said her mother as soon as Lily walked in.

'And?'

'He reckons there'll be a few empty houses coming up, and if Roger goes to see him he'll let him know when one becomes available.'

'That's good. Did he say where?'

'No, but I don't think his round goes too far away.'

'Mum, I'm gonna write to Will and tell him about me scar.'

Her mother stopped stirring the dinner and looked at her daughter. 'I'm so pleased. What's brought this on?'

'It was Rose. She told me to stop being sorry for myself and tell him. She said he was a nice bloke and would understand.'

'Didn't I say that?'

'Yes.'

'I'm so pleased. I know things will work out for all of you.'

Lily smiled at her mother, who was singing softly to herself.

'I still can't believe that Rose could be living near us,' Amy said. 'Even your father has changed towards them. Why do we always have to have a crisis for people to come to their senses?'

That evening Lily wrote to Will. She didn't tell him

how she got the scar, but she hoped he would still come to
see her when he came home.

A week or two later, Rose and Roger were still looking for
a cheaper place to live.

'I don't know what we're gonna do, Mum,' Rose said
on Sunday when they were all having dinner.

'When are you leaving your house?' Amy asked.

'We've got till the end of November,' said Roger. 'I
thought we could manage to stay a bit longer, but the land-
lord's putting up the rent then, and what with the hospital
to pay for . . .' He had suddenly begun to look tired.

'That's not very nice of him,' said Amy. 'A month
before Christmas and with the baby on the way.'

'I'm afraid that profit comes before everything,' said
Roger.

'Mum, could they have my room till things get settled?'

'And where will you sleep?' asked Rose.

'We can't do that. We'll manage,' said Roger.

'We could bring Lily's bed down into the front room
for a while,' said Amy.

'Thank you, but no. No. We couldn't put you out.'
Roger looked at his father-in-law, waiting for him to say
something. He still couldn't believe the change in this
man, but would it last?

'Ron, what have you got to say about this?'

Everyone waited for his answer. Rose kept her fingers
crossed and Lily just sat staring at him. They all knew that
whatever he said would be the last word in the discussion.

'Well your mother would skin me alive if I said no. But if Lily doesn't mind and Rose thinks she could stay here for a little while, it's all right with me.'

A great whoop went up and they all began talking at once.

Lily held her mother and Rose held Roger.

'Thank you, Dad,' said Rose, going over and kissing his cheek.

Lily smiled. She'd never thought this day would come.

Amy sat back and smiled at her husband. Soon they would all be together again. She just hoped that things would work out well for Lily too.

After the goodbyes, Rose got into the car knowing that this would be the last ride she was going to have in it. James was taking it tomorrow. She knew Roger had been hoping for a better price for it, but now at least, thanks to the family, they were going to have a roof over their heads. She smiled to herself. It would seem funny being back in her own bedroom with Roger beside her and Lily downstairs. She just hoped it would only be for a short while. Perhaps they would soon find a house and Roger would get a job, and everything would work out fine.

It was late November, and over the last few days a thick London fog had settled all around them. Lily found walking home from work very difficult; she lost her way so many times and it seemed to take for ever. Amy worried constantly about her family and would only relax when Ron and Lily were home. Roger was hoping that the weather would improve so that he could hire some sort of transport and begin to move into Enfield Road. Rose was also worried that the baby might come early and she would have a job getting to the hospital, as many of the buses stopped running when the fog got bad.

That morning Lily had a postcard from Will telling her that her letters would be taking a bit longer to catch up with him as he would be at sea for weeks. But he should be home in time for Christmas.

'If he wants to spend Christmas with us, he'll be more than welcome,' said Amy.

'I'll ask him, but I expect he'll want to be with his sister.'

Amy only smiled.

That afternoon Miss Tucker told Lily that she could go early, as the thick yellow fog had descended quickly.

'Do you think you will be all right?' she asked her.

'I would think so. I've been doing this journey for years.'

'I know, but it's all very different in the fog. You can quickly lose your bearings. Crossing the road is worst. You think you're going straight but then you find you've gone right off course.'

'I'm sure I'll be all right.'

'I'm sure you will. I'm sorry, I shouldn't be frightening you.'

'Good night. I'll see you in the morning.' Lily wrapped her scarf round her mouth and set off.

She had only gone a short distance when she realised this was the worst fog she'd ever been out in. Very soon she had no idea where she was. The shops she could make out in the gloom were unfamiliar. She was standing in the road when a man carrying a flaming torch came towards her.

'Excuse me,' she said.

He stopped.

'Please. Can you tell me where I am?'

'Where yer trying ter git to?'

'Enfield Road.'

'Where's that?'

'Off Rotherhithe New Road.'

'Blimey, yer way off course. This is Surrey Street.'

'Thank you, I know where I am now.'

'Well be careful.'

Roger was also lost. He had collected the hired van that morning but he was having trouble with it. First it wouldn't start, then the brakes were useless. He had to get home. This fog was a real peasouper and he knew Rose would be worried about him. He had to get to her.

Amy kept going to the front room and looking out of the window, not that she could see anything. She wandered back into the kitchen.

'Ron, I'm really worried about Lily. She should be home by now.'

'It's very bad out there. I'd go and meet her but I'd be sure to miss her.'

'I know you would.'

'She might have stayed on at the shop. She could always get her head down in there for the night.'

'I hope so.'

It was very late when Amy looked out to see that a slight breeze was helping the fog to lift. 'She might come home now.'

'Sit yourself down, woman. She's not silly. She's got a good head on her shoulders.'

Rose was also going to the window, but she couldn't see a thing. Where was Roger? He should have been back with the van ages ago.

It was almost midnight and she was still sitting waiting for him to come home when a policeman knocked on the door.

Rose sat in a daze while he told her that her husband had been badly injured in a road accident.

'Is he dead?'

The policeman just sat and stared at the helmet he was holding on his lap.

Rose began to sob.

'Are you alone?'

She nodded.

'Do you have any family near?'

'Me mum and dad live over Rotherhithe,' she gasped.

He looked at her swollen stomach. 'Look, I'll go back to the station and get someone to take you to them. Will you be all right for a while?'

Rose only nodded; she couldn't answer. When the

policeman had left, she sank to the floor, thinking of all the happiness they'd had together. Why did life have to be so cruel?

Lily felt such relief when she finally turned in to Enfield Road.

Amy hurried to the door when she heard the key being pulled through the letter box.

'Mum,' said Lily, falling into her mother's arms. 'I was so frightened.'

'Come on into the warm, love.'

As she walked into the kitchen, her father jumped up and held her close. 'Thank God you're all right. We was worried sick about you.'

As Lily sat in front of the fire with a cup of tea, she said, 'I hope Rose is all right.'

'Of course she is,' said Amy. 'She's got Roger to look after her.'

'She did say they were going to bring some of their stuff over today,' said Lily.

'Yes, I know,' said Amy. 'But he's got more sense than to be out in this weather.'

Chapter 42

THE RAT-TAT-TAT ON the front door woke everybody up. Lily was first out of bed. Grabbing her dressing gown, she hurried down the stairs and opened the door, expecting Roger to be standing there to tell her that Rose had had the baby. Amy was right behind her, and they were shocked to see Rose and a policeman standing there. Rose fell into her sister's arms, weeping uncontrollably.

'Come in,' said Amy, quickly gathering her senses.

The policeman came in and Amy closed the door just as Ron came down the stairs. Lily gently eased her sister into the kitchen.

Ron put his hand on the policeman's arm. 'Is it her husband?'

The policeman nodded as they made their way into the kitchen. When they were all seated, he told them what had happened.

Lily sat dreamlike as she held Rose tight. Her sister's sobs were heartbreaking.

After the policeman had told them what they had to do next, he left. When Ron came back into the room, he sat with his head in his hands. How he wished he could turn the clock back.

They sat talking for most of the night, and it was almost time for Ron and Lily to go to work when they finally persuaded Rose to go upstairs to bed. As soon as her head touched the pillow, she fell asleep.

'I'll just go in to the warehouse and tell them I have to see to the arrangements, then I'll go along to the hospital and find out when we can do things,' said Ron. 'I'll be home as soon as I can.'

'Don't worry. I'll look after her,' said Amy, whose eyes were red from crying.

'I'll go and tell Miss Tucker what's happened,' said Lily. She felt so sad for her sister.

The following week everything seemed happen at once. The family helped Rose to move into Enfield Road, and when James heard the news, he and Nora came to offer their condolences. It didn't upset Rose that they now knew where her family lived, but it did upset her to see them in Roger's car.

On the morning of Roger's funeral, Lily received a letter from Will telling her that he was really looking forward to spending Christmas with them. He also said that she just had to remember that looks weren't everything. She knew then that she had found love; she also knew that life could be snatched away at any time and you had to make the most of what you had.

Rose walked down the stairs. The heavy veil over her face hid her sad expression. She held on to the banister as another pain gripped her. She knew the baby was on its way, but nothing was going to stop her going to bury her husband.

'Are you all right?' Lily asked her sister.

Rose just nodded.

At the graveside, she leaned heavily on her father's arm. The silence was broken only by her sobs and the sound of the earth hitting Roger's coffin. Rose lifted her head to see her mother wiping away the tears that had trickled down her cheeks. Lily squeezed her hand. She was so lucky she had her sister close to her, and with the family's help she knew she would overcome all that was in front of her. She would stay with her family till after the baby was born, and then she would look for work. Together she knew they would get through this. She held on to Lily as another pain came.

'Are you all right?' her sister gently whispered.

Rose gave her a weak smile and nodded. She wasn't going to let her husband down. She was determined she was going to stay with him till the end.

Twelve hours later, at eleven o'clock on the night of December the eighteenth, little Roger yelled his way into the world.

When Lily saw her nephew, she just stood looking at him in amazement. 'He's so beautiful.' She took his tiny hand and he held on to it. She kissed his perfect fingers.

Rose looked at her sister and smiled through her tears. After all the problems and heartache they had shared, it upset her that her husband wasn't here to see his namesake. 'Roger would have loved him,' she said softly.

'I know, I know. And I promise that we will do everything we can to make his life a happy one. Mum and Dad are waiting outside.'

Rose wiped away her tears. 'Well, let them come and see their first grandson. Who knows, perhaps this time next year they may have another one.'

Lily smiled as she left the room.

Lights Out Till Dawn

Dee Williams

Before World War II has even been officially declared, ten-year-old Hazel Morgan and her eight-year-old brother Peter are evacuated, leaving London for the safety of the Sussex countryside.

With her children gone and her husband John in the army, Rene Morgan misses her family terribly. When she learns that John has become a prisoner of war, she has to take on the highly dangerous job of firewatcher.

Meanwhile, Hazel and Peter are desperate to go back home. Returning to the city, they are overjoyed to be reunited with their mother and Gran. But their father is still far away and the worst of the war is yet to come. As the air raids increase, the Morgans must face the terror of the Blitz together . . .

Warm acclaim for *Sunday Times* bestseller Dee Williams's novels:

'An inspiring tale' *Woman's Weekly*

'Harsh times, brave hearts and always a hint of hope' *Northern Echo*

978 0 7553 5891 5

headline

A Moment to Remember

Dee Williams

High hopes and shattered dreams . . .

Milly Ash is born into terrible poverty in the backstreets of London's East End. One of a huge family in which there is never enough food to go round, Milly has always dreamed of escape.

Her chance comes when she lands a position as a lady's companion to Jane Green, the disabled daughter of a well-to-do family. The Greens take Milly into their home and their hearts, and she even starts to develop feelings for Jane's older brother, Richard.

But then a tragic accident means Milly must suddenly leave the Green household and the life she so loved. As Milly tries to piece her world back together, will she ever find happiness, and love, again?

Warm acclaim for *Sunday Times* bestseller Dee Williams's novels:

'An inspiring tale' *Woman's Weekly*

'Harsh times, brave hearts and always a hint of hope' *Northern Echo*

978 0 7553 5889 2

headline

This Time for Keeps

Dee Williams

Love and war. Passion and heartache . . .

When Babs Scott loses her beloved parents in an air raid, she finds herself homeless and alone in Rotherhithe. The Land Army offers her an escape and, despite the backbreaking toil, Babs loves the peaceful green fields and the fresh, clean air of Sussex.

With the support of fellow Land Girl Lydi Wells, Babs forges a new life for herself. But, still haunted by her parents' death, her resolve gives way to resentment when two Italian prisoners of war are sent to the farm. And when her new RAF sweetheart Pete dies on his return to the skies, Babs is grief-stricken once more.

After the war and back in her home town, a foolish mistake changes Babs' life for ever. She fears she has lost her one chance for happiness, but then a letter from abroad arrives, offering an unexpected ray of hope . . .

Sunday Times bestseller Dee Williams' novels have been warmly acclaimed:

'An inspiring tale' *Woman's Weekly*

'Harsh times, brave hearts and always a hint of hope' *Northern Echo*

978 0 7553 3958 7

headline

Now you can buy any of these other bestselling books by **Dee Williams** from your bookshop or *direct from the publisher*.

FREE P&P AND UK DELIVERY
(Overseas and Ireland £3.50 per book)

Lights Out Till Dawn	£6.99
A Moment to Remember	£6.99
This Time for Keeps	£6.99
All That Jazz	£6.99
After the Dance	£6.99
Sunshine After Rain	£6.99
Love and War	£6.99
Pride and Joy	£6.99
Hope and Dreams	£6.99

TO ORDER SIMPLY CALL THIS NUMBER

01235 400 414

or visit our website: www.headline.co.uk

Prices and availability subject to change without notice